FAIR SHINE

REDBAT
BOOKS
PACIFIC
NORTHWEST
WRITERS
SERIES

FAIR SHINE

a novel

LLAWREN BIRD

redbat
books

redbat books
2017

Printed in the United States of America

First Edition: September 5, 2017

Trade Paperback ISBN: 978-0-9971549-5-5
Laminated Hardcover ISBN: 978-1-946970-99-2
E-book ISBN: 978-1-946970-00-8

Library of Congress Control Number: 2017950508

Published by
redbat books
2901 Gekeler Lane
La Grande, OR 97850
www.redbatbooks.com

Text set in Garamond Premier Pro and Souvenir

Book design by
Kristin Summers, redbat design | www.redbatdesign.com

For my children, with love.

PLACE NAMES FOR SPECIFIC GEOGRAPHICAL LOCATIONS
IN *FAIR SHINE* ARE FICTIONALIZED.

2/13

Trust her; she knows what she's doing. She's a wreck at the moment; she's struggling, but she has a plan. It's the most sensible thing to do. When you lose it all and feel like a failure, when there's nowhere to go but down, and you're thinking and feeling there's not one single soul on earth to appreciate you because there's no life left in you, it's time for the funny side. Sunny won't work: positive thinking *will not work* when things look this bleak. No, funny is all that will work. There is humor in everything.

Well, where might we look? She looked. She picked the wall in front of her and searched for the funny side of this wall. Maybe it was behind the wallpaper. A door through the wallpaper emerged in her mind. He was walking through it, and he exclaimed, "You aren't doing well! I am here to cheer you up! I've been terribly preoccupied with my projects, my new little book is out, you know, and I need time for my other women, but I'm here for you now." That was funny. That would never happen. If it did, she would laugh. It wouldn't mean anything. He didn't mean anything by what he said. He didn't.

He was a wonderful, intelligent, handsome, gifted man, a writer, and the other women were Faceboobs, Twitts and e-molls. He didn't sleep with them because he'd never met any of them, and the latest one, a wealthy, famous, international publisher—intimating that she would turn his career around because he was positively brilliant—finally confessed to being "happily" married with "lovely" children. She nonetheless *sought* a long-term affair with real sex in real time and proposed a luncheon: she would be most willing to travel some distance just to "be with him." He broke off communication with her in a gentle but firm email, citing his loyalty to his long-term partner, to his own self-respect and to the sanctity of her marriage and family. He asserted that he kept no secrets from his partner; secrets hurt relationships because lying was necessary to preserve those secrets. When this upstanding woman of the world, a handsome blonde, received the message, she was apparently standing up in her office. In the shock of rejection, she suffered a sprained wrist as she threw her laptop across the room, or so she claimed.

This was all passably funny—yet another injury in the workplace—the whole thing was funny, because Gifted One didn't even live with his partner. They loved each other and had been together faithfully, in the apart way, for years, nursing a funny twenty-five year age difference. The physical expression of sexual passion necessarily waned as the gap widened without hormone replacement therapy, and they had agreed that he would be moving into more viable relationship exploration *at some point*. For now, he claimed he was giving up on women, and with his youthful vitality, his giftedness and his freedom, he spent the evening watching a documentary on head lice instead of reading the final chapter of his old love's latest manuscript. She was a writer, too, you see. That might seem funny to some people.

Shakespeare, another truly desperate segue: now there was a writer. What about reading some Shakespeare? He can be funny, with or without the comedy and the errors and the light plasticity of lyrical, metaphorical speech and big, archetypal death and families gone awry and Macbeth and Macduff and, goodness, well, he can be serious, but he can be funny. She had written a critical review in college of a performance of a Shakespearean play and she began the paper with this sentence: *There was so much to talk about, even by intermission.* She was trying to be funny. Forget Shakespeare: he's not *accessible* at a time like this.

What about this? Was there humor to be found in the difference between night and day? Why not? Hear this: the day ended in a sloggy noodle backdrop of feigned poise, no noise and helpless driveling behind the screen of not feeling well and going to bed early. Tomorrow was Valentine's Day, the king-sized version of lovestir in the gut, poison in the arrow, hearts dripping sacrificially from greeting cards, bed linens and slimy cones of week-old roses from the grocery store, the heart box of chocolates set ceremoniously in the center of that big bed. My heart belongs to you. Very funny. It certainly does not.

So, you say: she hates Valentine's Day. It's hard for her; it makes her depressed. Maybe she lost a lover, a husband. Maybe the guy walking through the wallpaper was imaginary. Maybe her pet just died. Perhaps someone in her family she dearly loves is ill. Obviously, her current relationship with her boyfriend, or whatever he is, if he even exists, isn't romantic. She's a writer, so he probably doesn't exist; he's just a character. Whichever, this might make her sad about Valentine's Day. Maybe Valentine's Day this year is just too much for her. You say: you are funny.

A distant girlfriend sends a pentacostal post: Abba loves you. Abba god and abba father and abba-dabba-do. Hey! Kick in here, Abba! Super trouper needs you. Funny. Have a laugh on that. Or do as the slickie-foodie magazine implored: get up in the middle of the night and excitedly make shortbread with orange zest and poppy seeds. Do that. Hey! It's hilarious: I have no zest! I don't have pine nuts and asparagus to make a vegetarian linguine dish! I do not! Hilarious! What I do have is a pillow to dream on; I will dream funny. I will dream of being an improv comedienne who brings down the house by taking off her clothes, or not being able to find her underwear, or her bed, or her head. I won't have to say a thing.

2/14

Well, now. What *was* her problem, do you think? Was it simply a matter of getting through Valentine's Day? No, it wasn't that simple, and, as a matter of fact, she loved Valentine's Day, always had and always would. She wrote an email to a friend saying she felt it was the only decent holiday: she loved hearts and she believed in love. She would tell you this, then hug you. She was funny that way. She was a serious-minded intellectual who had a streak of romantic frivolity which surprised people. They found it funny that such a quiet, conservative little woman was capable of such flamboyance. They found it funny, and sometimes laughed at her. It might be the only funny thing about her. She wasn't funny. She felt unfunny to the point of despair, remember?

Oh, for heaven's sake! I say it, she says it, you say it, we all say it: get out of your own head! You're not special, you're not so important, you're not alone. Think about the whole, wide, wonderful world! Yes, well. I think about that and have to stop; things aren't going so well. It isn't looking good. Well, then, just look at the big picture: it passes. Natural disasters, war, poverty, racism, political scandal, violence, destruction, upheaval: all temporary. See timeline, see history, lighten up! Modern men and women are fortunate: so many improvements, so much progress, so much more hope than ever before. You're funny. Really, you are. Think about it.

So, what's the matter with this woman? Is she in pain? Is pain frying her brain? Is she terminal with pancreatic cancer? It's nice of you to ask, but no, she isn't dying, she isn't even ill. She isn't depressed and she isn't insane. She's just black: moody black, color chart black. All colors mixed into nothing, a dark hole with no light in it. Goodness, she is a dire old broad! She sounds, well, hopelessly, unattractively, self-absorbed. Tell me, does she have a name? Do you want to know? I doubt it; this doesn't sound like someone you'd walk across the street to meet, but you may be indulged. You might need a name to tack on this bundle of misery, which, by the way, I can label for you. It's called grieving. She lost sixteen people and three animals three days ago and she's destitute. She's pissed. She *is* hopeless. I think that covers it. Pretty funny, wouldn't you say?

You ask. Her name: Babette Bouche. Fake. Pulled out of nowhere on a dime. Babette Bouche. She isn't French. She's more than capable of indiscretion, not predictably charming and certainly not bourgeois.

She isn't a surrealist and she doesn't go out to dinner. She isn't a character in a novel or a play or a bar scene in a sit-com. No, she's just a woman who needed a name, a pretty skirt to hide behind while she sucked her thumb and her mother did all the work raising her. Babette Bouche. Some people know this name, but very few people see much of her or, obviously, would care to. What is she, you ask? Is she a gnarly, unpleasant bitch? She certainly sounds like one. I don't think so: very funny. No, she's reasonably pleasant. Reasonably pleasant is funny, don't you think? In this day and age? It's so beyond the ken, wouldn't you say? Funny lady. Lady is so beyond the ken, wouldn't you say?

Good God: what is wrong with Babette? She lost all those people and animals—what animals? I think you are wondering: how can she think about herself so much when all those people are dead? Is she empty-headed entirely? Yes! Empty! Vapid! You are absolutely right! Very good! That is helpful. That is a step beyond total despair: empty headed. Addled brain, maybe a slide. Slightly funny. A step. Empty Head Buries Dead. The Moon Also Rises. Heart of Lightness. Sometimes An Addled Notion. Bitches of Eastfuck. Tipping News. Interpreter of Fatalities. Would Take Any Damn Thing for My Journey Now. Limited Zest. The Tragic Mood. To Kill a Mocking Word. Blame Meridian. Boom, boom, boom, big feet, marching down the hall: I'm going to get you, I'm going to get you. It's a step, probably in the wrong direction, but hey, wrong directions can be funny. Look at Shakespeare.

It passed. The holiday trundled past midnight. It rained itself away. Her holiday haul consisted of a baked pottery heart magnet for her fridge, painted blue by her three year-old grandson, who is the only living soul who thinks Babette is normal. She received a midmorning phone call from her son who says Valentine's Day is special because it's the very day four years ago when he and his wife learned that this little paragon of virtue and wisdom was coming. Her daughter calls saying she has self-diagnosed her mental problems as passive dependency. This daughter is extraordinarily talented, independent and resourceful in more directions than Babette has ever even imagined being. Babette keeps her mouth shut as her daughter says: Oh, and by the way, Happy Valentine's Day. The charming gentleman friend appears, explaining that he is in withdrawal from videogames, his twenty-seventh day, and wasn't able to get *to* anything except Facebook, napping and a bite or two from the porn channel. He isn't doing so well. His sinuses are killing him. They kill him every day. His name is Will.

An older man, who lives down the street, a gentleman, we would have to call him, who has allergies, three cats and no luck in life whatever, on any front, shows up with a pizza and leaves it on her porch. He doesn't know she's pretty much vegetarian and that she will call immediately to feed it to her charming partner and his bitterly non-conjugal female roommate (isn't that so very *modern* of them?), also close neighbors. This roommate person is not doing well. She is worried about making a little more money and getting married before she turns fifty and wonders if she's ADD, or INFP or what? By the way, these neighbors all have names, but they aren't nearly as interesting as Babette's, so I'm not giving them out, at least not right now. Uninteresting names are a bore. These people are not, however, boorish, even though they have boorish sinuses and boorish bronchial tubes, respectively, and the female is a technical writer in the field of education. This could be funny. Both these neighbors, at forty and forty-one, are accomplished, just as Babette is accomplished. You are frowning and saying who cares. I see you; I can hear you.

You, a conscionable individual with a brain, you are more interested in hearing about all these people and animals who died, aren't you? You don't care about pizza and ADD, or Mr. Allergic Luckless. Or Valentine's Day: it's over, it's pointless, it's commercial, who cares? It's probably Christmas of the following year as you read this, anyway. You want drama. Comedy drama is your preference, is it not? Well, OK. Let's try to give you what you came for: edifying explication of the human condition. Something new, something you haven't heard before, something you can wear on your sleeve as a badge of courage, something you can talk about on Facebook or Twitter, something decent you can write home about, or use as a doorstop or never forget. Something real that isn't real. That something is called fiction. Isn't that funny?

2/15

They died of terminal punctuation. It's called a period, a tiny dot that ends a sentence. In this case, it was the dot ending the last sentence of a 90,000 word novel. It signified the end for them. They croaked. All dead. Sixteen people and three animals killed by a tiny spot of ink. You are quick: you are shaking your head. You are saying: god, is this what she's so upset about? That she finished writing a book and her characters are dead? Doesn't she realize that if she's a good writer, maybe even if she's only a marginal writer, these people will live on in other people's minds? That is the point? What's the deal? Is she a novice? Doesn't she have any experience with this? Is this her first novel and she doesn't know how it works? Is she stupid? Is this writer's block? You've heard about that, I'm sure. Or is it merely that she can't imagine loving new characters as much as the she loved the ones who just died? That might be a terrible feeling. You wouldn't know. It isn't funny.

I am telling you. It's funny, but she isn't stupid and she isn't a novice and she doesn't get writer's block. She wrote the last novel in twenty-five days. This is her seventh novel and it will be successful, just as all of them have been. She's quite good, actually, just ask her. So, what? So what? Write another one. How hard can it be? Your husband, Buck, leaves you for another woman, get going. Go out, have a drink, network, change your status on Facebook, have a make-over for heaven's sake. Get back out there and live your life. So long, Bucky, been bad to know you. But, you see, the funny thing about this is that you loved Bucky. Bucky talked to you in your sleep, Bucky brought you flowers and cried with you at your many losses. Bucky had a soul and a good mind and Bucky understood you. You understood Bucky: his every move, gesture, word, deed and laugh. You knew every piece of clothing in his closet. You shared war stories and friends. You even knew he would have an affair. You knew her name and how she came to *exist*.

Well, my god. You have to wonder: can't this woman see the line, the big fat boundary between fiction and real life? Is she damaged by watching too much reality TV? Is this a mental problem? You know, as in *mental*? Is she blurred beyond hope? Can't she just realize that Bucky is gone and sit down and type out another name, Harold or Jake, or something, and start again? How did she get through this before? How did she start with Bucky in the first place? You have read about this; writers do research, they have ideas, they make outlines, they develop a story, they begin to construct characters and events to advance the narrative. They travel to get the feel of a setting. They take notes while they travel: facts from which to create marvelous descriptive passages. They imagine the tale. They don't have to imagine the actual writing; that just happens. Yeah, right. Very funny. They begin this "actual writing" with a hook, a punch. An opening with teeth. Something riveting, arresting, desperately compelling: a grabber. Funny words, aren't they, for engaging the mind? It sounds brutal.

Babette knows all about this. It's called invention strategy. It's the culmination of positive exploratory heuristics. It's blah, blah, blah. She taught it, at a university. She taught students. She helped them with fluency. She advised them of the excitement of the process of writing: how valuable it is to learn how to communicate effectively, winsomely, and well. What a gift language itself is!

How exciting! You can do it! You have something to say! You have a unique contribution to make! You have a Voice! You will discover it! Use your imagination! How funny. If they could see her now, wouldn't they laugh?

She feels she would like to tell the truth. I would like, for a change, to tell the truth about fiction. You might like to hear it. Isn't that novel? Not really: the library is filled with books about this very thing. Great minds have addressed this subject at so much length, for so many years, that it's a wonder anybody is interested in reading anything. Anymore. Funny. That's what seems to be happening, actually. May be a link there. A stinky link: a horse that's been beaten to death stinks eventually. Lit crit is an ancient weapon with three spikes: what is it, what does it mean, how long will it last in the canon. The chain rattling on the end of the big round iron ball with three spikes is the chain of undoing: is it worth a damn? Maybe, maybe not. Funny how we often can't decide. Even more funny is this: how often we don't give a damn.

Well, now. There you see: you've reached the level of knowing required for empathy. Perhaps you are able to empathize with Babette Bouche. You know all about not giving a damn. You've read reviews. You've read bad books. You've fallen asleep in movies. You've turned to pubs, videogames and online lit whoredom instead of bookstores. You've watched serial shows on TV, just to keep from gagging on something long and challenging. Like a novel. You see what Babette feels she's up against, especially right now when she's grieving over the loss of her previous characters.

But, hey, I remember you asking: how did she start these other phenomenal books, which she whizzed through so capably in a flash with so little effort (less than a month!)? Talk about a zone, man! Funny as hell.

How did Babette begin her first novel? What is her invention strategy? You will laugh, but I'll tell you. She decided one day to begin to write. She had coffee and she turned on her computer. I'm going to write a book! She smoked half a cigarette and drank coffee. She sat down at the keyboard and said: Write. Put something down. She took her middle finger of her right hand and punched a random key. It was the dash. The line sat on the snow-field of a very large Microsoft word document like a track left by a wee, one-legged creature, whatever that might be. You see that her creativity was emerging! She left the computer and went out the back door and finished the cigarette. She came back and sat down and decided to translate the symbol into a word: dash. She looked at it and decided to capitalize the word: DASH. It had some energy, but not enough, so she put it in bold and increased its size to 24 pt.

DASH.

She claimed it: this was the title. Now. What happened next? Who knew? She walked around outside and made another decision. She needed a character doing something: a woman at a restaurant. She needed a name. Babette typed in random letters *danhsanahard* and quickly rearranged them: Sandahar. Easy. Now what? What is Sandahar doing in the restaurant? Probably eating, or drinking or paying the check. Eating. Now what?

You are laughing. You don't believe this. Surely a serious novelist doesn't begin this way! What is her premise? What is she writing about? What's the story? I'm telling you the truth: there isn't a premise and there isn't a story. There are no developed characters, there's no plot, there's nothing. We have DASH, a novel which begins with a random woman named Sandahar in a random restaurant. That's it. A month later, you will be asked to read a novel called DASH. It is finished. It does something. It's quite engaging. The "thing" happened, each chapter, each event, each character, "happened" in exactly the way the title and the name of Sandahar happened: brain nudge, finger to key.

You don't believe this. I understand that you think this whole thing is a little funny, a little not-square with the world of high-minded literary effort. The craft, and all. I empathize and I have an idea. I propose that you sit right here beside me as I begin this new novel, the post-Bucky affair novel, and you can actually experience it yourself. You may come and go as you please, invest whatever amount of time you wish in this project; I know you have a life. You may have better things to do, granted, but it's an opportunity you perhaps shouldn't miss. It's not a writer's workshop, but that can be nothing but a *good* thing. If you've ever been to one, you understand this; I've attended them and I've instructed in them myself, so I know all about it. This is so much more relevant; most writers wouldn't give you the chance to experience their process so intimately. You smoke? Good. We'll get along. What did you say? You said "Fine by me?" Excellent! There's our title. Now, as we go along, if you have anything to say—it's apparent that you're going to be good at this—just speak up. I take encouragement well. Let's have another ciggie and begin.

* * * * *

FINE BY ME

*An intuitive novel by Babette
and her hapless friend Arnold,
the only person left from a "crowd" of three
who gathered around Babette
at the beginning of this thing on 2/13.
She's a mixed metaphor:
something's wrong, but we'll catch up with her.*

1

NOT A NICKEL

. . . .

Painting and sculpture have ruined me...It would have been better if in my youth I had hired out to make sulfur matches.
—MICHELANGELO BUONARROTI

He was ruined. Who was ruined? His name was Dodd Boon and that was, perhaps, the very source of his ruination, the severing of the roots of his genius, which occurred moments after his birth. Surely the name itself *was* a large part of his difficulty. Dodd Boon was laughable, just by name, and no one could say why. When he introduced himself, "Hello, I'm Dodd Boon," people laughed. It was very curious. He finally figured it out, at about fifteen, and decided another syllable or two might help. He added son and K: Doddson K. Boon. It didn't help. All that happened was that people laughed and then asked what the K stood for. He told them it was Kooper, with a K. He added a hyphen. Doddson Kooper-Boon. They still laughed. Boon. Boon was the problem. Boondoggle, Daniel Boone. They didn't seem to understand that boon was a good thing, a world of good, a gift.

That's OK, Babette, but what's the severing of his roots of genius? Just his name? It sounds more serious than that. It sounds serious. I thought we were writing something funny. How old is this guy?

Precisely the questions you should be asking, Arnold. Let's continue.

Doddson Kooper-Boon was thirty. He was forty. He was fifty. He wrestled with this procession of decades. He wanted to be twenty, thank you very much, but he was actually 50. Tough business. He wore jeans and t-shirts and sandals. His hair was long and could still pass for blonde and he *could* look twenty, from the back. When he turned around however, there was a paunch, ever so slight, and a face worn by thundering around trying so hard to be a genius that one might wonder: was he 55? No. He was just worn. He was thin. He was talkative. He understood that speed, volume and flair worked. Many people allowed him a great deal of space. He wasn't often alone in the existential sense, but he wasn't often connected. The distance was great: thunder, far away, rolling up there in the clouds, gray clouds. He called himself a force of nature.

Enough of that stuff, that nature crap. What's happening? What's he up to?

You ask. That's exactly the thing: what's he up to? I have no idea. What do you think, Arnold? What's Doddson Kooper-Boon up to?

I don't know. He thinks he's a genius, thwarted. He's looking for an opportunity. Never too late, never too old. Still has it. But what is it?

Doddson is looking for love.

That's stupid. I hate that.
Just wait, Arnold. Let's see where it goes.

Doddson is looking for love. He isn't looking for a woman. He's had women and he likes women, but he's not looking for a woman. He's looking for objects, actual objects which signify love, either with a visual dynamic or with the actual word.

He's a collector?
Now, Arnold, that's just four sentences. I suggest you wait to interject until a bit more development of an idea has occurred. It's rather distracting to be interrupted after four sentences.
Sorry.

These objects are to be used in collages. Doddson Kooper-Boon is a bricolage artist. He creates enormous sculptures with found objects. His current project is "Love." His previous project was "Reason" and he had found it too challenging. It had taken him four years to complete and install. He has chosen "Love," thinking that it might be a more accessible topic and take less time and be more rewarding. It might sell; "Reason" has not sold. It is installed behind a library in a suburb. It is being used for the utilitarian purpose of accompanying the reading of books outside in a courtyard. The primary appreciators of the piece are children under six, since the courtyard is used for the weekly summer reading hour with preschoolers.

That's sad. Has he sold anything? Is he really any good? How long has he been doing this?
Ah, yes. Those would be the questions, Arnold. Is this the source of genius thwarted? You want to know.

I guess so.

We must go back in time and review the life of a man who wants to be twenty again and wishes to sell his art. How keenly are these desires presenting? One would have to say this: quite keenly. There is, in fact, some desperation, on rare occasions, to the keenness of desire. Boon lives on not much. He hasn't rubbed two nickels together in quite some time. He gets food stamps and lives in his car, which has been parked in a back row at Target for six months. And for how long has he been in this state of marginality? One would have to say this: since he left college at twenty, where he was majoring in business, and began collecting objects and creating sculptures.

He has a room in the back of an automotive repair shop where he assembles his sculptures. He doesn't pay rent; instead he cleans the shop, including the bathroom and office once a week for the privilege of using the backroom which has no windows. He has been in this particular situation, in this backroom, for twenty-one years. He has never sold anything, except his skill as a janitor. When it's cold, he sleeps in this room, but he has been cautioned against it. He is not to live there; he is to live in his car. There is one important perk associated with this alliance with the automotive shop. When a sculpture is finished and Boon has found a place for it, the owner allows him to borrow a truck to transport it to the site. How many sculptures has he created? Sixteen. They are placed around the city of 340,000 in barely visible locations which have required that Boon beg on bended knee to secure.

This is pathetic. Why doesn't somebody help him? Are these things that he creates junk or what? What's the problem?

Yes, well Arnold, we'll have to see. Tell you what. Let's just wait until the end of the book and chat about it then. I think we have enough here to move through a story. Let's concentrate and give it our full attention.

I'll try, but if I have to sit here, I might need to say something once in a while. I have ideas, too, you know, Babette. You aren't the only brain on fire.

2

SALT AND PEPPER IN THE WOUND

· ·

Why should we be in such desperate haste to succeed
and in such desperate enterprises?
—Henry David Thoreau

He flunked a final exam. He called home at Thanksgiving and his father yelled at him on the phone, after Boon explained that the term had not gone well. He would be on academic probation. He had earned a D in statistics. His father yelled a bit longer until Boon hung up. He withdrew from school and started his first sculpture, which he titled "Success." He had no interest in doing marketing analysis as a profession. It was his father's profession, not his. He had no interest in a profession of any sort. He decided he was an artist. He was also in love, at the time, with a woman and with cannabis, a stage in his development which lasted another two years, until he finally graduated with an advanced degree in hashish. Gradually, he gave up the light-up and gave up intense love affairs, although he had an occasional dalliance, and focused on his art. By the time he was thirty he was doing nothing else.

Boon didn't spend much time thinking about this past, especially now that he was past fifty, but this morning he was thinking about it. He was scanning through everything he knew about marketing, thinking about ways to garner interest in his work. He did it for pure joy, but he also felt he was good at what he did and should be compensated. Boon was not happy, any longer at least, with being an amateur. He needed to sell something. He didn't receive the vast illumination from the universe he expected that morning, so he went about his business. He put it out there and went to work.

He entered an antique shop, a misnomer really, because what it really sold was junk. Boon had found an ashtray on a park bench and thought he'd try to trade it for a love object. Helen, the woman who ran the shop, sometimes did this bit of business with him.

"Yo, Helen, you look like fine rice paper with a hint of mint this morning." She was 69 and wearing a green scarf choked around a withered neck.

"Yes, Boon. Whatever that means. What do you need?"

"Have an ashtray here, perfectly luminous red: firestorm on Christmas. One of the wise men wore red. You could put it with your holiday display. Might add something." It was July, so the ashtray would be adding something for several months, possibly forever. He held it up to the light so she could see it. "I'm fond of it myself, but I can't use it. Need a love object. Do you think we might trade?"

"Oh, I suppose, but check with me first. Look around. See if you can find something." She took the ashtray and set it down by the cash register, "I like this ashtray, Boon, but it's worth about fifty cents, so keep that in mind."

Yes! Boon took off, wandering down the messy aisles of three dank rooms, digging through plastic junk and dirty junk and worthless junk. He returned to the first room and was holding a pair of salt and pepper shakers, one the bride, one the groom, probably out of his price range, when a man, another customer, spoke to him.

"Those things are quite trite, I must say."

"Trite." Boon looked at them, and looked at the man. He was a short, bald, older fellow, with a nice face, dressed rather well, Boon thought, for being in Helen's junk shop. He was wearing a suit and tie, for starters.

"Yes. Isn't it amazing what our culture mass-produces? Thousands of those deplorable things were made and sprinkled around the landscape of consumerism. I simply cannot imagine what provokes such an endeavor. What is your interest in these salt and pepper shakers, if I might ask?"

Boon held out his hand, "I'm Doddson Kooper-Boon. Artist. I collect found objects of interest to create sculpture. The theme currently is love."

"I'm Jerald Redding. You have a fortunate name: Doddson, implying lineage which diminishes overwhelming ego, Kooper with a K, I would imagine, which signifies the renegade spirit, and Boon, the gift. This is fascinating. You are considering then, purchasing these items for your work-in-progress?"

"I'm trading, but yes."

"And what, if I may ask, are you trading for these salt and pepper shakers?"

"A red glass ashtray. It's up at the cash register with Helen."

"Might I see this ashtray? Would you mind going to the front and bringing it back here? I'd like to look at it in physical proximity to these salt and pepper shakers, if I may."

Something terrible is going to happen. Someone outside shooting pigeons is going to miss and the bullet will come through the window and kill Boon.

Arnold, don't be a dolt. Nobody's shooting pigeons. We can't kill our hero! What's the matter with you?

Then something good is going to happen. This guy, Jerald, is an art collector who will buy all the sculptures and Boon will become rich and famous.

Arnold, for heaven's sake. We have to have a story. We can't have that happen. This is a book, Arnold, a long book. Stay with that. It's a good thing I'm writing this and not you. This isn't flash fiction, Arnold, this is a serious novel. Now let's get back to business.

I don't want a serious novel. You promised a funny novel.

Jerald and Boon looked at the ashtray and they looked at the bride and groom. Helen was there, too, wondering what these two might be doing with her merchandise. Both men came in on occasion and neither one of them had ever, not once, purchased one thing. In this, however, they weren't really all that unusual. Very few people actually bought things. Helen felt she ran a shop where people could spend an hour handling things. That's what they did. They picked things up, they put things down and they left, most usually without a thank you. She did feel fortunate in one way, however: no one ever stole anything, either.

"I'm wondering, Boon—I choose to call you Boon, if I may, since it's the most interesting of your names—I'm wondering about the value of this ashtray. I also wish to know its history."

"I found it on a park bench yesterday at Ginn and Dayview. It's glass. It's not worth much."

Helen offered, "Five dollars. It's a good piece. I haven't tagged it yet, but it's five dollars."

It's worth a fortune! I knew it!

Jerald picked up the ashtray and looked at the bottom of it and replied, "This ashtray is worth about fifty cents, Helen, but I'm happy to give you five dollars for it. It's a pleasing shape and color." He handed over a five dollar bill.

"Could you wrap it in some way for me, please, perhaps a bag of some sort? I don't want to put it into my suit pocket. The fabric would be stretched. Thank you."

"What are you doing? Why did you want to see the ashtray with the salt and pepper shakers?" Boon had picked up the bride and was looking at her bottom.

"There's information to be gathered, always. In this case, the idea that I wanted to explore was whether or not it might be true that you are an artist. That was your claim, the label you used to describe yourself to me, is that correct?"

Boon nodded.

"This is merely a claim. I wished to validate it."

Boon was interested. "And you paid five dollars for an ashtray worth fifty cents and now light shines brightly on this question, apparently. I'm interested: how did it work out?"

"It worked out quite well. It is apparent to me that an individual who sees creative potential in the salt and pepper shakers, which are less than exquisite, actually offensively mundane, as opposed to the ashtray, which is intrinsically rather beautiful, is assuredly an artist. You see something in the salt and pepper shakers those of us who are not artists cannot see. And you are also an artist because you chose *not* to work with something that is already quite artistically designed."

He sounds like Sherlock Holmes.
Arnold! Please!

Jerald now had his ashtray in a brown bag and walked down the aisle to leave. "Have a wonderful, wonderful day!"

Boon stood there holding the bride. He picked up the groom. He put one in each pocket of his coat, turned to Helen and said, "May your day be filled with ashtrays and your pockets be filled with sunshine, Helen. I dig this shop. You should rename it."

"What's wrong with Helen's Antiques? It's worked for fourteen years, more or less."

"You should get a new sign, a new name. I'd be willing to help you with it. I think it's time for a change. Never too late, Helen. Let's rock the joint."

"Boon, you are crazy. I've always thought so. Go. Take your salt and pepper shakers and go."

"Don't you want to hear my suggestion for a new name?"

"Not especially, Boon. My arthritis is kicking up and I need to take some Motrin. This has been a busy morning for me."

"Well, you do that, but here's the name; you think about it. Might shoot you into stardom, Helen. Good Fortune Antiques. What do you think?"

"I think you're crazy. Go. See you later."

3

THE SIGN

. . . .

I always go up a back alley.
—Joyce Cary

Arnold, what are you doing? Get in here. We're starting the third chapter. You might show a little more interest. Aren't you curious about the sign?

I'm thinking about something else at the moment, if you don't mind. You know, Babette, there's more happening in the world than your current book. You get obsessive.

That's exactly what it takes, Arnold. That's what it takes: focus. Let's do this.

I have a question. These quotes you use to begin chapters. I'm looking at your bookshelf here and I can't figure out what you read. This looks like the cart at the library of books recently re-

turned, which some page person has to put back on the shelves. There's no rhyme or reason to any of these books. I just saw you come over here and pull out a book of student poetry and art from Reed College, turn to a bookmarked page, walk to the computer and type in a quote. You just did that, didn't you?

Yes. That's how I do it, but I deleted that quote. Not quite right. I'm thinking of something else now, but yes, I just go to my bookshelf and pull something out and open it and use it, but the stocking cart analogy is apt: books come and go here, just as they do at a library.

But it's still just three short shelves of random stuff at any given time! This is all you work with as a resource for quotes? For all your books? Don't you go online or try to find other things?

No, Arnold. You know I don't have internet and I don't go online more than once a month to do emails. You know that. I don't waste time, which is what is happening right now. I'm going to work.

Boon felt pretty stoked. He decided he needed to celebrate; he needed a shower, since it had been maybe a couple of weeks since soap and water had occurred to him. He went to his car at Target to get his rucksack of a clean set of clothes. Then he would go over to his friend Jake's house and clean up so he would feel refreshed for the day's creative work on "Love."

The car was gone. The car wasn't there. He looked. It wasn't in the row. It wasn't on the lot. It wasn't in the parking space he had chosen. It wasn't at Target. It was nowhere to be seen. Boon was an intelligent person, of course, and had no difficulty knowing what had happened to his vehicle. He knew it hadn't been stolen, since it was a thirty-year-old Chevy Nova with a duct-taped back window, several dents in inauspicious places, such as the door to the driver's seat, which was permanently scrunched into place and locked because it took twenty minutes to close it. Or open it. Boon always entered the car through the passenger door. The hood was held down with a bungee cord and the car wasn't drivable, or at least he assumed it wasn't. He had limped into the lot with it, the thing spewing smoke and coughing asthmatically and he hadn't tried to start it since. The car had been towed. His apartment, as Boon called it, was on its way to the graveyard. He wouldn't even inquire. It was impounded. It was dead and it was gone.

Good day, bad day, whatever. That's what Boon thought about this presenting dilemma. Move on out, say goodbye to the landlord, Mr. Towhappy Target and realign, man. Go figure something else out. He walked away in his jeans, t-shirt and sandals, reassured by the fact that he had his food stamp card in his wallet and had none of his art supplies or tools in the car. He'd lost very little. He'd lost his home, some clothes, some food, but that could be remedied. How? That was the thought in Boon's creative brain: how?

The first person who came to mind was Jake, since Jake's shower had been on his mind earlier. What about Jake? It took Boon about thirty seconds to decide against Jake. Jake had a wife and kids and Jake took enough shit about the showering. Jake's wife, Chris, called Boon a vagrant, to his face, and seriously had problems with Boon using "her" bathroom. She suggested he get a job and use the Y for showers. When she asked, several times, how her husband had "found" Boon, Jake wisely said nothing. Jake had discovered Boon in a line at a coffee shop trying to use his food stamp card, to no avail, and Jake had bought his coffee and muffin. They talked that day and Boon found out where Jake worked, at a copy center nearby, and they had become friends, a quite loosely defined construct as far as both men were concerned. They really didn't know each other very well. Boon showered at Jake's house when his wife wasn't home. That was it.

OK. Lou. No, too damn far up to his house and Lou wasn't in a good space after a break-up with his gay partner. The guy had ditched Lou after eleven years for a woman, probably a Q, something that was all new to Boon. He'd never heard of such a thing

happening and didn't know what to say to Lou. Worst case scenario. Too heart-breaking. What about Bobby? No. Messy deal,
Bobby. Drunk at sunrise and lived in a dump with his mother.
Too sad, too depressing. Walt, the owner of the automotive shop
was not an option. Walt had put it to Boon this way: you cannot
live here. Ever. Never. Get that straight. I'm running a business
not a goddamn motel. Walt was nearing seventy and had two
sons who worked for him, so the place was crawling with Walt
spies. Not possible.

> *It's gotta be a woman. He's going to have to find a woman.*
> *Why do you say that, Arnold?*
> *Well, because. Women are more nurturing. A woman would*
> *feel sorry for him and help him out.*

Boon knew he would have to find a woman. Women were
more nurturing and would commiserate with his dilemma. A
woman would respond. Which woman?

Boon's mind catalogued the beauties on his contact list for
emails, his vast network of Facebook friends and made another
quick decision: go to work. Boon, of course, had no email account
and was not on Facebook and never used a computer for anything
whatever. He knew about it, the whole cyberspace thing, but he'd
never had time to learn anything about it. When one guy who
saw his art one day at the shop remarked that a website would be
a good idea, Boon had nodded and stayed with the task at hand.
Website. The word waltzed into Boon's brain and it jigged out.

> *So he doesn't have any women in his life? I thought he liked*
> *women, had women, that's what we said earlier.*
> *Yes, Arnold, we did. Let's just see.*

Boon spent the afternoon in the backroom arranging pieces.
Arranging found items. Arranging his thoughts around the idea

of a sign. He hated to use some of his "Love" objects for a sign, but he also hated Helen's current sign. It was a gray rectangle which proclaimed that the store sold Helen's Antiques in black block lettering, followed by the address. It had bothered Boon from the first moment he saw it. It was such a terrible sign that he'd almost passed on going into the shop. Very bad sign. He would make her a new one, whether she wanted one or not, and he would solve the home loss problem by working all night. As long as the light was on and there was activity behind his door, he could stay the night in the backroom, claiming a deadline on a project. He'd done it before, he could do it now.

He began to assemble pieces and quite quickly found himself feeling just that: a deadline. He pushed himself. He would get this thing done. It would be phenomenal. Helen would be ecstatic. He amended that: Helen was too old for ecstatic. Helen would begrudgingly let him hang it. Boon was not a bad judge of character and neither was Helen. They got along. They didn't go far or tread very deeply on each other's turf, but they got along.

I'm sorry, Babette, but it's bothering me that Jerald what's-his-name hasn't been in Boon's thoughts. Wouldn't he think a little more about that guy? The guy who actually seemed to understand that he was an artist? The Sherlock Holmes guy? The guy in a suit and tie who obviously had money and brains? And some interest?

Boon's sign was a red metal heart-shaped tray, an enormous tray he had found ten years ago at the landfill. He used it to hold his adhesives and fixatives, but now he dumped them into a cardboard box and saw the tray as a sign. He would have to work with both sides of the tray, and wisely decided that one side would be sculpted with objects and the new name, and the back side would be just the name: Good Fortune Antiques. As the sign began to take shape, and the bride and groom salt and pepper shakers were in consideration as objects to be affixed to the sign in a prominent way, incorporated with a ceramic love letter, a glass bouquet of miniature roses, a glass cupid, a set of three gold hearts and a real arrow, which would, of course point to the entrance, downward, at a slant, since the sign hung high over the sidewalk, visible from both directions, Boon couldn't help thinking about Jerald Redding. He wished he had asked more about him: he obviously had money and brains and some interest. He'd been the first person who had liked Boon's name. He worked with the bride and groom and chided himself for having missed, perhaps, his one golden opportunity. Oh well, maybe he would run into him again. Next time he would pay more attention, get his business card, find out more.

He did the lettering on the sign himself, an easy task for Boon who had a sure hand and excellent design sense. He made a grid and created the sculpted lettering in less than an hour. He outlined each letter in gold and decided to make the shaft of the arrow gold. He also added filigree and small triangles of gold and outlined each love object to give the sign continuity. The name was perfect. The sign was perfect, but he felt it needed a slogan under the name, something to really encourage people to go in. He considered "Something old, something new, something borrowed, something blue" to incorporate the bride and groom idea, but didn't like the limitation presented by the word blue. And the limitation of wedding wasn't good, either. He couldn't imagine anyone purchasing anything from Helen's shop as a wedding gift. He felt trepidation: what was the idea here? He was sweating by four in the morning, concerned now about the whole project. It looked good, but it was missing something. What was the concept? Love. Stick with Love. He wrote slogan notes on a Taco Bell bag: For the love of junk. Perfect match. You and this shop. You love junk. Come on. Intelligent, Boon. Lift the concept, lift it up. Marriage. Use your brain; you shop here. Think. He liked people who appreciated junk. He appreciated junk. He was an artist. He married junk and art and created sculptures. Intelligent, Boon, you're not pitching tacos, you're pitching an idea. Junk? You'll love this place. Wedded bliss. As he wrote and worked, he felt increasingly burdened by the bride and groom. Did he have to use them? What had Jerald called them? Trite. Deplorable. Offensively mundane. This did it for Boon: he had to use them. It was a gauntlet which had been thrown: you're an artist. Prove it. OK. What sort of slogan would work to get people like Redding into Helen's shop? That was the question. Jerald Redding was the first person Boon had ever seen actually buying something in Helen's shop. OK. Target audience. People with money who see value in junk. Intelligent people, refined, educated people. Jerald Redding.

He finally had it. Under Good Fortune Antiques he quickly painted in a lively, scripted hand: To the Marriage of True Minds. Of course it didn't occur to Boon that this wasn't original, that William Shakespeare had written these very words in a sonnet. The other words Bill had written following these words would have been instructive and timely for Boon on this new day, now dawning: "admit no impediments."

What do you think, Arnold? Are you awake?

Of course I'm awake. I'm just closing my eyes to think.

Well, what do you think?

I don't like it. I liked it fine until the last three words. I just don't understand why writers do this. They do this in movies too: just when things are looking up, they put in something that slaps you down, something creepy, something not looking too swift up ahead. I hate that.

So you don't like the implication that Boon may encounter some impediments?

No. He's had enough. It's time for things to go right for him. He just lost his home. He's worked for years at this. He's brilliant. He's thoughtful. He's doing this sign with a great deal of care. His heart is in the right place. He needs a break.

You sound as if you care what happens to him.

Well, of course, I care; what if it was me?

I see. So what would you like to see happen to Boon, or by transference, Arnold?

Well, he takes the sign to Helen and she loves it so much she pays him a thousand dollars for it. No, better yet, let's say two thousand. It's worth that.

On the spot? She has that kind of money in her drawer of the cash register?

Yes, she does. She's closet loaded.

I see. Then what happens?

Well, Jerald Redding sees it and he wants to see Boon's other work and Boon is taken around town with Boon driving Jerald's BMW and Jerald is thrilled. He buys all of it and puts it into a gallery, Lucia maybe, and there's a rep there from MoMA and the rest is history.

You do realize that the kind of art Boon does is considered outsider art? And that he lives in a town of only 350,000 people on the west coast?

I don't care. He's an exception. He makes it. Oh, and I forgot, there's a love interest. Her name is Mathilda and she's European and she has a villa in Italy and they move there. She's extremely keen on Boon's art and has shipped one of his pieces, "Food for Thought," a free-standing columnar thing shaped like a fork, to the villa and installed it in their kitchen. She's hot and makes him feel like he's twenty again. That's the last line of the book.

I see. And this all happens rather quickly, I imagine? This fantasy?

A week. I think a week; it could all happen in a week, but I don't have a week.

Pardon?

I don't have a week to see Boon through this.

Why not?

Well, Sarah called and I have the kids for the week, unscheduled. I don't understand why it has to be this week, of all weeks, but I'm always happy to have my kids, but the timing is a little bad. No, make that really bad. Never fails.

So you won't be here, that's what you're saying?

Yeah, it's been good, I appreciate it Babette, it's been interesting, but I wasn't going to be here anyway because I finally got the jazz thing put together, for Saturday, with Hellitt and Frey, finally, finally, at night, with three rehearsals and a gig, with Cira drumming, meaning action. I cleaned up my apartment and everything, finally looked like the move was on, but I'll be putting kids to bed at 8 and watching TV instead. I love my kids, but I needed this Saturday, Babette, in more ways than one. Long dry spell all around me since the divorce. Frosts me. Especially since I know damn good and well that Sarah's unscheduled work demands are pretty much scheduled sex demands with a new doctor she's dating. She gets it and I don't. Sucks.

Well, then. You have commitments. Let's have a smoke and you can get on with what looks like a wonderfully challenging week ahead. Children are so inspirational. You got a light? My lighter died.

Yeah. Here. Keep it. I have another one in the car. Consider it my contribution to the great American novel.

Thank you, Arnold, you are certainly helpful. I'll grant you that, and Arnold, I might make a suggestion.

Yeah?

Your kids have babysitters, someone they know who stays with them when Sarah is out. They're older: just ask her to arrange for a sitter for rehearsals and for Saturday night. All night. They could even have a friend each for a sleepover, to make it more fun for them. Then you can do your thing.

Do you think?

I think.

4

HELEN OF TRY

· ·

Days of absence, sad and dreary,
cloth'd in sorrow's dark array;
days of absence, I am weary.
—SONG LYRICS FROM A *NEW STANDARD HARMONICA COURSE*
SONGBOOK, PUBLISHED IN 1927, WITH THE ORIGINAL PRICE OF
25 CENTS PRINTED ON THE COVER. IT RESTS ON THE SHELF BEHIND
HELEN AT THE CASH REGISTER. SHE REGARDS IT AS TOO VALUABLE TO
BE IN THE STACKS. SHE DOESN'T WANT PEOPLE HANDLING IT.

Helen was glad for the five bucks. She locked up at noon and went to the grocery store three blocks down and bought an apple, an orange, a banana, an avocado and a cucumber. These were thrilling treats. Helen lived on rice, beans, eggs, bread and oatmeal, and rarely had an appetite, understandably. She spent the afternoon eating halves of each of her purchases, slipping the other halves into Ziploc bags. She took another Motrin at two o'clock and sat behind her cash register thinking.

What was Helen thinking? She was thinking she should give up. Trenton had been gone twelve years, leaving her money in the bank and the shop which he had lovingly named after his wife. That money was gone. She had given up her apartment and lived in the back of the shop with a three-legged cat named Fox. She received a skimpy Social Security check each month, which barely covered utilities, food, toilet paper, cat food and Motrin. She had never told another living soul how skimpy it was; it was embarrassing. But Trenton had passed on after only two years of running the shop, taking his good heart, which was really a very bad heart, with him. It was tragic; he was still so young when he died—years her junior! They'd been married only seven years, a second marriage for each of them.

With Trenton's death, Helen's social circle dwindled. She knew everyone had loved Trenton; he was interesting and conversationally adept. He was handsome; he had energy and passion. People came to the shop just to chat with him; business in those days was good. Trenton went out on buying trips in the valley and came back with wonderful things. People waited and watched for Trenton's new purchases.

Helen was none of those things. She was plain, and had never worked at anything for more than a couple of months. She hadn't even been a mother. She was a shop owner who had never been out on a trip to secure new items to sell. She waited for people to bring things in, primarily because she didn't have a car—her eyesight wasn't great anymore, which meant she shouldn't drive anyway—and she was terrified of buses. She was a failed shop owner. She was hanging on to the shop because she was hanging on to Trenton. She owned it; she could sell it. She had no idea how she would pay the property taxes this year; each year, the income had decreased and there was no way she could do it. She should move on. But at her age? Where would she go? What would she do? Moving on surely meant moving out. She had actually considered hanging herself from the ceiling fan in the room with the holiday antiques. In more reasonable moments, she felt it was the single most perverse, disturbing idea she had ever had in her life. She would get her check in three days; the fourth Wednesday of the month was approaching. She would just wait for her check and keep unlocking the door in the morning and locking it at night, after which she watched television. That was her life. She should try to lift her spirits. She had Fox. She needed to buy cat food.

5

CHAIN MALE

· ·

*Congratulations, you have reached
the next step of your education.*
—STANISLAVSKY, TO HIS ACTING STUDENTS

Boon left the automotive shop early, before Walt and his boys arrived. He went to Jive Joe's for coffee. He had the drill down. He walked confidently in, ordered coffee and sat down. As he drank it slowly, he watched for someone who looked like a feasible source of assistance to pay for it. This morning, carrying his sign, he was dismayed at his prospects. There was no one in Jive Joe's. He ordered coffee and used more cream and sugar than usual. He was out of food stamp money, and his food stash in the car was gone. He was hungry. He waited.

Two young women came in, dressed for office work, ordered

lattes and left, carrying their nice purses and their traveler cups of brew. A man came in who looked surly and quite unpleasant, also ordering a coffee to go. An elderly man came in and sat down with a cup of tea and talked to himself. He was severely palsied, shabbily dressed and drooling. Boon put his hand on the man's shoulder and nodded to him, smiling, then took his seat again at a back table.

Boon knew the minute he saw him. Here's my guy. He was tall and thin, with long, very dark, brown hair, wearing black pants, a black t-shirt and a chain mail vest, a long vest. Boon instantly knew the younger man had made it himself. Boon knew his art history. He could tell a Morisot from a Renoir, and his knowledge was so profound that he was assured that if someone walked in with prints of a Berthe or an Auguste, he would be able to tell them which was which, and, very specifically, why. He could also expostulate quite thoroughly about the personal character of the artist who had done a certain piece. He knew the younger man at the counter, maybe he was 40, was an artist and that he had made the vest himself. This man would pay for his coffee. Boon reached down for the heart sign propped against his leg and put it on the table top in front of him.

The man sat across the aisle from Boon and nodded, acknowledging his presence.

Boon responded, "Good, fair day!"

"It is! I see you have a creation."

"Yes. My most recent project. You're the first to see it. I usually do sculptures; this is my one and only sign. Sixteen sculptures and one sign, cast into the richness that is Portland. The name's Boon."

"Donovan. Well now, let's have a look." He got up, coffee in hand and walked across to peruse the heart sign. "Very strong. The gold is powerful, especially in conjunction with the whimsy and sentimental aspects. The balance here is refreshing. There's a compositional integrity which compels the viewer to relate quite specifically to the message. It's unusual to link the heart motif and the mind. The partial quote from a Shakespearean sonnet is inspired, since most viewers will complete the line and feel there are no impediments to buying. It works. I am assuming this is a sign for a business. Is the antique store real or imagined?"

"It's real. I'm on my way to install it as soon as I finish this cup of coffee and get it paid for. I've been up all night working on this, start to finish, and I feel some urgency about getting it hung. Star-studded banner, it is."

"Let me pay for your coffee, Boon. I like to support the arts."

"Why, thank you, the community of like-minded souls thanks you, Donovan. And you do belong to that community, don't you? The vest. It's noteworthy: tangled vines of shining tines, woven as if Mother Nature herself embroidered it."

"Thank you. I do mail when I'm in transition."

"And are you in transition now?"

"Yes. I am looking at the day and seeing a wonderfully open book."

"Well, I have just the thing. Why don't you come with me and help me hang this sign? I also have adjunct plans to paint the trim on the windows of the shop red; I have half a pint of paint with me. I'm also going to wash the windows, since they are the eyes to the soul of the newly named shop. It's maybe two hours of work, and I would enjoy having help with the project."

"So this is your shop! Of course! Well, I'm delighted to help."

"No, no. This isn't my shop; I just have a studio where I've done sixteen or so sculptures. No shop for me. It belongs to a superlative individual whom I admire. She's quite elderly and suffers from arthritis. These sorts of tasks are difficult for her and I am volunteering my services. I have plans to also assist her inside and clean and rearrange, if she's amenable. She thinks I'm crazy, but she puts up with me. I think she'll be able to see the wisdom of my plan."

"Maybe having me along will help. I've never been to this shop, but I'm interested in antiques. This is intriguing, but I have to eat something first. Have you eaten?"

"No, actually, I haven't."

"Then let's go have breakfast, my buy, and get onto this project."

"That's a plan, Donovan. I'm curious. What do you think you would have done with this fair day had you not met me?"

"I have no idea. I never have two days alike and I never plan anything."

"So you don't have a job, or responsibilities which preclude doing whatever comes along? Breezin' free?"

"No, I don't. I have designed my life to flow. I admit no impediments."

"Well, water, my friend, flows freely under our bridge of friendship. Where should we eat? Ardelle's Kitchen is half a block down; I might recommend that."

* * * * *

They ordered at Ardelle's and ate, Boon trying to slow down and not look like the ravaged empty gut he really was, and asked, "This is the well-defined breakfast; I thank you, Donovan. Tell me something; you say you like antiques. You know all the shops here; which is the favored house of old?"

Donovan paused, eating the orange slice garnish, rind and all, "I just arrived yesterday." This wasn't true, since Donovan had been working away at projects in Portland for over three months. What he meant was that on this trip he had arrived yesterday.

"From which multiverse?" Boon laughed.

"From San Francisco."

"Ah, San Fran. The end all and the being of all historic. You probably know your antiques, then."

Donovan looked down. He didn't reply.

Boon took note of the recalcitrance and moved on. "Well, let's go hang a sign and brighten some eyes and lift a spirit or three."

"Where is the shop located, Boon?"

"The Langlois Historical District. It's down by..."

"I know where it is. There are five shops there, none of them named Good Fortune Antiques."

"That's right! You have found the jewel in our city's crown on your first day! That's impressive! And there isn't a shop named Good Fortune Antiques until we hang this sign. It's a new name for an old, tired lady. The shop and the owner have seen better days and it's my intention to significantly rebirth the entire scene."

"Which shop are you renaming?"

"Helen's Antiques. A name that isn't a name for excitement, I'm sure you agree."

Donovan was standing. He'd abruptly gotten up and put money on the table for the check. "Let's go."

Boon felt the wave, the scent, the undulation of spirit, the nod from the unknown sailor at the end of the pier. There wasn't a sailor and there wasn't a pier, but there was a nod, nonetheless. Boon saw an eagle in the sky, screaming. It wasn't an eagle, of course, it was only a silent pigeon, but Boon always saw eagles. Everything that flew was an eagle to Boon. He picked up the sign and watched the waitress clearing the table. She stuffed all of the bills in her pocket, as if the whole thing was her tip. Boon moved his feet toward the door, while his body resisted. Something felt funny.

6

FULL DAY'S WORK WITH PAY

. . . .

He loved this and he loved nothing but this, to the point
of forgetting everything that was not this, of remaining
for hours...and days, before the same spectacle determined
to penetrate within, to understand it, to express it—
an obstinate creature, a seeker, diligent in the manner of the
shepherds who discovered in the solitude of the fields
the beginning of art, of astronomy, of poetry.
—THE CRITIC GEFFROY ASSESSING PAUL CEZANNE

Jerald Redding had a difficult time deciding what to do with
his thumb. He had stricken it with a hammer and the nail was
sore and turning black. It bothered him. This was a man who
found a loose thread dismaying to the extreme. This was a man
who couldn't bear to see a mote, even a mote of dust, on any-

thing whatever. This was a man who washed a glass out of his cupboard, in the dishwasher, before using it. This was a man who brushed his teeth for sixty seconds three times a day. He used a stop watch to make certain the timing was precise. The thumb bothered him and he considered going to the emergency room and having the nail removed. He considered it and he rejected it. It seemed morally wrong to ask professionals who dealt with emergencies to perform such a task. He reassured himself: this is not an emergency and the coagulated blood under the nail will disperse. The verb phrase 'will disperse,' implicating the future, eventually troubled Jerald so much that he didn't use it, even in his private thoughts.

Jerald left his condominium and drove to work in his spotless vehicle, a perversely black, one decade-old Lincoln Continental. He had purchased it new and the odometer read 64,000 miles. It was professionally serviced monthly and the interior was detailed, also professionally, weekly. He drove the 2.39 miles to his workplace, parked, and arrived at exactly the appointed hour: 8AM. He worked until noon, lunched at his desk, and resumed work at 1:00 sharp, finishing his work day at 5:00. He then returned to his condominium and resumed this same work, now without pay, until 10:00 PM, when he went to bed.

Jerald was a gemologist. He rented office space in the Langlois Historical District, a delightful walk-up with a view. He had retired to this spot, following years of work in New York City and in Brussels. He was retained by a firm called Grand Select Gemology, GSG, Inc., an international gemstone resource center. He now called himself an emeritus research gemologist, and Jerald was always quite specific with people who asked what he did: he was a gemologist, to which the reply was often, so you're a jeweler, to which Jerald replied that he certainly was not a jeweler. He was a scientist. This was inarguably true. Jerald did not own or wear jewelry. He had little interest in jewelry, only in an occasional gem which was set in a mounting, which he carefully removed.

His interest was in gems, a lifelong interest, his only interest, which had begun at the age of five with a treasure box of stones his aunt gave him. These stones were agates, or, more precisely, chalcedony quartz, displaying concentric layers in a stunning array of colors and textures. The wooden box containing these original stones, which was actually a recipe box, still sat on Jerald's desk. It had been in precisely the same position, on the left front corner of the huge desk—everywhere Jerald had been he always had a huge desk—for fifty years.

There was one important fact surrounding Jerald and his gemstone fascination, which, of course, was an obsession. This fact was unknown, even to Jerald. No one in the entire world knew more about gemstones than Jerald Redding. No one single person could recite the history of each stone, nor identify stones and assess their quality as competently as Jerald Redding. Although the depth of his expertise was not recognized, his services were much in demand. He was regarded as an expert. In truth, he was *the* expert. Jerald had never once in his life erred in the arena of gemology. It was quite easy to imagine how hitting his thumb with a hammer while hanging a painting would disturb such a man. He worshipped perfection. Beauty was his passion.

Arnold! What are you doing here? You're back!

I am. I brought you a mocha. How's it going. How's Boon doing?

Well, Boon did the sign and has finally had a decent meal and has met someone to help hang the sign.

Is it a chick?

No, no. Just another guy. Donovan.

Sounds like you're poking along. That's not much to have happened since I left. You have to pick up the pace, Babette. Christ, I've made a million meals, had kid conversations, rehearsed, performed, slid under the sheets with a stellar woman and scheduled two new gigs since we last spoke. You have to get Boon moving.

Well, point taken. I was just beginning chapter seven when you walked in. Why don't you give me a title and a quote, since you're such a fast mover?

Well, I can't do that, I don't know what's happening next. Besides, I can't hang around. I'm on my way to the library.

Neither do I, remember? I have no idea what's happening next, Arnold. What difference does it make? Give me a title and a quote and then you can go.

7

DRUM ROLL

. . . .

The right woman moves a man through life
as music moves the soul.
—ARNOLD WILLIAM NEWTON, JAZZ PIANIST

"What are you boys doing? You get down from there, Boon."
Helen stood on the sidewalk looking up at Boon who had the
old sign, which hung from an overhanging roof, off its hinges. It
swung forlornly from a rusty chain.

"Mornin' fair Helen of the rocket ship! You must get on board;
we're soon to blast off into the atmosphere. This is Donovan. Donovan, here you go." He handed Donovan the old sign. "Now hand
up the priceless work of art by the grand master of new impressions."

"Boon, so help me! Trenton put up that sign and it means too
much to me. I want you to put it back up right this minute."

Donovan engaged the strident tone and the woman as well. "Helen, if I may call you Helen, it might be advisable to allow Boon to hang the sign he made for you, even if for only a few moments. He's crazy, a little crazy about this sign, and I'm afraid of the scene which might commence if we don't allow him this small courtesy. Let's indulge him, you and I, and then I will personally assist with reinstalling your previous sign if that's what you prefer." He smiled so endearingly and put his hand out so kindly to steady her nerves, that she stopped yapping and just stood there.

The Good Fortune Antiques sign was installed. The golden arrow pointed at the door. Boon came down from the ladder and left to return it, to the store three doors down, from which he had borrowed it.

Donovan took Helen by the hand, "Miss Helen, let's step back a few feet, down the sidewalk, and have a longer look at this sign. We might pretend that we are tourists, seeing it for the first time. What would we think? Would we want to go inside and see what might be available for sale?"

Helen stood there and stared, then began sniffling. "It's beautiful, isn't it?"

"Yes. I do believe Trenton would have admired it, just as you do. I admire it, as well."

"Did you know Trenton? You seem too young..."

"I did not, and that is unfortunate, truly."

"It really is! He was so wonderful. He said I was his rudder, that I guided him through his life. He said he had a difficult time of it before he met me, and he always said I had saved him. He was very romantic, just like the sign. I do think you're right. He would have loved this sign. I want to keep it. Where's Boon?"

Boon was gone. The pint of red paint and a brush sat on the sidewalk. A spray bottle of Windex and a half roll of paper towels sat on the sidewalk. Donovan escorted Helen back into the shop and exited, looking up and down the sidewalk for Boon.

He waited, thinking the talkative Boon might be engaged in a conversation in the shop down the street. He waited ten minutes, after which he decided to begin washing the windows. He began inside, explaining to Helen that it was Boon's idea to clean the eyes of the shop's soul. He cleaned inside and then did the outside windows, amazed at the depth of the grime. He waited again, but now realized that Boon was gone. He picked up the brush and the paint and painted the window trim on the three front windows. When he finished, he went in to see Helen, hauling the old sign inside.

She was sitting behind the cash register, red-eyed from crying, but stood and attempted composure when she heard him enter. "Donovan, it looks nice. You did such a nice job. I wish I could pay you something for your hard work. And Boon, too. I wish I could pay him for the sign, but I can't."

"Oh, no! That would detract from the whole purpose, Helen! Even if you could pay us, we wouldn't be able to take it. Good fortune will accrue in other ways for us. You musn't worry. This is something that requires that money not be exchanged. This is a very firm rule, which we dare not break."

"I think you are giving me a line, young man, but it's nice of you."

"I am most certainly not giving you a line, Helen. Do I look like that kind of man?"

"Well, no..."

"Then it's settled. You're happy. That's the payment. Now, I would like to have a look around. I'd like to see what Good Fortune Antiques has to offer."

Helen's head dropped as she frowned, "I'm not proud of how this place looks. Trenton kept it up, and I tried for a few years, but I just haven't had much energy. I've let things go. I know I have."

"Well, that's not the end of the world, Helen. With just a few days of effort, this entire place could be transformed."

"It would take money. I'd have to hire someone and there are repairs. You see the floor. The plumbing in the bathroom doesn't work in the sink and the whole place is run down. There's a roof leak in the back room. It's just too far gone."

"No, it isn't. Tell you what. I can volunteer some time and energy. I like this place. I can help. Let me look around. What you could do for me is make a list of repairs that need to be done. I'm handy at things like that, but I don't know the place like you do. Just prepare a list and I can work away at it. No time like the present. I'm going to wander around a bit, if that's OK with you."

"I guess. Go ahead."

Donovan was out of sight but not out of Helen's mind, certainly, for forty-three minutes. She kept looking at the clock. She had trouble thinking about anything except time and what Donovan might be thinking as he wandered through the dingy aisles.

"This place is tremendous, Helen! I'm excited! I must leave for now, but I'll be back in the morning and get started. Please try to have a list ready for me, if you would. That's essential. I'll see you then. I'm so pleased to have met you."

Helen knew she'd never see him again. Of course she wouldn't. No one in his right mind would take on the renovation of her shop, and Donovan, unlike Boon, seemed perfectly sane to her. No, she wouldn't see him again, but she was still pleased. She had a new sign and the windows were clean and she would have to go look at the red-trimmed windows. Just this much was a vast improvement.

Donovan left the shop and started up the street when he noticed the planter box in front of Good Fortune Antiques. He had noticed it while Boon was fussing with the sign because it was ugly. It was a large brick planter filled with dirt and the entire top edge of the thing was destroyed and the bricks were scattered around in the dirt. Donovan had thought it was a shame someone didn't repair it and plant flowers in it. He stood staring at the planter box now and was thoroughly confused. Someone had smoothed the dirt and arranged the bricks in three interlocking hearts. As Donovan looked at it, he realized that the person who did this had not had to spend much time doing it, but the effect was a tremendous improvement and very pleasing. He knew who had done it. No one else would be able to imagine this improvement and make the change this quickly. It had to be Boon. Where was he?

8

WATCHING MR. TRANSITION

· ·

Sometimes, you are drawn to things and you don't know why.
—JODIE FOSTER

Boon was no dummy. Boon was at the end of a hall on the third floor of a building down the street admiring his new sign out the window and watching for Donovan to leave. He had watched him cleaning windows and painting trim. He had waited nearly an hour while Donovan was inside. He had watched Donovan notice the planter box he had sneaked back to fix, before finding his viewing spot.

Boon felt the urge to know. He wasn't a naturally suspicious person and he wasn't suspicious now, but he was feeling short of the entire cosmic deck, that's how he put it to himself. Screw loose in Thunder Bay, hidden agenda in the tricycle, something not right in the left hemisphere, puzzle time in the glory day, chain letter stuck in the mail. He'd just had this happen with Jerald, the man with the pin-striped satin tie. He would not let it happen again with the man in the chain mail vest. He would follow him. He wanted to get back to work on his "Love" sculpture, but something more pressing had arisen: woodpecker, woodpecker, pecking away, Donovan, Donovan, Donovan.

Boon left the building as Donovan walked quickly toward the next section of Langlois Historical District. He was talking on a cell phone as he walked, but Boon was too far back to hear the conversation. It appeared that Donovan was headed for Jive Joe's, but at the beginning of the block, Donovan entered a hardware store. Boon waited twenty minutes until Donovan came out, carrying three bags of merchandise he had purchased. Boon followed as Donovan did, in fact, go directly toward Jive Joe's, but surprised Boon by walking to a small, black pickup truck parked in front, unlocking the door to the passenger side and placing the bags inside. As Donovan went around the back of the truck and was opening the driver's door, Boon approached.

"Donovan. We meet at the Jive for the denouement. What's up?"

"Where have you been? Helen loved the sign. She cried, Boon. She loves it, and I finished the windows and looked around. I'm going to help her get the place in shape, your idea. That's where I've been. Other than fixing the planter box, which is ingenious, where have you been?"

"I've been following you, stepping through each step to here."

"Why would you do that, Boon? It seems unfriendly, frankly, which seems out of character."

"True words, by the book of Sunday, but there's a bookmark in the book that wasn't there when I woke up and I want to know where it came from. Who put it there? What's it worth?"

"I see. You don't trust me."

"I am a very trusting person, Donovan. I trust the sky, the weather, the whole world, every human on the planet, each leaf on every tree. I trust God and little kids and dogs, green apples and nursery rhymes. I trust every damn thing you can name, but I mostly trust my instincts which, as you know, are artistically grounded in a reality few can see. You may feel that way about yourself. I'm wondering what the reality I am seeing in the aura folds around that chain mail means. That's all. It seems obvious that I trust you, since I have no experience not trusting another human being. It seems unwise and childish not to, and I'm a grown man."

"You know, Boon, you might consider getting into my truck and taking a ride with me. Let's see about your operative level of trust."

"Where are we going?"

"You are trusting, you are creative, you flow freely as water under a bridge, remember? I'll put these bags in the back. Get in."

9

FIRST CUSTOMER

. . . .

And they shall be mine, sayeth the Lord of hosts, in that day
when I make up my jewels, and I will spare them, as a man
spareth his own son that serveth him.
—MALACHI 3:17

Jerald Redding had watched the sign exchange from his walk-up. His office was down the street, across the street and on the second floor. He kept working. He kept looking out his window. It was lunchtime. He debated about changing his routine and walking down to have a look at the sign. No, he should have his lunch and wait for the fax he was expecting. He had a long report from London to read. There was an inexplicable query about larimar, a rare pectolite, from a young chemist in Helsinki which required further attention and a reply. He was waiting for

FedEx and a delivery of three raw clinohumites from Tajikistan, about which he was inordinately excited. He shouldn't leave.

He had to. He had thoroughly gone through all the relevant items for sale in the other four antique stores in Langlois, but he hadn't finished the task at Helen's Antiques. He had stopped in a few times, but had never perused the back rooms; Helen's Antiques was the least pleasing of the five shops and what he had seen was not exciting. He was a thorough man, however, and he now felt the pressure of a task not completed. Of course, the only thing of interest to Jerald in any shop of this sort was rocks, stones and jewels. He wasn't interested in the jewelry, but he always assessed the gems. He had been fortunate, on three occasions over the years, to find hidden gems of value in antique shops. This was work; he had to go. He would be back at 1:00, on schedule.

Helen greeted him, "Welcome. How are you today?"

"I am most well, thank you. I have noticed your new sign, created and installed by Mr. Doddson Kooper-Boon. It is quite magnificent. It has inspired me to take my lunch time and do a bit of shopping. Perhaps you could assist me?"

"Of course. What is it you're looking for?"

"Rocks, stones, gems, jewelry, inlays. Certainly any stones which are engraved."

"Well, I don't have much, but let me show you." She left the cash register and motioned for him to follow. "This is a muslin bag of rocks. As you see it's unopened. The tag is still on it. I suspect it's nothing but river stones. It's sold, as you see, as 'spirit rocks.'"

"Yes. We may pass on the bag. What other specimens might you have?"

"Well, here's a tray of things my late husband collected along the way. I have no idea." The tray held an assortment of raw stones, which Jerald quickly assessed, picking up one of them, a dumortierite quartz.

"I might purchase this, if you are willing to allow me to choose just one from this tray."

"Sure. Is it valuable?"

"It's quartz, a unique quartz. When polished it is a deep blue color caused by intergrowth of the mineral dumortierite. What else might you show me?" He put it down.

"Well, here is a display of turquoise. I'm sorry it's so dusty. These have been here for years and no one seems to have an interest in turquoise anymore. When I was a kid, turquoise was big, but not anymore."

"Yes, lapis lazuli, a cousin to turquoise has been in favor, but turquoise has diminished somewhat in popularity, although it has been valued for thousands of years. The earliest mines in Sinai, Egypt were already depleted in 2000 B.C."

"So it isn't worth much, is it?"

"Let me look at these pieces." His hand went immediately to one stone which differed from the others. "This is variscite, relatively rare. It is enhanced with traces of chromium and is used for carvings."

"Is it valuable?"

"It's quite a large piece. What else do you have?" He put the rock down.

She took him to another room and pointed at a piece of tiger's eye, about the size of a loaf of bread. "I like this. Trenton said it was worth something, but it's never sold; no one has even looked at it, really. I can't imagine what anyone would do with it, but I like it."

"People often buy this kind of piece as a simple natural sculpture. It's quite pleasing just as it is, but if cut and polished, it would be a resource. Do you have other items?"

"Well, we'll need to go back through here. I have a case with jewelry. I'll show you, but I'll have to go back to the cash register to get my key."

She returned and unlocked the case. Jerald took out his glasses and looked at the jewelry tacked onto a piece of red velvet. "Interesting."

"You may take anything out, if you want to handle it and look more closely."

"That won't be necessary. I will purchase the bracelet on the left and the necklace there in the center."

"Are they valuable?" Helen was tingling now with excitement. He had said the magic word.

"The bracelet is jadeite. My interest is the color, which I've not seen before except in photographs. This is a very luminous violet. Exceptional."

"And the necklace?"

"The necklace, my dear, displays a sphalerite; dispersion is rated three times higher than the diamond and the quality is superb. It's surprising to find it here, especially in a mounting. It is extremely fortunate that you have stored it in a locked case. It's rarely, rarely set."

Helen was stuck on the word diamond. "Does that mean it's worth three times more than a diamond?"

Jerald smiled at Helen's logic, "Let's simply say I will purchase it. I'm delighted. Now, I have little time. If you would please help me gather the bracelet, the necklace, the tiger's eye, the variscite, and the quartz, I will pay you and get back to work." He handed her a clean folded handkerchief from his suit pocket, "Please carefully wrap the necklace in this and place it in a small box or bag of its own. It's very fragile."

They stood at the cash register, with Helen focused on one thing: get enough to buy Fox's cat food.

"Now, m'am, what might I pay you for these items?"

"Well, I must say you certainly know more about rocks than I do, so why don't you make me an offer? I have no idea."

"Are you willing to accept a personal check? I work, perhaps you know, just across the way, in the Underwood Building, suite 212. I will require a receipt, if I may trouble you."

"Yes. You've been in before." She had no concern about accepting a check from a man dressed as he was.

Jerald wrote out the check and handed it to her, then picked up the brown grocery bag parcel, which Helen had secured with a piece of blue masking tape.

He waited for his receipt.

Helen stood there looking at the check. "This isn't right." She felt faint.

"Yes, it is quite correct. I feel it's an appropriate amount. It's quite what I'm willing to pay, but you understand my need for a receipt."

Helen was in a daze. She wrote out a receipt by hand and gave it to him. She sat down, holding the check again, staring at it. She looked up at Jerald with tears in her eyes and whispered "Thank you."

"Thank *you*, my dear. I am so pleased with our transaction. And please advise Mr. Boon that I admire his sign a great deal. Have a wonderful afternoon." He walked out.

Helen sat there. She was crying. She would lock up. She would go tell Fox she had to go out. She had to get to the bank. It wouldn't wait. She felt wobbly and frightened. She had to go, right now, to the bank. The check she held as she talked to Fox, holding it up to his face so he could see it, was written out for $5900 and signed with a flourish by Jerald J. Redding.

10

TATTOO TINABELLE

· ·

Don't be so old.
—ANDREW KNOWLTON

Donovan drove silently and Boon talked nonstop about scenery and roadside attractions and the air they were breathing. He felt nervous about the destination, increasingly nervous, as Donovan turned off the highway and headed down a county road, then turned onto a rough dirt road which snaked precariously through huge trees. They drove into a clearing with three big yurts placed in a pleasing arrangement with decks and landscaping. Several vehicles were parked in a row along one side.

"Get out. We'll do this. I'll get the bags. They're waiting for the hardware store haul." Donovan nodded his head at Boon who just sat there, showing no compunction to obey. Donovan shook his open palm toward the door of the pickup. "Come on, Boon, let's go. Don't be a puss. Move."

Just the numbers were intimidating, as twenty people streamed out of the yurts and came toward them. They were led by a woman, who hugged Donovan and took the bags, "Thanks, man, you save us from certain death for tonight's show. Sold out! For a midnight show! We just did dress, as you can see, but we need this stuff bad. This is totally app, Donovan. Who's the foil?"

"This is Boon. Artist, Tinabelle, as we say, as we say. He's usually not shy, but we'll give him a ten-second rearrange and see." He looked over at Boon, "Now Boon, this is Tinabelle and she's the consort."

"Your girlfriend?"

"No, no. By consort I mean that she consorts with all, on a higher level than the one you're referencing."

Boon looked at these people. They spanned the unknown, they shadowed the shadow, they might as well have been horned beasts with golden fleece from the Himalayas: creatures rarely seen. They had elastic faces, tattooed bodies, piercings of such range and depth that Boon wondered if all the metal made them feel chilly. None of them stood still. They were wrestling and leaping and cuffing and talking and making faces. One was juggling and another did somersaults and back flips. They wore skimpy, ragged clothing. Bottom line on the scene for Boon was this: he was old. This group was dipped in youthful energy the way a bon-bon is dipped in chocolate: a thick coating. Boon's chocolate analogy held in another way. There was a great deal of black in evidence. An approximate half of the twenty people had dark skin, and all of them had black, heavily kohl-rimmed eyes. All of them had black hair in a studied array of styles, from buzz to braids to dreads to spikes to curls to straight to Mohawk. All skin in evidence on every single one of them was tattooed.

"What happens here? Light needs to shine, Donovan." Boon again felt the need to know.

"Well, Tinabelle is the grand mistress of Circus Tantamount, based in San Francisco. They come here in the summer to work on new acts for fall, do a performance now and then. I try to come up occasionally, and this year I had to be here on other business, so here we are. I thought it might be an experience a man like you wouldn't want to miss."

Tinabelle enthused, "You two have to come in. Y3. Food all over the place. Lamb kebab barb out back. Beers. Keilly made a cake! Come on! You're with me."

She waltzed—literally waltzed—away from Boon with a liquidity of movement which made Boon wonder if she actually had a skeletal system. She was the oldest of the bunch, in her late thirties and there was no possible way that any man from any planet would find her anything less than beautiful, sexy and, well, motivational. She could have held up a hoop of fire and Boon would have leapt through it, head first, to land on his face on the ground if necessary. He was led to the yurt, tethered by prospect, even though Tinabelle was two yards ahead of him.

Donovan was laughing. He laughed and he laughed. He drank beer. He ate kebabs. He sat over sheets of paper with three of the guys, having a conversation of some length about art. He watched two guys do a routine with a bar stool and two glasses and rose at one point to move around the stool himself, showing them a revision on the routine. He looked at a wig and shook his head, then put it on. He was Gilda Radner. He put on headphones and listened to something from a recorder. He sat at a laptop and looked at a video. Boon watched this with a third of an eye, not the third eye, but with the third of the one eye he felt he could afford to invest in surrounding activity. He was watching Tinabelle. He wondered: did she or did she not seem to dig him? She was friendly and affectionate with everyone, but she seemed thoroughly focused on Doddson Kooper-Boon. She had asked his full name, and after she heard it, she called him Doddson Kooper-Boon.

He finally asked her: "Do you call everyone by their full names?"

"I do. It's a matter of respect and inclusion."

"What's your full name?"

"Tina Rothchild Halle Breon. All mine. Born to it."

Boon asked what she called Donovan: "Donovan Trenton King."

Boon stood immediately. The circus was over. He walked up to Donovan and said, "Donovan Trenton King. Step away, right now. We have a conversation beyond multitudinous coming right up. It's snagging your rear end, Donovan, teeth stuck in your back pocket. Blood might be drawn. Now."

Donovan excused himself and followed Boon to the parking area. "You figured it out. Good for you. So what?"

"What are you doing here?"

"I teach directing, Boon, at Payne Institute of the Arts. These are some of my former students, all except nine of them. One of those exceptions is Tina, unfortunately. I'd certainly like to be able to say I helped train her, but she's a natural, I'm afraid, not in the slightest in need of direction of any kind whatever."

"I'm not talking about the circus, or film, Donovan, and you know it. Read the clouds, man, speak to the fog rising around you. Dublin in winter dreary."

"What? The shop? The name? What? Where do you suggest I begin?"

"Let's do the same name. Helen King. Let's do the King thing."

"King. My name. Her name. Not related."

"Oh, no? And I suppose it's coincidence that your middle name is Trenton and her late husband's first name was Trenton? That pickle's too big to fit in the jar, Donovan. Gonna have to eat it."

"Trenton King was my father."

"But Helen isn't your mother."

"No. I've never met Helen before today. Actually, I thank you for that, Boon; it was something I found challenging to consider doing on my own for a number of reasons."

"Does she know Trenton had a son?"

"No. Trenton didn't know he had a son."

"So you never met him? No matching thread."

"No."

"Let's see. Why would you show up here, now, when Helen is almost 70 and Trenton's been gone, what, twelve years, thirteen? Something. What's the purpose? It ain't the show and tell of antiques, no shine on that dime."

"Backstory. Could we just say that?"

"You can say that, but I'm still not hearing the lead line in this piece of music, Donovan. A chord or two does not satisfy the appetite for a meaningful riff. Need more than rafters. Where's the roof? Where's the mother?"

Donovan stood there and became a statue. Every muscle stopped, nerves halted, he didn't seem to be breathing.

At first Boon thought it was an act, something stupendous Donovan could do, something theatrical, but then he realized his question had made it happen. What he saw on Donovan's face was either fear or pain, both of which Boon recognized and had felt himself. He spoke, "Listen, my friend, I need more Tina and the bells, if you know what I mean. I am rolling to thunderous applause and I am getting back to my audience." He walked away.

* * * * *

Poor old Boon. He ate chips and spinach dip and drank four beers and then had too much barbequed lamb kebab and a big bowl of rice pilaf. He inhaled a huge slab of carrot cake with cream cheese frosting and found himself flat on his back on the couch, mumbling to the exquisite Tinabelle that he needed to take a break, that he had done an all-nighter. He felt her lift his dead head and put a pillow under it and felt the soft weight of a blanket over his body and he was gone.

When he awakened at two in the morning, stepping outside to pee, there wasn't a person in sight. The cars were gone. He declined to use the porta potty parked in the trees and watered a big, old hemlock instead. He looked around in the dark and saw an outdoor shower installation illuminated by a porch light on Yurt 2.

Water. Thirst. He went inside and drank two green plastic tumblers of water and looked around. He thought one thing: money, money, money, honey. He couldn't help it; he was noticing things no man could notice with Tinabelle in the room. He saw art and expensive rugs and fancy kitchen appliances and a wine rack. He went to the couch and picked up the blanket and wrapped it around his shoulders to take off the chill; it was mohair, purple and brown striped with long fringe. He summed it up: not your usual summer camp cottage for the circus kids. No, even with the porta potty and the shower deal, this set-up smacked of the get-go and the more to come.

But we know Boon. He was thinking gladness, happy go glad for Tinabelle and her retinue: they did a fair job on any fair day. He took a shower. He hoped he might see these people again, most specifically, Tinabelle, of course; he had an interest in seeing the tattoos he hadn't seen. However, we know Boon. Boon was inspired and Boon, though he admittedly had thunder thoughts, especially in the groin and the heart regions, probably in that order, Boon needed to get back to the "Love" sculpture. He saw a glass container filled with granola bars. He lifted the stainless steel lid, took two and walked out, down the lane, down the road, all the way to the highway and hitched a ride for Walt's.

He left the mohair blanket behind, folded neatly on top of the pillow at the end of the couch. He leaned down to kiss this blanket before leaving.

Arnold! You always show up at the strangest times! What's up?

Thought I'd pop by and see how it's going. I just have a minute. Is it going? What chapter are you on?

Eleven.

How's Boon doing? Has he gotten laid yet?

My God, Arnold, do you think of nothing else? What's with you and Boon getting a woman? Wait. Cira. You're in love. Oh, no. Don't tell me.

Well, I might be, what's wrong with that?

Nothing, except that with your track record it might be a dead end, frankly.

That's mean-spirited of you, Babette. How do you know this isn't the one?

Oh, god, tiresome. I don't, Arnold. Maybe this is the one, maybe you've found your destined soulmate.

You don't believe in it, do you?

Love? Of course I do, Arnold. Why not. Makes the world go 'round. Etc.

Cynical, cynical, cynical. Unattractive, unattractive, unattractive.

Now, Arnold, that's not true. I'm a big believer, actually, but I'm a realist. Big magic wands: that's what I don't believe in.

And you call yourself a novelist. Hey. I gotta go. My car's been in the shop and it's ready for me to pick it up. I'll be back later and we can see about this. Man, I think I have a responsibility here to see Boon through the woman thing. You certainly aren't on his team. See you later, Babette. Go eleven.

11

BLITZ

· ·

SO STRANGE!—UNCANNY.
—Joyce Carol Oates

Helen King unlocked the front door of Good Fortune Antiques and was met by twenty-one sets of eyes peering at her from
the sidewalk. It was a quiet group and Donovan stepped forward
to greet her.

"Good morning, Helen! I'm here to begin renovation and
reorganization. I've brought workers with me. They are a circus
troupe who performed at midnight over at RainDrop Theatre
and they've had naps in the green rooms there. We're ready to
roll. Do you have the list?"

"What list?"

"The list. You were going to make me a list of repairs. We have trucks of supplies." He pointed to three pickups parked across the street. "I'm telling you, Helen, we are ready to do this. In a day. This particular day. Can we come in and get started?"

Helen stepped aside and everyone filed in. Tinabelle was last. "I'm Tinabelle, and I am happy to meet you, Helen. I will make sure everything goes smashingly and smoothly and softly. We will proceed with great respect for your lovely shop. The sign outside is darling, darling, darling."

"Boon did it. Where's Boon?"

"Doddson Kooper-Boon disappeared. He was with us, sleeping, and he skated. Do you know where he lives?"

"No. I kinda always imagined that he didn't live anywhere. He has that look."

"He has the look of a man who is at home in his world, Helen. He lives wherever he lives, I suspect. I want to find him."

"So do I. I owe him money. If you find him before I do, tell him I have money to pay him for the sign."

"Will do. Now I'm flying into this, Helen. Got troops to line out. Touch base later."

* * * * *

Helen was banished from her own quarters for the day and Fox was in a cat carrier at her feet while she manned the cash register, sneezing often, watching the blitz team bringing boxes in, taking trash out, hauling things through the back door, pounding, scrambling around on the roof. One customer came in and Helen explained about renovation and the woman left, saying she would be back.

At five, she locked the front door and put up her closed sign and went to her apartment in back. It was transformed. New dark red carpet had been laid. The sink was fixed. The place was spotless. The light fixture, an old fake gold thing she'd always hated had been replaced with a beautiful chandelier. The walls of the studio room had been painted a soft creamy color with white trim. The dirty, old Venetian blinds, none of which worked properly, had been replaced with wide, vertical blinds. Her bed, one corner propped up with bricks, with the missing leg stored under the bed, was now repaired and the bricks were gone.

Two fans had been set up and the windows were open.

The final touch was a painting newly hung on the wall near her kitchen table. She stared at it, instantly convinced it was the oddest thing she had ever seen. It was uncanny. That was the word that came to Helen: it was uncanny and it was strange. It was also familiar. She liked it; it rang bells. What? She searched, but couldn't find the connection. It was a painting of two red croquet balls nestled in green grass; it was a lawn. In the background was a faint rainbow sky with a bird in flight.

She sat on her bed, the door shut, old Fox gimping around the room, wondering, wondering about the painting, when there was a knock on her door.

"Yes? Hi, Donovan. Goodness. This is just amazing. I don't know how you did this so fast. My room is so pretty! And the sink works!"

"Good deal. We're out of here, but I'd like to run you around the shop, just for a minute, so you can get your bearings. Can you leave Fox and come with me?"

It was too much. She started weeping, which Donovan ignored, as he led her through the shop. She was walking on new sisal runners. She saw every square inch of the place cleaned and organized. They hadn't missed anything. Nothing was the way it had been. When they came to the room where the bucket had been sitting to catch the roof leak, and she pointed, Donovan shook his head.

They had fixed the roof. All ceiling light fixtures in every room had been replaced with chandeliers, all lit. The holiday display was rearranged, with blue LED lights glowing on the Christmas tree. The paintings, prints and posters which had been stacked along the west wall in the back room had been hung throughout the shop. Tiny blue lights festooned display cases and had been threaded along the floor behind a display of old furniture, now in an inviting seating arrangement.

Helen collapsed into one of the overstuffed chairs, hanky at her nose, and began mumbling about money. "This is so much work. You spent so much money. I will pay you. It's so much work. You had to have spent so much, Donovan. I need to go write you a check."

He sat beside her in a brown chair with curved hardwood arms. "Helen. You are not paying us. We talked about this. It can't happen that way. You are intelligent. You know it can't happen that way. You have to say thank you. That's it. I'm leaving. I'll be back. You say thank you and you go about your business, which is selling wonderful old things to people who appreciate them. That's it. You do the work, Helen. We did ours; you do yours."

Helen stood. She put her arms out, beckoning to Donovan. They embraced and she said, "Thank you, Donovan, and thank Tinabelle and the others. You must come back, each and every one of you. You must come back. That's all I ask."

"You got it. We love this place." He started to walk away, then turned back toward her, "And Helen, one more thing."

"Yes?"

"Trenton would be pleased with you, with your shop. He would love this, don't you think?"

Helen was crying again. All she could manage was a nod in the affirmative.

12

SPY MOVE

· ·

Well, there's something to be said for putting yourself
in a little bit of danger.

—Sarah McLachlan

Boon stood. Boon looked. Boon turned around in a circle. He didn't scratch his head. He hit it with the heel of his hand. He walked back and forth. He sat down on the ground and pulled out a granola bar and ate it. He got up and walked to the door of his studio, the back room at Walt's Automotive, and yanked the piece of paper folded and taped on the door off that door and unfolded it and read. Eviction. Failure to perform. New ownership. Effective immediately. It was signed by Timothy, the evil son of Walt, the eldest son, the devil in a pair of coveralls. Boon envisioned him naked, painted red head to foot, holding a screaming baby. He and his wife had a new baby, number four.

Boon had missed the office cleaning chores by taking off with Donovan and experiencing Circus Tantamountism in a yurt in the country. He had forgotten it was his night to clean. The apparent consequence of this lapse was in front of him. Everything had been removed from his studio and now sat scattered around outside the door, quite haphazardly removed. The partial "Love" sculpture lay on its side. His toaster sat there on the ground with a note attached: you were told no food.

"Boon." It was chubby TimBoy in a suit. "Where have you been? Thought you'd ditched. As you can see, that's what's happening. Need the space. Old Pa finally decided to retire; he's gone in two weeks and fur is already flying around here. I'm taking over and the first thing to go is you and your wastoid garbage. Get this shit outta here, like last week. I cannot begin to tell you how happy I am to see you get the hell on down the road, Boon. Never liked you, and now I can say it and do something about it."

"Tim, you are the big man now, look at the rags. Wow! Power move by the man. Congratulations. Fixing cars is a business of great significance in our culture, Tim. You should be proud."

"Don't give me your hippie bullshit, Boon. Get a life, get a job, cut your goddamn hair and wear a decent pair of shoes. But before you do all that, haul this crap outta my line of sight. Not good for business. I have a decorator coming from DeCor Furniture, steamy little number with the biggest jugs on her I've ever seen, and I don't want her to see this junk strewn everywhere. Makes a bad impression. She's coming to set up an office for me, and said she'll show me how it's done." He laughed and ramped his groin toward Boon. "You have an hour. Haul ass."

Boon knew what to do, of course. He walked to the nearest grocery store and asked to borrow a cart for a few hours, promising to return it. He took the largest variety of moving van the store had available, a blue plastic affair, checking the wheels to make sure the thing would roll right, and went back to load his art supplies and the sculpture. He slipped into the bathroom and stole four large garbage bags from the cabinet of cleaning supplies, returning to bag everything. He threw the toaster, two extra cups and two boxes into the trash, along with a bag of broken pieces of things he knew he'd never use. He thought of throwing the sculpture itself out, since it was the biggest thing to handle, but after assessing his progress on it carefully, he decided to keep it. He liked it and he felt it was important to finish it. Love, after all, was important.

He stood there, one bag filled with lighter stuff over his shoulder, the rest of the cart bulging precariously with the sure sign of overload, ready to roll away. The question, of course, was simple: where was he going? He pushed the cart toward Jive Joe's. He needed a cup of coffee and time to think things through. Get organized in his mind. Coffee was needed. A whole lot of things were needed at this singular moment in time, Boon did realize that, but he focused readily on number one: coffee.

No one was there to pay for it, so he told the girl who had served him, "Hit a snag, had to move," he pointed at the unseemly cart, "I'll have to come back and pay later."

She nodded, took change from her tip jar, and put it in the cash register drawer,

"Don't worry about it. It's on me."

"You are a precious gem, little one. I thank you!" He downed the entire thing and placed the empty paper cup in the full trash bin.

He was moving down the street in a direction he hadn't chosen, when he heard a shout. He stopped and looked behind him.

Coffee girl was running toward him. "Hey!"

"Hey! You hate your job? Shouldn't just run out the door on it, might slam shut."

"No, I got Alicia to take over. I just wanted to know if you have somewhere to go."

"Interesting question. I'm Boon. Who are you?"

"Cindy."

"Cindy. You ask a particularly well-imagined question given the ley lines on the sparkle points of this day of opportunity. I am going, that's where."

"I mean, are you OK?"

"Oh, surely, that would be the case in point of perfect fact. Sun always rises, Cindy. You can count on it."

"But do you have a place to go? It looks like you maybe don't have a place to go."

"This concerns you?"

"Well, yeah."

"Tell me why?"

"Well, what if it was me? What if I came in and you bought me a cup of coffee from the tip jar and I went away with a cart of my things saying I'd hit a snag and had to move and looked like I had no place to go, since I obviously had no money to pay for coffee and didn't even have, well, you know. A place. You would probably ask if you could help me, wouldn't you?"

"I would."

"I'm a girl. You're a guy, but same difference to me. You either got a place or you don't."

"And if I don't?"

"Well, we find you one."

"We?"

"We. I can help you find a place."

"You can."

"Yes. Do you need a place?"

"I do."

"OK. Geez. Now. What's all this stuff? Clothes, food?"

"No. Art supplies. I'm an artist. These are my supplies and one of my sculptures."

"I want to see it."

"Right here? Now?"

"Yes."

"OK. We shall display the inner workings of the artistic mind on this sidewalk in the broadest light of the possible day. Prepare yourself, Cindy."

He took out the stump of sculpture, a two foot tall partial column about sixteen inches in diameter. He set it down by a fire hydrant. "There you go. It's called 'Love' and will be about double this when I finish. Tall, not around."

Cindy looked at it carefully, from all sides. "I like it. Put it back in the bag."

"You have an interest in art?" He had the piece back into the bag and reloaded onto the cart.

"Not especially, but my Mom does."

"Your Mom."

"My Mom. That's where you can go, but you'll have to come back to Jive's and put this stuff in my car and wait an hour until I get off. Then I can take you to our house."

"Now, Cindy, you are a visibly kind-hearted little soul, but your Mom should have some say in this, I feel, if it should happen at all. I regard you highly, you are a radiant one, but I must consider the fair soul, surely she is that, who is the mother of Cindy."

"Oh, no, don't worry. She's fine with it."

"You called her then, and asked her? Already? When did you do that?"

"No, no. She doesn't answer. She won't care."

"Cindy. I cannot just show up at a sterling woman's home with these droll black bags and feel right about it. I may not strike you as a man who would care, especially at this swing of the weathervane, but I do. It's not the sum of the things I can do, Cindy."

She started to cry. "Please. You have to."

Boon saw the coming nightmare. He felt the pulse of the broken heart, beating a jagged rhythm with this young girl's tears. He sensed the trouble, he felt the rub, he knew the drill. "Tell me what you mean, Cindy. Don't cry. Let's just sit right here on the grass and I'll hear you out. What gives, girl?"

"I can't do it anymore. She's so bad now. I can't stand it."

"What."

"She's depressed. She's been really, really depressed for ten months, since Dad left. She was depressed before; that's why he left us. I think he found someone else, that's my guess, and I don't blame him. He couldn't take it anymore, but she's worse and no one can help her. She sees people and they give her pills and try to talk to her, but she's just dead inside. Just dead. It's awful."

"You and your Mom live alone?"

"Yes. My brother Sam is in college, in South Carolina. He's a junior."

"How old are you, Cindy?"

"Sixteen."

"Aren't you in high school?"

"I dropped out for now, but I do four classes online and will go back, I think. I'm a terrible student, not like Sam, but I'll graduate early, if I can. I hate school. I take care of Mom and I work."

"Is there enough income for you to support yourselves?"

"Dad pays the mortgage and sends money every month. Mom's on SSI. It comes up for review and it'll be OK, I think. She's worse now than when they gave it to her, well, alive after suicide attempts, but worse. I make my own spending money. We do fine that way."

"OK. Tell you what, I would like to meet your mother. What's her name?"

"Susan."

"Susan. I would like to meet Susan. I will store my things in your car and wait for you to finish your shift. Then we will go meet your mother, but I don't want her to think I've arrived to move in, Cindy. That's not good. It's threatening, to her and to me. I meet her. We talk. We consider things, we let light shine on the subject, no more, no less. Agreed?"

"Fine. I guess so."

"OK. Show me your car, I'll unload and then take this cart back. I'll just wait in the parking lot, sing myself awake."

"No, no. You have to come in. I'll buy you some food and another coffee. Anything you want."

The "anything you want" part did it for Boon. He knew he was in trouble, but true to form, he walked resolutely into the midst of it. He had theories about these sorts of scenarios, of course he would. He recited these theories to himself now: storms pass, disasters never last, release your grasp, never gasp a last breath.

Ask. He was asking: what possible brilliance in the lovelight of human affairs would he encounter at the house of Susan and her fragile little opal named Cindy?

He took the cart back and waited by the car. He was not going into hock mode for "anything you want." He waited by the car.

Cindy came out bawling and got into the car. "Get in. That little bitch, so help me, I cannot believe she did that. She is such a snotty..." She turned to back out, hitting the gas way too hard for Boon's liking.

He grabbed the steering wheel. "Stop. I'm driving. I don't know what's wrong, but the day isn't long enough for me to sit here and risk my life over snotty. Get out and get in. Damn it, Cindy."

He drove. "Where to?"

"Left at the light, then to Yost Road, then right at Woburn. It's a gray house, 2714."

"What happened?"

"I'm fired. Alicia called the boss and told her I took tips and bought you coffee. We're never supposed to do that; Mrs. Lanner says it draws bums. I say, it's my money, I can do what I want with it. She didn't actually fire me; I quit."

"Peachy fine time. So this is news for your mother, depressed and all, might help, is that what you're thinking here, Cindy?"

"You don't have to be mean to me. I know it will upset my mom, Boon. Don't be mean."

"I'm not being mean. I'm seeing the handwriting on the sad wall of 2714."

"Don't."

"It's OK. We handle this like we handle everything else."

"How's that?"

"We get creative. We can't help ourselves. We're artists. Art reigns, it rules, it informs the masses, it attacks the dreary and the forlorn with light sabers in the night and in the day. Whoosh, whoosh, quickest fix on the planet."

"I'm not an artist."

"Yes, you are. You're creative or you wouldn't have some bum driving you home in your car asking if you have any money on you, now would you?"

"You're going to rob me?"

"No. I need some cash. Need to buy some flowers."

"What?"

"Hand over your cash, young lady, the knight errant needs flowers to take to the lady of his dreams. Come on. Play."

"OK. Here's ten. That's all I have."

"That'll do for the three yellow roses which signify the intent, the dream and the happy ending. I'll try to get the blooms they sprinkle with gold dust. They work best."

"Are you crazy?"

"Should be. Hope so. Try to be." He pulled into a supermarket at the corner of Woburn and Isaac. "Sit tight and meditate. I'll be right back, blooms in tow."

* * * * *

The house was gray. Inside and out. Boon tried, he really did, to find some color, some sign of life, but didn't succeed. The roses he held in his hand were it: color. He handed them over. "Susan,

I am Boon and I have brought you flowers for the sunshine in your heart."

"Who the hell are you?"

"Boon."

"Get out."

"Well, we're getting along. I like that. Honesty, and all. I think I'll just have a seat and watch you smell the flowers."

Susan threw them on the floor.

Boon picked them up and handed them to Cindy, "Cindy, put these in some water, if you would. We need them hydrated and safe from women who cast them about as if they have no *significance*." He turned back to Susan. "Now, we should get to the bottom of the murky load that is your mind, Susan, and lighten that load. Shine the flashlight around, see what we can find as a foothold to crawl out."

"Who the hell are you and where did you come from?"

"Pluto. Took a flying leap just in the last twenty minutes and landed on my feet in Susan's neighborhood. Heard some moanin' and came over. What seems to be your problem?"

"My problem? You don't *see* my problem?"

"I so far see these things. I see a pretty woman who has let herself go to shit. I see this woman's daughter who is a delightful little thing who probably has an eating disorder and needs help with her education. She's a dandy. I see a woman named Susan who has probably thankfully been left behind by a man who found something he thinks is better. He is mistaken, of course, but that's to Susan's advantage. He pays the mortgage and sends monthly money because he's feeling guilty. All good. No woman needs a man around who is somewhere else, even if he's a good man, which I assume this man is. Now, I also see a dump of a house which not enough people give a damn about and I see a wasting away in a muddle of pity party that's pathetic. That's what I see for starters. Haven't looked around, but I suspect I'll find unmade beds and a dirty bathroom and no food in the fridge. I see the TV's on, which is a clear sign that this place is in the throes of death itself. That's what I see."

"And I suppose you have a recommendation. Such an asshole."

"I do and I can be. Orifices are good for releasing festering putridity of the soul, Susan."

Susan shuddered. "Disgusting."

"Recommendations. Yes. I have them. I say shut off the TV. I say shower. Put on clean clothes. Put on some classical music. Cindy and I will make dinner." He stood, grabbed Cindy's hand and headed for the kitchen. "I say, let's party."

Boon whispered to Cindy, "I don't cook. Find something. I'll clean up around here."

They worked away at the place together, until Cindy said she had dinner ready. The table was set for a macaroni and cheese and salad meal with a bunch of grapes and pecan cookies from a package. Susan appeared, but had not showered. The roses were in a vase in the center of the table, gold sparkles and all.

Boon was tickled. "This is the superb deal, mac and cheese is exactly what I'd have ordered tonight in a fine restaurant, which is generally where I have my evening meal, independently wealthy gentleman that I am."

Susan countered, "You're some bum Cindy picked up off the damn street to come over here and help her out."

"To come over here and help you out. Give the kid credit, Susan. She knows when she can't handle something by herself anymore. She's a brainy little number, the Cindy is."

"That's a sick joke. She's as dumb and desperate as I am."

Boon stood, clanging on the edge of the plate with his fork. "I have a speech. Hear ye, hear ye."

"You are nuts. God, Cindy, what were you thinking?"

"Sorry, Mom."

"No sorry now, ladies. Let's do this. I speak to you now as an emissary from the planet Pluto. This is how we dress and speak on Pluto."

"Jeans and a t-shirt?" Cindy had to ask.

"Yup, regulation. We all look just like this and we speak thusly: The time has come. We are taking over. There will be no more dumb and no more dumber and no more TV and no more of no more. No morose. No more depressed desperation dished out in dollops of dolorous diphthong. There are lives to live on this planet and only three of them are in this room as I speak to you. We need to reach out. Embrace your Plutonian friends and your fellow Earthians. Let's cut the crap, here, Susan. I'm going to finish my mac and cheese, and then have four or five cookies and some grapes, if you don't mind."

"Then what?" Susan shook her head in dismay.

"Then I need a place to stay. I want my things brought in from the car—Cindy, that's you, girl—and I'd like to be given a room where I can work on my sculpture. In exchange, I will contribute food, my entire food stamp allotment, which is available tomorrow. Should I find a wad of bills on the sidewalk, I'll hand that over, too, after I tie it up with a red satin ribbon. But, I make this clear: I cannot create in a negative space. I expect a positive environment for creation. It's essential and I must have that firmly in place or I'll leave now. I am an artist of some note, my sculptures are installed all over this city, and I must have a clean-spirited, enlivened space. The taint so far has been rather severe and I must protect the aura." He stood and took his plate to the sink, washed it, put it in the rack and returned to the table. "Well, has the assembly voted?"

Cindy got up and headed for the front door, on her way to the car.

Susan sat there staring at him. "I..." she stopped, shaking her head.

"That's good. That's a start. You have a kid to raise. I'm not a parent, but it's always been my understanding that the other way around doesn't work too well. Be strong, Susan. We might end up together some day, you never know."

"You don't even know me! What are you talking about? You're crazy!"

"Should be. Hope so. Try to be."

13

DONOVAN'S ROOF

. . . .

So yo then man what's your story?
—DAVID FOSTER WALLACE

It came to pass, of course it had to. The day came, a week later, when Donovan Trenton King embraced his mission. He appeared at Good Fortune Antiques as Helen was unlocking the front door. He had someone with him, a man named Frank Hunt. He had rehearsed the meeting with Helen King many, many times. He knew what he had to say. He knew it would be the most difficult conversation of his life, and hers. He had explained to Frank that he needed maybe an hour with Helen before Frank could talk business. Frank claimed he needed to look around anyway and intended to be on the roof. They had an extension ladder in the back of Donovan's pickup: he would carry on.

"Good morning, Helen. You look really lovely today. Is that a new dress?"

"It is! Donovan! I'm so glad to see you. You wouldn't believe the interest I've had in this place! Business has been much better. It's just made such a difference!"

"Well, that's good. That's what I hoped would happen. Now, Helen, we need to talk. Can we go back where the furniture is and have a chat? You can hear people come in from back there. I have some things to discuss. While we do that, I have a man on the roof, assessing some things. His name is Frank Hunt. You'll meet him later."

"What's going on?"

"Let's go back." They went to the couch and to the same chair they'd occupied following the blitz and Donovan began, "Helen, my full name is Donovan Trenton King. I am legally your stepson, or would be if my father were still alive."

"What? You're what?"

"Trenton had a son. He didn't know it. I never met him. I am that son."

"How is that possible?"

Donovan scooted his chair closer and took her hand. "This is complicated, but I thought you would want to know. You need to know because I've found you and you and I...well, let me explain first."

Helen had a look of terror, "No! What is this?"

"Helen, just listen. I was adopted after my mother, Katherine Townes Bennett, Trenton's cousin, gave birth to me and I was put up for adoption. Trenton was the father, who was sent to Africa for missionary work when his parents, devout Christians, discovered a sexual alliance between the cousins had developed. He was gone six years and was never told Katherine was pregnant with his child. She died two weeks after delivering me and I was put up for adoption. She gave me life and my father's name; that's what she was able to do."

"This is horrible! He didn't tell me any of this!"

"He didn't know, Helen. I'm sure of this. As far as I can find out, he never knew of Katherine's death, even. He was told she had moved away; in fact her family did move away, to Canada.

"When Trenton returned from Africa, he became involved with a man of disreputable character, a Bob Vicker, Robert Yost Vicker, and his daughter Pauline. Trenton was working at a halfway house, he was a social worker, and became connected in some way that I can't really explicate, in criminal activity. He was arrested as an accessory in a money laundering operation, extortion, and sentenced to six years in prison. He was given early release after four years due to health reasons; he had to have heart surgery and a long convalescence. Pauline, of course, was in this picture, and at first I thought she was my mother."

"Prison! Pauline! Can't be! I don't know anything about any of this, except the heart thing. I know about that. How do you know all this?"

"It has taken me a long time to unravel this. I began researching my adoption only a year ago. I was adopted as a seven-month-old by the Reinharts, Richard and Evelyn, of San Francisco, who encouraged my research. They are corporate attorneys, both of them, and helped me through it."

"But you would be a Reinhart, then."

"I was Donovan Trenton Reinhart until about six months ago, when I changed my name back to King. My parents supported that, knowing that I've wanted to find my birth parents all my life. It took me a great deal of time and effort to find you, Helen. Apparently, my father took considerable care to erase his past and the ability to track him, which seems obvious now, since you know nothing of his history."

"He was such a good man, Donovan. He wasn't a criminal! I loved him so much." She was crying.

"I know he was. I know that."

"Have you found anyone else who knew him?"

"No. His parents are deceased. He had no siblings. You and I are the only connections left."

"How did you find me?"

"Medical records. He had another surgery in this state, the year before he died. Your name was on the hospital records as his wife, but it took me a long time to actually find you. There was a different address, a different town, Haines, listed as domicile, and no mention of an antique store, of course. All I had was your name and there's very scanty information on you. I couldn't access Social Security records, so I had no address and couldn't locate you in Haines. It's by sheer luck that I found you."

"How did you find me?"

"Well, I teach at a film school in San Francisco and the circus performers you met come up here for a kind of summer camp. Some of them have been my students. I visit on occasion, and I was walking around in Langlois Historical District one day, a little over three months ago, and saw Helen's Antiques. It was the oddest moment. Something came over me; I wasn't thinking about my father or anything, but the sign stopped me dead in my tracks on the sidewalk and I wondered: could it be? I knew Trenton had died, that was easy to find, but I wanted to find you. I researched property records and found Trenton King as the owner of this shop. You haven't transferred the deed, Helen. I'm surprised they haven't had you do that. It's been so long. Anyway, I realized that you, Helen, are my father's widow. I wanted to meet you, and I am very glad I did. It's taken me some time to get to this meeting, but I'm here." He leaned over and hugged her. "You are family to me; the only connection I've ever had to my father. He must have loved you so much."

"Oh, my. This confuses me. He didn't tell me. I don't know. I don't understand why you've done so much here..."

"Why wouldn't I, Helen? It's what I can do, something I can do for you, and for his memory. As I said, I think he would have been pleased."

"I still have a feeling, something else..."

"There is something else."

"What? What is it?"

"My father died young, too, too young."

"His heart. He had a bad heart."

"I know. I have the same kind of heart."

She stared at him. "No! You..."

"Yes. One of the reasons I began the research for my father is because of a congenital heart defect, which may shorten my life as well. The doctors were insistent that I find birth records and possible inherited tendencies in an effort to historically analyze my condition, which is quite rare. My father also suffered from it. You know all about this. There is not one case on record of anyone with this condition living as long as Trenton King did."

"You are dying."

"No, Helen, I am not dying. However, my father's records have been increasingly important as I've grown older, and they have been helpful. Everything is being done to assure me a longer life. I've had two successful surgeries. I will be on medication and monitored for the rest of my life. Trenton King's records have been invaluable for research, and for my treatment."

She had her head in her hands. "This is too much. I don't understand."

"Yes, you do understand, Helen. He loved you. You loved him. His memory is secure and powerful in your life and now I'm here. I want to get to know you, I want to be in your life. That's why I'm here."

She leaned over and hugged him. "Donovan, you are just like him, you know. You don't look like him, you don't look anything like him, but you are just like him."

Donovan teared up. "Thank you, Helen. Thank you, for telling me that. It means so much to me." In truth, it was a mix of feelings for Donovan, not all pleasant, and he stood and walked around in the small space, regaining his composure. "We need to go talk to Frank. I heard the door. I think he's up front waiting for us." He reached down and helped her up. "You might be interested in what Frank has to say." He winked at her.

Frank was standing with a folder in front of him, reviewing papers at the cash register. "There you are. Helen King? I'm Frank Hunt, architect."

"Architect?"

"Architect. Hunt, Jackman and Pierce, local."

"Why are you here?"

"I'm here to ask your permission to install a glass-roofed gallery on top of your building."

"A what?"

Donovan filled her in, "Over the last couple of months, I've taken some liberties, no question. I did the historical research, secured a building permit, have approval from the committee in charge of renovation in this district, and propose, with your permission, to install a second floor art gallery, a sculpture gallery, above your shop. At a later date, we may install shades for easel shows."

"I live here! Cleaning up was one thing, but I hate building, all the noise and disruption. I don't know anything about art galleries, Donovan! What are you thinking? This is not what I want! It's an antique store!"

Donovan nodded at Frank. "Show her the specs, Frank."

Frank pulled out a huge sheet and unfolded it. "Here you go, Helen. This is what it would look like."

Helen stared at the drawing of her flat-roofed shop. It now had a second floor, a four-sided glass structure with a pitched roof. "There's no way to get to it! This is high!"

"There would be an interior spiral staircase, wrought iron. It's ready." Frank pointed to the sheet.

"This is too much. Too much of a big deal. I don't have any art. This is ridiculous. Too much work, a mess. Too much money. I don't have this kind of money."

Donovan motioned for them all to sit down in the three chairs he'd dragged over.

"Sit, Helen. I can explain. It won't cost you a dime."

"I doubt that. This is ridiculous."

Donovan ignored the comment. "Now. Here's what this means. One. The structure has been built. It's in five pieces, plus a prefab floor. Cranes will come in back and it can be assembled and placed on the roof of this building in one day. That's why Frank is here. We've been working on this for three months. He has hired the contractors to build the structure and to secure it. He has the spiral staircase ready for installation, which requires an afternoon to create an opening in the ceiling, right there." He pointed to the ceiling to the left of the cash register. The noise and disarray will commence for about two hours, during which you and Fox will have to be elsewhere. I'll take you to lunch, whatever. You'll have to close the shop for that short time."

"But I don't want to close the shop, Donovan. I don't want to go to lunch. Fox will hate this!"

"Fox will be fine, Helen, and it wouldn't hurt you to get out of here once in awhile."

"But what art? There will be a big glass thing up there with nothing in it!"

"Not so. It will be filled. I have several pieces in a warehouse ready to install. A docent from Payne..."

"What's Payne? What's a docent? God, Donovan."

"Where I teach. A gallery volunteer will come and place the pieces in the gallery. You won't have to do a thing except take the money when they sell and split it with the artist."

"I don't know any artists."

"I know plenty of sculpture artists and have things all lined out."

Arnold! Do you never knock? God, I sit back here typing away in the dark and there you are, lurking. Knock, for Christ's sake. Scare me to death.

You knew I was coming back.

Did you get it? Your car?

I did and I am seriously pissed.

What happened?

Well, I go to pick it up, it took them three days longer than they said it would, and now I know why. They did every damn thing they could think of and didn't even call me first. The bill was $650 fucking dollars and should have been $300, in fact that's what they quoted.

Where was this? Let me guess. Ben's Automotive.

Yes. Never goin' back there; I'll tell you that.

Yeah. It's bad. I had it happen, too. When Ben retired, his son and daughter took over and they are crooked. Just not running the place the way their Dad did. I can't stand the oldest one, Ken. Creepy and crooked. I go to Jay Chevrolet. Much better. Go there.

Do you ever change your clothes?

What?

Change your clothes. You are always wearing the same thing. That hat, the vest, that gray fleece shirt, the jeans with bleach stains, the slipper socks. Do you sleep in those clothes?

No. I have my pajamas underneath. I just take off a couple of layers to sleep and put them back on in the morning. I change if I go to town, when I go to sit my grandson. What's it to you, Arnold?

Nothin'. Fine. Eccentric writer. Goofy. Fine. Sleep in your clothes. Wear your pajamas 24/7. Whatever. How's it going? The hilarious antics of Boon?

Next question out of Arnold's mouth will be: does Boon have a woman yet?

Well, does he?

He does.

Well, finally fuckin' finally. What's she like?

Is she hot? That's your next question. You are the most pre-dictable man I've ever met, Arnold. The most.

Yeah, so what? What's she look like?

Well, she's got dirty hair, she's in the toilet with clinical de-pression, she's on SSI, she lives in a tacky, messy gray house. Her husband left her for another woman, which means she's way married, and she has a kid, a teenager.

Yuk! Who wants to read about that? Nobody, Babette. God, there's enough of that shit in the world, I don't need to pick up a book and have to read about more of it. Besides. This is sup-posed to be funny and this is supposed to be the story of our hero, Boon. Sounds like he's doing more and more of the loser routine to me. It's bad, Babette. Rethink yourself. Maybe you should start over.

Out. Go. Be gone. Arnold, you are not helping. I appreciate the advice, but I am working. Just go. Live your stupendously exciting, glorious, funny life.

Cira and I had a big argument.

Well, great. Go deal with Cira. Sounds like that script needs a little work. You do your thing and I'll do mine.

Helen was getting impatient. "What does that mean?"

"Well, I've decided to just choose one artist for the gala opening and do a retrospective. It makes a stronger initial impression."

"Gala? Retrospective? I don't know what any of that means, Donovan, and I can't see why I need to. And when is this all sup-posed to happen?"

"Right away. All that's needed is your signature on several documents; Frank will go through them with you. It's just ap-proval from the owner of the property to make these changes. No money, I repeat, no money involved. Permission. That's what we need from you, Helen, this very morning, in the next ten minutes if possible. I have worked hard on this and I'd appreciate your encouragement." He walked outside and stood under the sign.

Frank began, "Now, Helen, do you want to read through these yourself or would you like me to just tell you what you're signing?"

"Neither. I'll just sign. It won't mean anything to me, anyway. Pointless. I'll just sign. He reminds me so much of Trenton. This is exactly the kind of thing Trenton would do. In fact, this is how he bought the shop, just came in one day and had a whole new life outlined for us. I went along then; I'll go along now. I don't see how any of this is going to work, but I'll go along with it. What choice do I have?"

14

RAISING CINDY RAISING BOON

· ·

Art saved my life.
—SHARON D. WISE

Poor Boon had never experienced so much slog and woe in his life. Susan was the source, Susan was the nemesis, Susan was the constant niggling detail in Boon's environment which drove him crazier than he thought it sane to be driven. She rode him.

"Boon. I can't stand that noise; what are you doing?"

"I'm sanding a ceramic shard with a sheet of sandpaper on a block. I am not making much noise, Susan, but I'll shut the door. Maybe if you didn't stand right there in the hall watching me, it wouldn't bother the silken linings of your pretty ears."

"It's not bothering my ears, it's bothering my brain."

Everything, it seemed, bothered Susan's brain. "Well, move your brain basket into the next room, Susan, you silly old squirrel." There was an edge to this remark, the edge produced by the eighth day of Susan's bothered brain.

"Don't call me old and silly. I am not old and silly. That would be you, Boon. Old fart who thinks he's a big artist. This is junk. I don't see art and I don't see any point to it. You say you have stuff installed all over town. Sure you do. This crap wouldn't be left behind the supermarket next to a dumpster for long. Somebody would throw it in and it would be hauled off to the dump, which is where it belongs. You're just wasting your life jacking off, Boon. This cobbled-up mess is drivel. I was a watercolorist at one time. Flowers and plants. I know art when I see it and this isn't art."

He stood there, considering this connection of a couple of things Boon thought about quite a bit. His instinctive response to Susan was to consider putting down the sandpaper, grabbing her and kissing her passionately, professing his love—of course, he would remember to do that—and flinging her onto the floor, right where she now stood, and ravishing the hell out of her, but we know Boon: he didn't do it. He didn't do it, not out of strong moral fiber, but because of fiber of another sort which lay limp and unresponsive to Susan in a skimpy nightgown. Boon was mad at her. She wasn't going to get his time of day, much less his precious light saber. No: she could go back to her bed and languish some more in self-pity and surliness. He was getting tired of Susan and often knew exactly why her husband had left. She was negative, with bells on, constantly. She complained, literally, about the air she breathed and when Boon opened a window, she complained that it was drafty. When he shut it, she said the sound hurt her brain. Boon decided she didn't have one. He also decided he would find somewhere else to live.

He decided to leave several times a day, but then Cindy would appear and in two seconds, Boon was recommitted. She didn't have a job. She worked hard cooking and cleaning. She spent time on the computer in her room, ostensibly doing school work, but every time Boon went in, she was watching music videos. She and her mother argued constantly about things which amazed Boon: the location of a sock, the proper way to fold a towel, the name for a cloud formation, the problem with a door, the apportionment of the money from the husband, the haircut Cindy got free from a girlfriend, the changing of channels on the TV which still enthroned itself in their lives.

A breakthrough conversation between the two women sent Boon into wild and crazy: instantly, totally, ruthlessly. He breathed fire at them, he was the dragon. He would consume these damsels. He would take this dwelling as his kingdom.

"I do, too."

"You do not."

"Yes, I do, Mom. I know more about this than you do."

"You certainly do not. He's closer to my age than yours, Cindy. I know."

"Yes, but it isn't about age, Mom. It's about style. Authenticity, it's called. You can't just turn him into Dad, Mom. He's not Dad."

"Well, fine, but we have to do something."

"I agree."

When Boon heard these two words, he knew he was hanging in the gallows. The rope was around his neck and there was a guy with his fat foot poised to kick the bucket out from under his feet. He had ten seconds, tops, to save his own life.

"I'm hearing the chatterbirds. I'm hearing the Boon name basketballed around on the court of linguistic fancy. I see death and fire and nonsense. What gives?"

"We think you should change your look." Cindy blurted it right out, quite forcibly.

"What's wrong with my look?"

Susan had her say. "It's tired. It's old. It's been done, Boon. It's what you were doing thirty years ago, Boon. It's like me if I walked around in a little pinafore and pigtails sucking on a lollipop."

Boon thought about this. The image kinda turned him on; it certainly was more evocative than the half-dressed, limp-breasted crone with stringy hair and no make-up standing before him. "It's not that bad. I just don't think packaging is the path to righteousness."

"Well, path to righteousness is one thing, path down a dead end is another. It's a dead end look, Boon. We want to help you with a make-over." Cindy clapped her hands lightly in mock excitement. In truth, she thought it might be a lot of work for nothing. Boon was pretty old. Cindy, being young and agile, was running full speed ahead of the dragon's fire. "Lexie is coming over and will cut your hair. And Dad left clothes, lots of clothes, which he said we should throw away. I think they'll fit. I don't know about the shoes, but we'll have to see."

The old dragon stood on his haunches and blurted out a final burst of flame, "You wouldn't do this to Boon."

"Oh, we aren't doing it *to* you; we're doing it *for* you. It will be fun! You won't recognize yourself."

Boon thought about this. He hadn't recognized himself since he'd set foot inside the door of this gray hen house.

"Come with me, Boon."

The dragon was led away. His scales were shorn, his whole beautiful green naked body was swathed in human being clothing so foreign to Boon that he felt he might have died. The way dead bodies look in caskets, so unreal, so much better than they ever looked in real life, came to him. Even the damn shoes fit: odd crocodile-nosed slip on things with a tassel.

The damsels squealed unattractively. They made him put this on, then that. They kept comparing him to various movie stars in an especially aggravating way: He was Brad Pitt, except older, thinner, taller and not as cute. He was Liam Neeson, except blonder and not as rugged, maybe not as handsome, maybe more handsome, without the tragic. He was Peter O'Toole, except better looking, though not as talented and not as dead. They thought maybe Lawrence of Arabia was dead. He could be an older, tougher version of Leonardo DiCaprio, but his eyes were wrong and he was too extroverted. They decided he looked most like a blonde George Clooney, but taller, with a sprinkle of Liam. They found consensus in this. Yes, George Neeson, a new breed, that's what Lexie called him.

He turned from the full-length mirror and addressed them, quickly, while there was a nanosecond pause in their chattering, "It's Doddson Kooper-Boon, ladies, at your service."

They shut up and stood there and stared at the clothing Boon himself had chosen. They had been so busy doing movie stars, they hadn't been paying attention. He was wearing black boots, tight black leather pants, and a flowing black silk shirt with pirate sleeves, hanging over the waistband of the pants. He'd unbuttoned it down two buttons and rolled up the cuffs. It had a mandarin collar.

"Well, doesn't anyone have anything brilliant and wondrous to say as Boon becomes a pirate of the Caribbean?"

They looked at each other. They didn't smile, they didn't speak. They didn't frown, they didn't say one thing.

"Man, you've been cast. I can see it. A spell was cast here! I'd better look around. Some evil necromancer lurks. He's cast a spell on my women! Where is he? I will find him and vanquish him." He left the room and went to what was now called Boon's studio and went to work.

Cindy was first. "Oh, my God."

"Incredible. What happened?" Lexie whispered.

Susan was the oldest and wisest, of course. "Tell you one thing, Lexie. I'm next. Give me a haircut. A facial. Cindy. Get into my room and lay out three outfits. Just three. Nothing black and nothing pastel. I'll do the underwear myself. And bring my make-up kit in for Lexie. It's in the bottom drawer in the bathroom; I think that's where I last saw it."

* * * * *

Boon didn't recognize himself, and not because his clothes were different. It was because he was driving a car on what Cindy called "a family outing." This was a sunny afternoon outing, with Boon in his black drama and Susan gussied up in a tight red dress with a deep V decolletage with a bit of black lace showing.

Her hair, now a burnt ochre color, was cut in a sharp blunt pageboy which had been blow-dried and swept to one side, held rigidly in place by a gallon of hair spray. She wore a great deal of makeup, including false eyelashes and bright red lipstick outlined in black. She wore long, dangly, fat red faux-pearl earrings and sling-back high heels with stockings. The final blow was a slit in the skirt up her thigh. She smelled like hair spray and looked like hell.

Cindy was also problematic. She wore a cropped tank top thing that looked more like a bra than anything else, at least to Boon's fashion sensibility, with tiny spaghetti straps. Her belly was showing. Her belly button was showing above tight hip-hugger jeans. Her toenails were painted black with silver stars on them. She had braided her short brown hair, with only two braids hanging on either side of her face like handles. Boon felt she belonged in her room, on Facebook.

Where were they going on this family outing? Well, it was Cindy's idea: an art tour. Boon was to take them around the city and show them his art installations and then they were going out to dinner: Chinese. Susan was buying. Boon, of course, had severe reservations, just about every which way from Sunday through Saturday about this tour, and said so, to himself in the mirror before leaving for the car. His art was buried in unlikely places. He didn't want to see it buried in unlikely places. He didn't want them to see it buried in unlikely places, like the entrance to a welding supply store in an industrial park. He didn't want to go to dinner with what looked and acted like Annie Sprinkle, dressed for a change in public, and a munchkin sex teen, who was chewing neon blue gum. George Clooney wouldn't be caught dead in this situation; he would not. Neither would Liam Neeson. Boon, caught alive in the situation, willed himself (temporarily) dead.

It went badly from the first turn of the key in the ignition. The car wouldn't start.

Boon got out, popped the hood and wiggled things. The distributor cap, the spark plugs, hoses, then had a thought. He put the hood down and turned the key again to see what the gas gauge did. Nothing. The car was out of gas.

"Cindy, the car is out of gas. This is fuel-injected. You can't let it run out of gas. Do you have a gas can?"

"Cindy, I've told you a hundred times. Keep the car gassed up. I might have an emergency. When you have someone ill in the house, you make sure you have a vehicle. You have to start using your head!"

"Well, now. No gas can, I take it. Yes, that's a no. OK. I'll go in the garage and look for one, then walk to a gas station."

Cindy handed over a ten dollar bill. "Here. I can go. You could stay here with Mom and I could go get it."

"No, no. I'll do it. Just sit tight." Ah, reprieve. A walk. Maybe he should just keep walking. He'd hit the ocean eventually.

They took off twenty minutes later, on their way to the closest installation, at the library. No sculpture. Boon explained that maybe it had been moved inside; they'd talked about it, and the library was closed. Too bad. The next one was gone, and the next, and the next. They were all gone. After the third no-show of the sixteen Boon sculptures, he stopped trying to explain what might have happened. He was glum, stricken dumb, stumped.

Susan, of course, called it as she saw it: no big loss, quite a gain, actually, because now she and her gullible daughter knew the truth about Boon. He was a fraud. He wasn't an artist; his work was slop, if it even existed. He had lied. He was an opportunist;

he was a snake. He was another slime-ball man who took women for *rides.*

Boon longed for the little girl in pinafore and pigtails sucking on a lollipop. At least the mouth would be engaged in something other than this diatribe against not only himself but his entire sex. He was sorely afraid that if she called his art "slop" one more time, he would park the car and get out. Maybe if she didn't say it one more time he would park the car and get out.

Cindy, of course, believed Boon. She felt sad; his art had been stolen. "I think it's amazing that someone liked every single one of your pieces so much that they stole *all* of them." She mumbled quietly in Boon's direction, "I think maybe you should be happy with this; it means someone really appreciates what you did."

Susan heard her. "I am telling you, Cindy, you are the dumbest little thing sometimes. I don't know why you have no common sense whatsoever. I just don't know what I'm going to do with you. Look at the mess you've gotten us into with this man. It's a *man*, Cindy. We have no idea what he's capable of. He lied. God, Cindy. I swear, you are just as clueless and stupid as your father."

Boon pulled over in front of KFC, shut off the engine and yanked on the parking brake. "I have something edging on important to say to you, Susan. Cindy, would you run in there and get yourself something grandiose—chicknugs, Coke, something—so I can talk to your Mom a minute?"

"Sure." She went inside.

Boon turned on Susan. "Susan. You should be ashamed of yourself. I mean it. I am madder than hell. I didn't lie to you and you know it; I've just lost thirty years of my work and all you can do is rant and riot about Cindy and men. You need to listen to me. You are a mean, spoiled brat. You are a nasty, negative bitch who somehow has done a beautiful job raising Cindy. She is exceptional, Susan. I never, ever want to hear you call her dumb or stupid or just like her father. I will not hear a man who fathered that child maligned. Not now, not ever. The way you've been acting, I'm positive Cindy is like her father and not like her mother. Her father must be great; her mother is awful." He caught his breath for a few seconds as Susan cried. "You need to get a grip, stop thinking with your wounded heart, your lame brain and your lonely cunt. Get over this fucking shit, Susan, and be decent. Depression is one thing, but I am sorry; most of your behavior has nothing to do with depression, it has to do with self-ishness. You are a beautiful, bright woman. I happen to dig you, or could if I could see my way through the shitstorm, but if you don't get straightened out and stop this bullshit, I'm gone. Like right this minute. I'll go in and say goodbye to the kid, which breaks my heart, and I'll let you drive your own sorry, snarly ass home. You can wear your red-tag rags to bed, for all I fucking care." He took a breath, blew it out and punch-lined, "You do have a nice ass, by the way." He reached for the door handle and had one leg out, when she grabbed him, yanked him back in, pulled him into her arms and clung to him, bawling, black mascara tears streaming down her face.

Cindy came back with three bags of food and three drinks and stood by the car, looking around to see if anyone might be witnessing this embarrassing scene. She waited a couple of minutes, crawled into the back seat and cheerfully exclaimed, "Let's go home! I have food for all of us! Even mashed potatoes and gravy!"

15

EXCEPTIONAL DISPERSION

· ·

When all is said and done, there is no advice to be given.
—WILLIAM JAMES

Jerald Redding rebelled. He ached. He stewed. He lost sleep. He spent more time looking out the window than he did working. His world had been rocked and he didn't have enough information. Not having enough information had never happened to Jerald before. Perfection in the gathering of knowledge was Jerald's edge in life, his specialty, his blanket, his thumb. He developed a headache which lasted days. He found it difficult to eat. The leap from small to gigantic was too much for Jerald.

Small changes he could handle: Boon's new sign and the name change on Helen's shop in his business neighborhood he could accommodate. He had dreams about it after it happened and did have to consciously adjust himself to the new sign, but he had done it. When they repainted the door to his building red instead of forest green, it had taken him two weeks, but he had accepted it.

When two men came in and cheerfully informed Jerald that his phone service was being upgraded to include voicemail and caller ID options, Jerald had, after three months, learned to like the improvements. He didn't like the slim modern handset, however, and never would.

The next new thing Jerald had watched happen was the arrival of a small white pickup with the Langlois Historical District logo on the door. It parked and a woman began unloading flowering bedding plants in a light rain, quickly planting them within and around the brick hearts in Good Fortune's outdoor planter. He noted the preponderance of what he assumed, from his distant viewing perch, must be geraniums, to which Jerald was allergic. That was one day.

The next day, two cars parked and two men went in to Helen's shop and came back out after a very few minutes with no purchase packages. They left, but then he saw them on Helen's roof. He had witnessed a man on the roof rather recently, but it was a different man. He had witnessed men on Helen's roof before: strange men in raggy clothes with a bucket of tar, obviously doing a repair. He had documented the day of twenty-one people, a day about which he was still having nightmares. He had watched carefully for Helen after they left; she was alive. He saw her lock the front door.

But now, something else was happening. Huge cranes were parked in back, in the alley. They were dropping enormous beige panels onto the roof. Now workmen were on the roof, lifting these panels and securing them. It was flooring. Another load of panels was dropped. It was top flooring. They secured it in sections. Then a glass panel appeared. Drills were heard. The panel hung there in the air. A second panel, a third, a fourth, and then

Jerald, anticipating a roof, of course, was still astonished when the huge structure came floating through the air and was positioned on the glass walls. It frightened him. He was sweating. It was too much. When a large truck with a flatbed trailer pulled up in front and four men hauled a huge black spiral object into the store, Jerald logged off his computer, stood up in a state of extreme agitation, and determined that he would go over and inquire. It was time for lunch; it was sitting on his desk, but he had no appetite. He was worried about Helen. Maybe she had sold the shop. Maybe she wasn't there anymore. Maybe she was gone. Maybe she didn't own the shop anymore. Maybe he would never see her again. These thoughts frightened Jerald as, for the first time, really, he admitted to himself that he cared about Helen. He admitted it: he fancied her.

Had Jerald felt this before? No. Jerald's experience with fancying was limited quite specifically to gems, selective art and even more selective nature. He was fond of inland bays, stands of white birch and the golden eagle. Gigantic, professionally custom-framed photographs of these three preferences were displayed in his office. As for the art, he would not be specific: he liked what he liked. He had frequented galleries around the world as a younger man, and regarded himself as uncommonly knowledgeable in this area, but he did not invest in art. He invested in gems. This investment task had been so consuming that Jerald had never invested in people. He had done rather well with gems; he couldn't say he'd done poorly with people, he had many friends and was regarded as a very nice man, but he had never had a relationship. Lovely opportunities had presented, but Jerald had stepped back, literally and figuratively, as many as a dozen times.

So what was it about Helen? She was his age and she didn't know anything about him, but she had cried when he bought the things in her shop. He couldn't forget how poignantly she had held his check, a rather modest check to Jerald. It was touching. She had moved him.

He moved in her direction. He was crossing the street when a black pickup pulled up and a slim, attractive man got out. He was met by Helen at the front door of the shop, carrying a cat carrier, which the man took. She was moving out! He knew it! This was the new owner! He had seen this man before, four times. This was the man who had helped Boon hang the sign! This was the man who came with the twenty people! And with another man who spent time on the roof doing nothing. Of course, this was the new owner. Jerald was dashed. He was taking her away. He stood there, half a block away, stopped in his forward progress by a chilling thought that this might be the very last time he would see Helen.

She saw him standing there and called out, "Mr. Redding, hello! Please come over here. I have someone for you to meet." She smiled and waved Jerald toward her.

"Helen, good morning, although I must amend that, since I believe the noon hour has passed. How are you today?"

"Well, as you can see, I am having quite a time of it. Mr. Redding, this is my step-son, Donovan Trenton King. Donovan, my favorite customer, Mr. Jerald Redding, the gemologist." Donovan had heard the Jerald story by now, of course, and hopped to it.

"Mr. Redding! I am delighted!" He shook his hand. "You must join us for lunch. I'm taking Helen out to Fiona's for Sicilian. You must, you really must come. Would you join us as my guest? We have exciting news to share with you as a most valued customer. Please come."

Helen added pressure. "You must join us, Jerald, you must. I never go out to lunch, and the whole prospect scares me. You would make me so much more comfortable. Fox and I are displaced for a couple of hours and I can't say I'm adjusting all that well to what's going on. Surely you've noticed. I could use some soul support. Please come."

The use of his first name added considerably to Jerald's confusion. He stood there a minute and then replied, "I'd be happy to join you. I will go get my car and meet you at Fiona's." He needed time. He didn't know if he could do it. He didn't eat in restaurants. They weren't assuredly clean. There was no way to know how sanitary the kitchen was. So many people handled the food. He felt sick, standing there, thinking about having this lunch, actually having to eat this lunch. The only saving grace was Sicilian. Jerald loved Sicilian cuisine; he knew about Fiona's but had never been there, of course. He'd stayed in Taormina for six months; one of his favorite sights on earth was Isola Bella. He loved Sicily, but he still felt sick.

"Wonderful! We'll see you there. We have reservations, so just come in and ask for the King party. I'll tell them we are expecting you."

* * * * *

"Mr. Redding?"

"Yes." How did this young man know his name? Jerald shook his head. This was difficult.

"The King party is just this way, sir. Welcome to Fiona's."

Donovan stood. "Hi, welcome, Mr. Redding, please." He pulled out a chair and seated Jerald himself.

"Thank you, son. I do believe you might call me Jerald."

"And I'm Donovan, remember. We've ordered wine." They sat quietly watching the wine steward present the bottle, open it, pour for the tasting and wait for Donovan's approval. "Superb! Really!" He smiled and nodded and three glasses were filled.

"Taste this! It's so full-bodied and fragrant! Perfect for Sicilian! I propose a toast." The glasses were dutifully lifted as Donovan proclaimed, "To good fortune all around, to my dear Mother, Helen, and to you, Jerald, for so graciously joining us today." He took a sip, set the glass down and picked up the menu. "What should we have?"

Jerald took a rather long swig of the wine. He had a theory that alcohol killed germs. He took another generous sip and picked up the menu. His eyes couldn't adjust to the four pages of offerings. He put the menu down and asked, "Donovan, you've been here before. Please order something that you recommend. If they offer a pesto Sicilian entrée, with basil, tomato and light tuna, I will have that. Sicilians excel at preparing fish."

Helen smiled. "Good idea, Jerald. Do that for me, too, Donovan. That sounds good. None of this means anything to me. Half of it's not in English. I have no idea. We're in your hands."

They ate. They reviewed the changes at the shop, the renovation, the gallery, the gala opening that was scheduled for the following weekend. They explained the spiral staircase. They told Jerald about Circus Tantamount, about Donovan's work at Payne. They did not discuss Helen's late husband or how Donovan happened to suddenly surface in Helen's life, although there was an admission that they had just met rather recently. They asked Jerald about his work in gemology and were suitably impressed by his travels and his knowledge of gems. They enthused that they were fascinated by every single thing he had to say. Helen loved the entrée she praised Jerald for recommending, and Donovan had a different fish entree which pleased him, as well.

Jerald ate the food and drank the wine. He was instantly and increasingly tipsy and felt a giddiness totally unfamiliar to him. Jerald didn't drink—only on the rarest of occasions, which this luncheon surely was. He hadn't had a drink in perhaps ten years. He didn't notice that Donovan had not touched his glass after the toast. Helen sipped cautiously and ate with delight: she was having a good time. It was soon obvious, even to Jerald, that he, too, had enjoyed the food and the conversation and that he, alone, had over-indulged in wine. He felt so suddenly exhausted, he didn't know what to do. He looked over at Helen and determined that he was fascinated with her. She was beautiful, she was charming, she was a delightful woman. He put his napkin down and wondered: what should he do? His world was turning, just slightly, just enough to make him realize he might have trouble walking. This distressed him, of course.

As they readied to leave, Donovan gave Helen a pointed stare and spoke to Jerald, "Jerald, I'll be calling you a cab. I realize you kindly brought a cab here so Fox wouldn't be disturbed by a third party in my small truck." He pulled out a cell phone and called. "We must get back to the shop; we're running rather late, so if we may excuse ourselves, we will see you back in the neighborhood. We have so much on our plate this afternoon, however, that maybe it would be best if you came by Good Fortune in the morning. Perhaps around 10:00. We will have coffee and bagels brought in and we can show you around. How does that sound?"

Helen stood for Donovan's invitation and reached over and patted Jerald's hand, which lay by his plate. "You are a dear, Jerald." She turned to leave.

Jerald was in shock, but somehow gathered together a few words of polite response. "Why, thank you, Donovan. That would be fine. I'd like that." That was it. Jerald Redding knew one thing for certain: Donovan Trenton King was a superlative step-son, yes he was. Immediately after this expansive, inebriated thought, another one came in, quite quickly and quite forcefully. He felt sick. He really did.

As a result, Jerald missed the morning bagels and the entire next day of work due to illness. Jerald J. Redding had never missed a day of work in his life. He was not only physically ill on this unusual day; he was psychologically ill. He was worrying himself sicker by the minute. She had a cat. She might want to be held, kissed. She had touched his hand. Jerald had avoided intermingling with humans and animals all his life. He knew this was a behavioral consequence of his condition, obsessive-compulsive disorder, first diagnosed when he was six as rigidity. He wasn't pleased with the old, or with the new, terminology.

He had been a difficult, yet perfectly affectionate, bright child. He began showing signs of OCD at three: his sock drawer was ordered by color, he was very particular about clothing choices, he was fussy and meticulous about food, especially its arrangement on one specific plate which only he used. His room had to be perfectly arranged at all times, his toys were rigidly compartmentalized, he became agitated with dirt on the floor from the sole of a shoe, a smear on the fish bowl, a spot of water on the mirror in the bathroom, a swipe of mud on his playsuit. He cleaned and disinfected his toys and books. He began doing the family dishes, by hand, at four, to be reassured that they were clean.

Everything had been done to address the troublesome condition which presented in the daily lives of his quite normal parents, a housewife and a high school science teacher, and his much older, capable and sympathetic sister, Alice. There was no precedent for this kind of behavior on either side of the family, and careful analysis revealed no discernible reason for the child's obsessive profile. He had been conceived, carried, birthed, nursed and weaned without complications and he had been extraordinarily easy, and early, to toilet train. He was extremely independent and capable from the time he began walking. He talked early, and was reading at three. Professionals reassured that perhaps it was a stage he would outgrow, that maturation would mitigate it, although they admitted its severity. He was gently therapied and medicated. He did not outgrow it, nor did it mitigate. The condition was exacerbated by allergies, asthma and panic attacks. Everyone who knew Jerald in the slightest noticed at least some of these presenting conditions; no one, not even the professionals, knew about all of them. His family kept in touch, as he dutifully did, but it was a euphemism, of course.

He majored in chemistry in college, graduated with honors and became a gemologist. His early childhood fascination had not diminished; the gem was the most perfect expression of beauty. He also felt so much security in gems partially because they were clean and exuded no fluids. He could handle them, literally and figuratively. He had always lived alone after leaving home at eighteen: he roomed alone at college, he traveled alone and he worked alone. Aloneness, therefore, was the issue with which Jerald Redding now struggled. Apparently, and only apparently, perhaps, and only perhaps, gems did not exude enough warmth, did not disperse enough fire, even for the elderly Jerald.

16

THE NAOMI CYCLE

. . . .

The spindle turned on the knees of necessity.
—PLATO'S ACCOUNT OF ER, RELATED BY SOCRATES

Boon slept with Susan. He made love to Susan. He did not profess his love, nor did he make any pretense about the fact that the alliance was practical, timely, beneficial, pleasant and temporary. Boon slept with women, but he respected them too much to make any promises. Boon knew Boon.

Susan had other ideas, such as filing for divorce, unbeknownst to Boon. Cindy knew and didn't tell him, primarily because Cindy had an agenda of her own and her mother's moves were helpful. Getting her mother married to Boon would be grand. Susan sleeping with Boon was grand. It finally allowed Cindy the luxury she had long not been able to afford:

she had a boyfriend. Her best friend Naomi had hooked her up with her brother, Pete, and the hook was set quite firmly into flesh. This hooking happened whenever and wherever the two could by chance engage, and Boon began, early on, to hear the signs and see the looks and catch the drift of sneaky teenagers getting laid. Of course, progressive male that he was, free love, open relationship advocate and all, he came unglued and was all over it. Not happening. No, no, no. They were too young. We needn't point out that Boon started having sex at thirteen and hadn't turned it down since, not once that he could recall. This historical fact escaped Boon.

It did not escape Susan. They argued. She took her daughter's side. "She's sixteen. It's her decision."

"She's a kid, Susan. She's sneaking around. She's lying. Just that is bad. Then pile on sex at all hours of the day and night with a punk that looks like he'll never amount to anything, and all I see is a barrel belly and two kids in two years."

"Oh, for heaven's sake, Boon. You said yourself that she's smart. She's using protection; she knows all about it. God, Boon, listen to you. Wow. Pete won't amount to much. Sure seems like an old pot calling a cute young kettle black to me."

"He's not cute, Susan. He's empty-headed and stoned all the time. That's not cute."

"I'll tell you what's not cute, Boon. What's not cute is a floppy old fart getting all knicker-twisted about youthful vitality in bed. Lick your wounds, Boon, but don't mess with my kid. She has a life; let her live it. Christ, Boon, she's never had a boyfriend. It's about time."

He slept in the studio. Chilly winds blew from both female quadrants. The quadrants had bonded and taken over the entire north forty of the house, east and west. They went places together, they sat up all night talking. They were great buds, suddenly, and Boon was left to gluing love objects on his sculpture, his one and only sculpture, which was getting on his nerves. He didn't like it. He kept trying to get a new direction with it, zap it with some startling flash, but it seemed dead to him. It wasn't working.

He was on his knees, sorting through items he had laid out on the old studio couch he'd dragged in from the garage, contemplating wringing Naomi's neck for starting the downward spiral—he had to blame someone—when a man stood in the doorway of his studio. This man was familiar to Boon. He had seen his picture and Boon was wearing this gentleman's clothes. Jim. This behemoth was Jim. Boon stood and offered his hand, "Boon. Friend of the family. You're Jim."

"Yup. Jim it is. You know who I am, then?"

"Well, of course. Cindy's Dad. Susan's husband."

"That's the deal, right there."

"So, the girls are gone. Didn't say when they'd be back. Might be late."

"I'll wait. I'm not planning on leaving at all, actually, Boon, and you seem like a savvy guy. You know what that means."

"I think it might be best if you just went ahead and told me what it means; oracle reading is sometimes a challenge for the old Boon."

"Is that a fact? Well, here's the deal. Susan plans to file for divorce and said she was marrying one Boon, the guy standing here wearing my clothes. Now what Susan doesn't know is that I am not going for the divorce and I am back here to put this family back together again. I've had counseling and I am in. I'm back and I'm staying back. I love Cindy and I love Susan. I am not losing my family to some guy who drifted in while I went through some shit."

Believe it or not, Boon had been in this situation before, twice, which as far as he was concerned, made him an expert on the subject. He smiled broadly and extended his hand. "Well, welcome home, Jim. This is great! I am happy for all of you! This is the best news! Fit to print!"

Jim was somewhat taken aback, but replied, "That means you're history."

"Of course. I'm gone already. Just give me time to gather up my things here and I'll be on my way. I'll leave the room shipshape; I'll take a bunch of this garbage out to the dumpster. You can explain everything to the girls, and they'll be excited. I'm telling you, Jim, this is best. You're a good man. I always said that."

"I'll bet you did. That's why you're wearing my clothes."

"I'll leave them behind; sure appreciate the loan."

"Please don't. Take whatever you've worn. I don't want them back. Jesus."

"I can understand that. OK. I'm on this. Ten minutes, maybe fifteen, and it's so long."

"I'll be in the kitchen. Let me know when you take off."

"Will do."

Boon grabbed the garbage bags tucked under the studio bed and filled them with everything art. Everything. He took them outside and put them into the neighborhood dumpster. He went back in and chose three of Jim's sets of casual clothes, including a jacket and a pair of tennis shoes. He packed them in a backpack Cindy had given him. He put on the jeans, t-shirt and the sandals he'd worn into the house that first day, walked through the kitchen saying "I'm outta here, good luck to you, man," and walked to the bus stop. He didn't have any money, so he decided to walk out to the highway, a considerable hike, and get a ride south. Anywhere south was fine, though San Francisco might be a possible destination, but anywhere would do. He was gone; he'd done this town and this town had done him. He wouldn't come back. New game. New roll of the dice. Let's see the snake eyes, that's what Boon was thinking. He was also thinking about Cindy and couldn't believe he was thanking God, the man himself, for, of all things, Pete.

* * * * *

God must have heard this prayer of gratitude through the bullhorn of Boon's hitchhiking thumb, because it was Pete who provided the truck and the ladder for a post-dark dive into the dumpster with a tearful Cindy, who had been informed by her father in a direct, but nonetheless sensitive way, that her friend Boon had moved out of the studio. When she ran to look and found the room empty, she asked if he had taken everything with him. She was told no, that Boon left with a back pack; he had taken his trash to the dumpster. Jim softened this news, which caused even more tears, by saying that Boon seemed "pretty sorry" he couldn't say goodbye.

It was Pete who set up the ladder and carefully removed the three garbage bags from the overflowing, rank dumpster and loaded them into his pickup. It was Pete who said he would store them in his parents' garage. In that garage, it was Pete who actually taped the three big signs Cindy made, which read "Property of Doddson Kooper-Boon, ARTIST," to the sides of those bags. It was Pete who supplied the duct tape to seal them up. He was more than happy to help. His parents were gone on an anniversary trip; he had five acres and a huge country house to himself. He had friends coming over. He had weed and beer and logs for a fire, and Cindy was spending the night. She needed him.

17

HUNTING BOON

· ·

Nobody's Fool.
—Print ad for Lincoln MKZ Hybrid

Everybody seemed to know who Doddson Kooper-Boon was. Nobody knew *where* he was, but they had ideas and were more than willing to share them with Donovan. Three consistent comments accrued from the many encounters Donovan made during his effort to locate Boon: he's a little crazy, he's harmless, he's around. Then there was a question: Is he in trouble? Donovan assured them that no, Boon wasn't in trouble, in fact, quite the contrary; Boon was the guest artist for a gallery opening and his presence was needed. Donovan put his own cell phone number out on the streets of Portland and waited. He had gone ahead and had a transport company locate and gather Boon's sixteen sculptures, which took some doing; two of them were so hidden, it took city maintenance crews to help locate them. He felt assured that he would locate Boon quickly and the whole plan would commence without a hitch. Donovan Trenton King was the sort of man for whom grand schemes proceeded without hitches, certainly. There was no reason whatever to assume that his vision in this instance would be thwarted.

Donovan was, in one way, at first, happy enough with the disappearance of Boon, because he was learning quite a bit about the man, just by roaming around following leads. He was told Boon called bingo at the armory. Boon swam at the Y. Boon had moved out of Walt's, where he had a studio and was a janitor. He'd been "around" for over twenty years. He was always at the food bank at 3:00 on Wednesdays; he picked up free food because he used much of his food stamp money to supply people who couldn't get food stamps—people with no address, no ability to process the appointments, the forms. He'd had a dog, but it was run over by a car and killed. He had a girlfriend, Kelley Swartz, a "looker," at one time, years ago, but she went off to Houston "for some reason." One person offered his opinion that maybe she had gone down to "dance," referencing the obvious equipment she possessed for success in that profession, using hand gestures and facial expressions Donovan vowed to share with Circus Tantamountians. A few people knew Boon lived in his car, but that he moved locations and they had no idea where it might be now. Donovan was told he might try Colora Collective on Yew Street.

The most frequently mentioned lead was, indeed, Colora Collective; a huge ramshackle warehouse buzzing with friendly volunteers representing many stripes of humanity, although an astute observer, as Donovan surely was, would, perhaps, conclude that some of the Colora people might live on the premises. Boon apparently volunteered at the collective doing weatherizing, recycling and plotting urban gardens for seniors and people on public assistance. It seemed the best place to dig for Boon.

A curmudgeon—Donovan quickly estimated 100 pounds and 100 years old—presented himself just inside the door of Colora and grabbed Donovan's elbow, escorting him back outside. "Nice day, friend, let's do this out here. What you need? I'm Willard."

"Pleased to meet you, Willard. I'm Donovan. I'm looking for Doddson Kooper-Boon. Do you know him?"

"Sure. Daniel Boon, I call him. He calls me Wee Willie. Been around a long time. Crazy around the edges, but a good young man. Does a lot for us. He isn't in trouble is he? Doesn't seem like it."

"No, I just have an art show set up for his work. He doesn't know about it and I think he'll be happy to see me. You know where I might find him?"

"Daniel? Art show?

"You know he's an artist?"

"Well, yeah, that's what he says. Never seen anything of it, but I guess so. I don't know art from a hole in the ground, but if you say so. Is there money in this?"

"Yes, there is."

"Well, that might be somethin'. Don't know about that. Daniel's nobody's fool."

"What does that mean?"

"You know, nobody's fool. Smart, Daniel Boon is."

"How so?"

"He has a five dollar rule."

"Now, we're talking about Doddson Kooper-Boon? I want to make sure."

"Yeah, yeah, tall, 50-some, long, gray, or blonde, I guess, girly hair. Artist. Lives in his car. Talks in bubbles, kinda like cartoons."

"Yes. Now, what's a five dollar rule?"

"Boon works at things, he's a good old worker; he'll help with most anything, for however long it takes, but never takes more than five dollars for his work."

Donovan politely asked, "Could you explain the wisdom of this rule?"

The weathered, cough-racked old derelict explained, "Daniel Boon is smart: he has figured it out."

"What has he figured out?"

The man coughed and spat on the ground. "That you don't need much."

* * * * *

Donovan waited, talked to Helen about the dilemma, and decided, reluctantly, to go to the police. He'd checked the hospitals and followed every lead imaginable: no Boon. The opening was in two days. He felt odd, to say the least, about opening without Boon's presence and his assent, and recalled a scrawled quote a student had tacked on a reader board at Payne: Don't depend too much on anyone, because even your own shadow leaves you when you are in darkness. Just where *was* Boon when he needed him? He knew Boon would be happy with the gallery and the opening, as was Helen, but still, they both wanted Boon. By now, both of them had begun to worry: where could he be? He was always around somewhere.

Donovan dressed conservatively in slacks and a sport coat and the only plain button-down collared shirt he owned. He pulled his long, black hair back into a severe, neat pony tail and braced for what he knew could be a challenge. He knew he might learn things he didn't want to learn by showing up at the police station.

"I'm Donovan King, from San Francisco. I'm on the faculty at Payne Institute of the Arts, and I would like to see someone about a missing person whose work I represent."

"The name?"

"Doddson Kooper-Boon."

"Ah, Boon," the woman at the desk smiled. "I seriously doubt he's missing, I can say that much."

"You know him?"

"Well, of course I know him. Everybody knows him. He's made a name for himself in Portland."

This did not sound at all reassuring to Donovan, of course. When the police say you've made a name for yourself, they generally don't mean it as a compliment. "Is there someone I might talk to?"

"Yeah. Should be Marc Fitz, CSI. He knows more about Boon than anyone else here."

Donovan cringed. CSI! No! "Is Mr. Fisk available?"

"I'll see."

"He's in his office, 110, through there. Go on back."

The man stood for Donovan's entrance. "Fisk. Have a seat."

"I'm Donovan King. I'm searching for Doddson Kooper-Boon. He seems to have disappeared."

Fisk laughed out loud. "Sorry, Mr. King, but Boon, well, Boon can disappear and be in the same room with you." He laughed again and seemed to struggle with gaining an appropriately serious demeanor to address a missing person request from a member of his public. "OK. OK. This is serious." He cracked up. "I'm sorry, I can't get past this. Excuse me." He got up and went out for a drink of water at the cooler in the hall, returned and sat down. "I work in the meanest, ugliest world, you have to understand, Mr. King. I do this work. It's difficult. I like it. But the Boon, well..."

"Apparently he makes you laugh. That's what you're saying? I can understand that; he's amusing in an offbeat way and I know what you mean about disappearing. He's disappeared on me three times, every time I've seen him, actually."

"You might say that," Fisk snorted and laughed again, but reined it in. "I'm laughing because if Boon were here he would find this hilarious, but I understand that it isn't funny to you. I guess maybe if you think Boon's missing, that's what Amanda said, I might tell you something about Boon and we'll see about having someone help you file a report. I don't handle that, but I'll pass you on. Now, how well do you know Boon?"

"I know his work, his art. The bricolage sculpture. That's about all I know." Donovan conveniently and quite easily lied, then asked the question most prominent in his mind, "Does he have a record?"

Fisk frowned. "Does he have a record. Oh, yes. I'll just bring it up here on the screen. Pages and pages of infractions. Great deal of taxpayer's dollars spent on keeping Boon in line, you know."

Donovan sighed and waited. He felt very much like leaving.

"Here we go. What the hell?"

"What?"

"Well, there's something that must have come in yesterday. I was off. Looks like two other people are looking for our Mr. Boon."

"How can that be?"

"SFPD."

"San Francisco? Police Department? Is he there? What did he do?"

"No, obviously he's not there. I said they're looking for him. They're assuming he's here. Looks like family, must be a brother or cousin; I guess it could be an uncle, Douglas Boon, address is Martinez, and an attorney, Yon Carter."

Donovan's first thought was son, but he didn't say anything. "Why are they looking for him?"

"Says death in the family, father, Sorel V. Boon. Died eight days ago."

"This explains it; he heard about this. He's in San Francisco."

"I'm telling you, no, I doubt that. This is current. This would go off if he surfaced. We cross it, several times a day. This is a function of law enforcement that is such an important public service, it all is, of course, but when someone passes away, we are very attentive to the needs of families. This is live. He hasn't been notified. He may have found out some way, but I seriously doubt it."

"So where is he?"

"Well, that's a good question. I'd say here. He's invested here."

"He has a record here. Maybe he decided to leave."

"Oh, yeah, that's what we were going to have a look at. His record. Let's see. It says here we impounded his car after two warnings from the Target parking lot. Indication that it was his domicile. Expired tags, like three years ago. Second impoundment of a vehicle. The other one was eleven years ago."

"I know about that, this last one. What else?"

"Warning for squeezing."

"Squeezing."

"Yeah, that's convincing someone to take you along on their shopping trip with your food stamp card, buying food for them, then having them give you cash. Squeezing: means wringing hard dollars out of a stipend intended only for food. You probably wouldn't know anything about this, but it's done most often so that food stamp recipients can buy alcohol, cigarettes, weed, whatever. In this case, however, Boon needed money to buy over-the-counter foot medication."

"Foot medication?"

Fisk laughed, "I know. It sounds ridiculous, but he has trouble with his feet. He walks everywhere, lives outside sometimes, doesn't have the best shoes or socks and gets these lesion things. We've seen them; he's shown us. That's what he did that day when we were called. The officer just shook her head and gave him a warning."

"What else?"

"This is the big one. This is how I met Boon. Vagrancy. Warning."

"What happened?"

"I was driving around one night, this was winter, so raining heavily, by the way, on duty, and there he was curled up on a bench in Elizabeth Park. I went over and told him he'd have to move along, find somewhere else to be. He sat right up and I could see he was sick. He told me he wasn't feeling very well and had just decided to rest a little bit. My buddies had picked him up before over the years and skated on logging, but I knew I had to report, mostly because a sheriff's vehicle passed me as I was talking to Boon. I offered to take him home."

"He doesn't have a home."

"No. But that's what we always say; it's a matter of respect. We usually take them to the mission, but we always ask if we can take them home."

"What did he say?"

"He said he would appreciate it, but he needed to get to K-Mart to buy some cold medicine. I could take him there. I knew that must be where his latest car was parked. I put him in my car; he was pretty wobbly and worn out. I offered to take him to ER, or the mission, but he said no. When we got to K-Mart, I told him I thought he might consider how long he'd been making the choice to live on the street and that he might consider how well it was working for him. As sick as he was, he perked up at this remark and laughed heartily, slapping his knee. Then he looked at my name on my jacket and said, "Fisk, you might consider how long you've been making the choice to do what you do; you might consider how well it's working for you." He laughed, thanked me and left my patrol car, walking directly for his vehicle, making no effort to make me think he was going into the store."

"You remember this so specifically."

"I do. You see, I had typed my resignation that morning and wanted to show it to my wife before I turned it in. I was disgusted with my job; I'd just finished with the wrap up on the Burton Granger case, I was CSI team for that, killed two kids, you know all about it, and I was sick of seeing innocent people victimized. I was through. I felt like an innocent myself, someone who shouldn't have to pick up the pieces. I felt damaged by it, and wanted to give up law enforcement and go into something else. I'd had it. And here I was on mindless night patrol, with all my training, taking a sick vagrant to his home in the K-Mart parking lot, issuing a warning for fucking vagrancy."

"I'm not sure I understand."

"Well, Boon used the word choice. He laughed. He was sick and he laughed. You said it; I'll never forget the conversation I had that night with Boon. I drove around for hours and finally realized I wasn't an innocent at all; I'd made a choice. I also realized that I took myself too seriously, that the way I was looking at my life and my job lacked dignity. I don't know exactly how to explain it, but a switch was flipped that night. I saw that man, sick as a dog, still walking with assurance to his illegally parked wreck of a car to sleep the night with no heat, and I went back and tore up my resignation and changed, somehow. I don't know. This probably makes no sense, but I stopped taking myself so damn seriously. Doddson Boon has something that's hard to nail down, but I knew I needed some of it."

"He's an artist. He's good at embracing what presents; people in my field might say he's a visionary. He's creative. In terms of law enforcement would you call that being an operator?"

"No, he's not opportunistic enough. He's more like, what, skillful in a practical sort of way. He never presents himself as a victim; he's not innocent. He has a certain dignity and he laughs at himself. He's *happy*. Who says that? I don't know. He's just someone I admire, that's about it, I guess. I run into him once in awhile and he always says, good choice, Fisk, my man, good choice. I don't know. He just encouraged me somehow when I needed it. I guess maybe that's all there is to it."

"That's great; that's quite a compelling story, but you said there was a long list. What else is on his record?"

"Nothing. He's been here probably 25 years, although 20 is all we have on record, maybe it's even 30, I don't know. And that's all we have on him. A few calls every year about trying to get customers to buy him coffee in coffee shops, but we don't even respond anymore. God, they can handle it. The last time we did send someone, to Mocha Momma's, the woman who bought his coffee read the officer out and screamed at him that she *loved* Boon and would buy his coffee *any day*. We're positive she'd never seen him before, but that's Boon. He just gets to people."

"That's how I met him. At Jive Joe's. I bought his coffee and then took him out to breakfast."

"He scammed you. So, tell me, do you feel like reporting that?"

"No, I certainly don't. I'm glad I met him. Very glad."

"See? That's what I'm talking about."

There you are, Babette. I knocked on the damn front door, like I'm supposed to, and no answer.

Smoke break. Arnold, you look like hell. What's the matter with you?

Let me have a drag and then I'll tell you.

Aren't you going to ask about Boon?

No. I don't care about Boon, Babette. You probably have him in some kind of your deep novelist shit, anyway, and I don't need to hear it.

I see. So things aren't going well for Arnold, real life hero. Are the kids OK?

You might say that, but the kids are fine.

Cira.

Cira and Sarah.

Let me guess. They've ditched you and the doctor and have fallen in love. They're sleeping together, have moved in with each other. Lesbians.

Don't joke about it, Babette. This is serious.

Sit down here on the steps and tell me what's going on.

Sarah and the doctor are getting married and moving to San Francisco. Some big hospital appointment for him, Dr. Do Big, I call him.

How do the kids feel about it?

Oh, they're excited. They're sick of boring Portland and are looking forward to living in a real city. Just great, two young teenage girls loose in San Francisco. Nightmare is what I call it.

Well, that's pretty negative, Arnold. Good God, they deserve to broaden their experience, you know.

Yeah, well, that's just it. They're both getting goofy about boys and I worry.

Uh-huh. You would. What about Cira?

Cira. It's over.

Over. What does that mean? You're still in the band with her?

Over over. I'm out. He's in.

Who?

Xavier.

Who is Xavier?

The ex.

You knew about this guy?

Sure. They were separated. I know him. He's a pianist.

Don't tell me: a jazz pianist.

Yes. How did you know that?

I didn't. I guessed.

He's back. She's taken him back, or, I guess, it's the other way around, whatever. He's in the band now. I'm out.

Wow. Clean sweep. What are you going to do?

Yeah, right. Like I can do anything about any of this. I tell you one thing, Babette, I am not interested in women. God damn it, it's too tough a business, falling in love. I'm over it. No more. Couldn't get me set up with a date no matter who she was. Sick of it. Gave it my damn all, and end up flushed bad.

Well, Arnold, I commiserate. This is all so unusual! Every last detail! I can't recall ever hearing of anything like this happening to anyone, even in a novel. Just bizarre! Such a totally rare set of circumstances. Probably never happened before.

Oh, Babette, stuff it. You don't have to be so sarcastic. I know this is a chapter that's been written zillions of times. I'm not stupid, Babette.

No, you aren't, Arnold. You might give yourself that. Change your status on Facebook.

That's your advice? Change my status on Facebook?

Yes. Now I have to get back to work, shoveling deep shit for Boon.

Donovan went to his rental suite at Miriemme Manor and logged onto Facebook. He was going with his hunch: a son. Douglas Boon. If he was the son of Doddson K. Boon, he would be the right age for Facebook. He would be there.

He was there, but Donovan was disappointed. He couldn't be a son. There was no picture and no age, but the guy was a doctor. Douglas Boon, MD, on part-time staff at a hospital. Too old for son, obviously. Could be a brother, a cousin, no relation whatever. There was nothing else to learn, except the list of schools he had attended, all back east. Donovan wondered why Douglas Boon had even bothered with a Facebook page. There was nothing there; it was no help whatever—no images, not even one photograph.

Donovan logged out, but then had an idea. The opening was in two days. Why not? He went back to his computer and punched in the hospital, found an email address for administration, since staff contact information wasn't listed, and typed out a quick email to be forwarded to Dr. Douglas Boon. He realized that it was entirely a long shot. He wasn't in administration, he was on consultant staff, whatever that meant. It didn't say what kind of medicine the man practiced, but Donovan wanted to try. He wrote carefully, extending condolences on the recent death of Mr. Sorel V. Boon, carefully not describing a relationship, either his own or Douglas's to the deceased. He stumbled; how did he know about this death? What could he say? He decided to tell the truth. He was handling a gallery opening featuring the sculpture art of Doddson Kooper-Boon, which commenced in two days. He added the address and the time. He considered referencing the police department, even Marc Fisk by name, but decided it was extraneous. He also considered issuing an invitation to Dr. Boon to attend, but decided it was inappropriate. He signed off, listing his credentials as film faculty at Payne Institute of the Arts, and hit send.

18

THE OPENING

· ·

An intriguing invitation. A revealing discovery.
A promise of adventure. A whispered romance.
A question answered. A secret kept.
—TIFFANY & CO. ADVERTISEMENT FOR JEWELRY

Boon's sculptures had signs at their bases: the title of the piece, his name and NFS. Donovan was dashed, but wouldn't let anything sell without Boon's permission. He still hoped Boon would show, that he would just walk in the door and be there. The room was wonderfully arranged and the sculptures were subtly lit. The largest piece, "Reason," was central to the exhibit. It was six feet tall and three feet in diameter, composed primarily of objects in three colors: black, metallic gray, sometimes represented by actual metal objects, and white. It was the most stunning piece. Donovan wanted to buy it for Payne. The sculpture he wanted to buy for himself was called "Creativity+," a beach ball-sized bricolage of pins, nails, magnets and copper wire. It was the only interactive sculpture, presenting paneled areas of moveable pieces. It fascinated Donovan; he played with it while he worried.

Donovan had worries of all kinds. He had advertised this event, of course. He had called the press. He had sent out emails to everyone he knew. He had asked Stephanie to post flyers at Payne. He had invited Stephanie. Helen was pestering him about Stephanie: was she or was she not his girlfriend? Donovan demurred. Stephanie was an enigma. Stephanie didn't do girl-friend. Donovan wasn't at all sure what Stephanie did; she was Stephanie. He explained that she was an actress in Hollywood and fully expected that even Helen would understand how sum-marily that answered every question. She had been his student. It was certainly understandable that more need not be said.

The caterer set up long tables and floral centerpieces and champagne. The cellist arrived and began to play. The street out-side was festooned with ribbons and a shiny gold sandwich board sat on the sidewalk proclaiming the opening of Good Fortune Sculpture Gallery.

Helen became a worry as the hour of the opening approached. Donovan explained to her that it would be "marvelous" if Helen could greet people and send them up the spiral stairway to the gallery, that he, Donovan, would be overwhelmingly occupied in that gallery and somebody needed to greet people. He felt that the lovely owner of the place would be appropriate. She could help out.

"I can't do that. What would I wear?"

"It doesn't matter. A nice dress. You always look wonderful. Anything. Not important." It was forty-five minutes to opening. Donovan could care less what she wore.

"What color?"

"Black."

"I don't look good in black."

"Yes, you do. Wear black. Always good."

"What about white?"

"White's good. Do that."

"No, I think maybe the light gray, with my hair."

"Light gray. Lovely. Great."

"I don't want to do this, Donovan."

"Oh, it'll be fun. You'll love it."

"I'll hate it, Donovan. I don't want to do this. I want to stay in my apartment with Fox."

"This is just like manning the cash register, Helen, you can do this. You just smile and say hello and direct people upstairs."

"I don't want to. My arthritis is killing me."

"Take something. You can do this. I need your help, Helen."

"I can't do it. It's too much for me. My feet hurt."

"Then you can sit down."

"No, that's rude."

"Well, stand, then, Helen. Do it however you'd like."

"I can't do it. I'm going to my apartment. I don't wear black."

"Oh, for heaven's sake, Helen! Wear anything! Take some Motrin. You know, it's one thing not to have the damn artist, but if I don't even have the shop owner, it's ridiculous. This isn't my show, Helen, it's yours and Boon's."

"It wasn't my idea."

"So what? It's a good damn idea, Helen."

"I don't care. I don't want to do this, Donovan." She walked away to her apartment and shut the door quietly behind her.

Jerald Redding walked into the shop to find Donovan standing there with an angry, pained look on his usually serene face. "Good afternoon, Donovan. We meet again. I am pleased to attend Helen's opening of the gallery."

"You're early. That's good, but Helen is in a snit. She doesn't want to participate."

"Well, you know how shy and sensitive she is. Going out to dinner with us concerned her. I'm certain this is a challenge for her, Donovan."

"Well, it's a challenge for me, too. No Boon. We can't find him, Jerald. It's distressing as hell, to tell you the truth. All this work and neither Boon nor Helen can get behind it. Flop in the making, Jerald, I'm telling you."

"Now, we'll just see about that. Why don't you do whatever it is you have to do and let me go in and visit Helen. I may have a technique or two to advance our purposes."

"Well, that would be nice. That's what we need here. If you can round up Boon in thirty minutes, I'd certainly applaud that as well. Thanks, Jerald. Come upstairs when you're ready to see fantastic art." He bounded up the stairs.

Jerald knocked on Helen's door and called out, "Helen?"

She answered, "I'm not doing it, Donovan. Leave me be."

"It's Jerald Redding, my dear; may I come in?"

She opened the door. "Jerald. What are you doing here? The shop's closed for this awful thing that's happening. It's just too much."

"May I come in?"

"To my apartment?"

"Yes. May I come in? I need to speak with you a moment."

"Please, of course. I'm sorry, I'm just not myself. I don't do things like this."

"Nor do I." He shut the door behind him and took the chair she offered him. "You look especially beautiful today, Helen. That's a wonderful hair styling for your face."

"I had it done this morning, thinking I'd be seeing all these people, but I can't do it. Stupid. They don't want to see an old biddy like me. I told Donovan to get young, pretty girls, the circus girls, Tinabelle, all those girls. And Stephanie. I'm sure she's attractive if Donovan's interested."

"You're attractive, Helen."

"Well, thank you Jerald, you're a dear, but I know what I see in the mirror every morning and it doesn't lie."

"Neither do I."

Helen paused, finally getting a tiny drift of something, something personal. Jerald looked mischievous. What was he doing? "What are you doing, Jerald?"

He fished a small gift-wrapped box out of his pocket and presented it to her. "I've come bearing a gift. You may open it now, if you would, please."

"What is it? Why are you bringing me a gift?"

"Please open it, Helen. I chose it especially for you."

She unwrapped the pink ribbon and unwrapped the pink foil paper and frowned, "Tiffany? Surely not!"

"Surely."

She opened it cautiously and squeaked, "Jerald! This is so beautiful! It's new, isn't it?"

"Yes, Helen, it is."

"What am I supposed to do with it?"

"Well, if you take it out, you'll see that the key is on a fine, white gold chain. You are to wear it around your neck, if you wish."

"It's diamonds! The whole thing is diamonds! This is worth a fortune!"

"No, Helen, it isn't worth a fortune, you are."

"What are you saying? Have you lost your mind?"

"I have not. Allow me to explain. The key, although it is a fine piece by one of the world's finest jewelry houses, and is set with high quality diamonds, is not worth a fortune. You, Helen, are worth a fortune."

"Today? You mean today? The show?"

"No, Helen, I mean every day. From now on. I intend to share the good fortune of having met you, my dear."

"With whom, for heaven's sake?"

"With you, Helen."

"Oh, my goodness. You don't mean..."

"I do mean exactly that, Helen. I propose a future alliance of companionship, the parameters of which we may define as time goes on."

"What does that mean?"

"It means, Helen, that I am fond of you and wish to formalize a commitment with you, hence the key. I do believe there is much we could share and I wish to get to know you better. You are a fascinating woman. I see no reason whatever that might preclude us from living out the rest of our lives companionably."

"Does Donovan know about this? Did he put you up to this?"

"He does not and he certainly did not. This is entirely my idea, Helen."

"You. You need. It's hard for me. I don't know what to say, except that I can't thank you enough, Jerald; this is the most beautiful gift I've ever received."

"Let's put it on you; let's see how it looks." He clasped it around her neck. "Lovely. You are lovely!"

Helen stood to look in the mirror. "It's so bright! It's just gorgeous, Jerald."

"You do like it, then?"

"Of course! I love it!"

"Then you do accept this gift from me?"

Helen didn't hesitate. "Yes, Jerald, I accept it. I do, of course I do."

Jerald stood. "Then I'm going upstairs. Should we meet up later, I trust you'll be wearing the key. The necklace might be shown off to its truest advantage against black, perhaps a black dress for this rather formal occasion."

When she just stood there, Fox in her arms, looking in the mirror, he left.

* * * * *

Donovan. So rarely was Donovan wrong. Donovan was always right, but on this day, he was wrong. The opening was not a flop; it was a huge success. Helen worked the event, wearing diamonds and black, thoroughly confident and charming. Tinabelle and a troupe of three entertained as mime artists, dressed in white Tencel jumpsuits embroidered on the pockets with Circus Tantamount in green satin floss. They wore white gloves, matching white Tencel berets and white face paint.

Guests were asked, by a ravishing Stephanie wearing a black shorts suit, Rolex and heels, to sign in and enjoy the exhibit, catered buffet, music and entertainment. She asked them to review a placard on the table which explained that the artist was not present and handed them a four-color brochure. Any interest in purchasing sculpture was to be noted with a check, after the name and contact information in the sign-in book, and they would be contacted. No financial transactions would transpire for the opening of Good Fortune Sculpture Gallery. They were to enjoy themselves and they were thanked for coming, all 312 of them in 5 hours, an hour past the designated closure of the gallery.

Donovan, Stephanie, Tinabelle, Helen and Jerald stood talking and drinking champagne while Donovan reviewed the guest book. He scanned the names, noting that an art critic had attended, and had not introduced himself, which might be good, might be bad. Donovan was on the ninth page, adding up the checks indicating purchase interest, which numbered thirty-nine, when he saw the name: Douglas Boon. There was a check beside the name.

"Look at this! What the hell! How did we miss him? Damn it!"

"Who? Who did we miss?" Tinabelle came to look at the signature. "Oh, Mighty Dog! How did he get in here and not one of us...this is terrible!"

"No address. No contact! Damn! The one person we needed to talk to!"

"One of us may have talked to him. We had so many people, but it's probable that one of us talked to him, don't you think? I had to have at least spoken to him when he came in downstairs," Helen was trying to reassure them.

Donovan added, "Well, we know one thing. He doesn't look anything like Boon, or we'd have recognized him."

"The only person who reminded me of Boon at all was that woman, the one in the dark brown sheath and high heels. Tall. You saw her, blonde, really tall. Silver bracelets. Who talked to her? Surely Donovan." Helen knew her stepson.

"I did talk to her! She liked 'Healing.' She...can't be. No woman is named Douglas. A woman doctor named Douglas Boon? She didn't strike me as a doctor in the slightest and I know doctors. She talked about small galleries. She likes small galleries which represent one artist at a time. I guess I did think she wasn't local; I did think that. She was very poised."

"She was built. She was very pretty and sexy, Donovan. You can say that." Stephanie helped him out.

"Yes, she was. Man! I can't believe she would come all this way and not tell me! She knew I was in charge of this thing, she asked me if I was Donovan King. Why didn't I get her name? I know why I didn't. Another woman came up and started talking about 'Healing.' The two of them started talking and I left." He paused, then stood, shaking his head, "No, this is off, way off. She can't be Douglas Boon, just because she's tall and blonde. We're off the mark here."

Jerald, ever logically inclined, asked, "Perhaps it would be constructive to imagine that this woman is Douglas Boon. What if she is by chance a doctor with a man's first name? This is not unheard of, historically speaking. I can immediately think of a number of women with male first names, such as George. The question I believe we might ask is this one: how would she be related to Boon? How old is she? What might be the relationship?"

All of them looked at Jerald as if he'd asked the most difficult question any of them had ever been asked and then started responding.

Helen said, "His wife."

Stephanie said, "No. No wife looks that much like her husband. She wasn't wearing wedding rings; I checked. She also didn't act married, Donovan, did she? It's a blood relationship. His sister."

Jerald said, "A cousin or an aunt."

Donovan said, "His daughter."

Stephanie said, "No way. She's too old."

Donovan said, "What if she was born when he was 15?"

Stephanie countered, "Maybe, I doubt it. Well, maybe. Could be, I guess."

Donovan was dismissive. "This is ridiculous. Douglas Boon is a man who slipped in here and we missed him. We're wasting time thinking about Douglas Boon as a woman. I can't get there. It's just not something in my brain bank. It's a guy. A brother, a cousin, something. What about the men? Anybody talk to anyone who mentioned Boon at all?" Donovan was intent on getting back on track.

"No, but one guy came up to me and said something strange."

"Tinabelle, I can't imagine. What on earth could anyone say to you that you would regard as strange? What did he say? What did he look like?" Donovan was shaking his head.

'Well, he was mid to late twenties, maybe thirty, but I doubt it. Cute. Curly dark hair, wearing a caftan shirt, red and orange. You must have noticed him. I thought he was coming on to me at first, but then he said it."

"Said what?"

"We were looking at 'Vision' with all that clear glass and he said, 'It's a star-splitter if ever there was one.'"

"What did you say to that?" Helen's face was crinkled up.

"Well, I looked at it and I asked why he called it that, of

course. And he said it's a telescope. You see the tripod, the shape, pointed at the sky. He said he thought it was profound and walked away."

Donovan smiled, "That's our man! I know it! The line is from a Robert Frost poem, actually titled 'The Star-Splitter' and he's right; it is profound. 'Vision' may be Boon's best work, I do think that, but I hadn't realized it was a telescope, but he's right. It *is* a telescope! Amazing! Only a Boon could get that, say that, I swear. But thirty? Are you sure, Tinabelle? Few twenty-somethings are doctors that I've ever met."

They discussed this young man and agreed that all of them had noticed him. They drank champagne and talked and spent a good deal of time looking at "Vision," finding it more and more pleasing as the champagne flowed, and then they dispersed. There was only one thing upon which they could all agree: the event had been a success. They couldn't agree on anything else regarding Boons, but there was one thing, expressed by Helen who had taken off her shoes, about which they all heartily concurred: they were exhausted.

As Donovan and Tinabelle left, she had a question for him on the way to the car, "Since when do you have obscure lines of poetry memorized, Donovan Trenton King?"

"I thought somebody would wonder about that, but I certainly wouldn't call any line Frost ever wrote obscure, Tinabelle," he laughed. "Believe it or not, I had to take English as an undergraduate. Saw no point in it, of course, since I truly believed I knew the language very well at the time, but I was assigned a paper on Robert Frost. I wasn't keen on it. I wanted to do T.S. Eliot. It's funny, Tinabelle; that Frost paper was one of the most important things I did in college, not because of that particular poem, I'm not saying that, but because it was my first intense experience with dramatic narrative. It's because of Frost that I took a modern drama class and studied plays and then went on to graduate school and began to work in film. I've told many people, especially my students, that poetry made a difference in my life and I recommend that they read it, study it, write it.

"Of course, I always recommend Frost, especially for the reluctant—he's accessible and probably the most American of all of our poets. It's interesting to me, that Boon's visual art is similar, although I doubt Boon knows Frost's work, knows much about poetry." He paused as he opened the car door for her. "I don't know, maybe he does. Maybe *he's* the star-splitter."

19

GLORY, GLORY BROCCOLI

· ·

Only so much can fit into a fine grasp.
—WILL JONES (BABETTE'S AFOREMENTIONED WRITER "BOYFRIEND")

Yes, well, Boon was doing Boon. He was in Santa Rosa. He was harvesting broccoli. He was working at a gardening collective and harvesting other things as well. He was doing trim. He was knocking down boxes at the food co-op. He was collecting trash. He was speaking to multitudes of young people on the run, on the make, on the dole and on the way to certain stardom. He was drenched in the recurrent, energizing pool of twenty-somethings doing twenty-some-thing and he had a hard time keeping up with them. He felt his grasp of life was, perhaps, a tad finer than theirs, meaning a bit more measured and refined, but at night, sleeping in a tent pitched up against a bank of trucks, watching them around the fire, playing hacky sack, staying up and working the next day, easily, with two or three hours of sleep, he had to admit it: he was getting old for this. It was on this night, this very night, that Boon changed his mind about a long-held life view: he admitted that he really did *not* want to be twenty again. Ever. Maybe he was just sick. His feet were festered and sore as hell and he felt bad. He was shivering. He had a fever. He decided, clear light of dark night illuminating, that he was miserable. He didn't like broccoli, never had. He was all for food not drones, but he still didn't like broccoli, dead or alive. He would leave tomorrow and get on to San Fran where there was certain civilization. He was close. He had forty bucks. He would head out.

He left at sun-up. He went to the highway and got a ride within ten minutes, taking that as a sure sign that things were looking up. "Yo, appreciate the ride, puts a shine on the day that outdoes the sun."

"Get in. I'm only going fifteen miles, but you can ride along if you keep your mouth shut. I don't want to have to pay for my good deed."

The pickup proceeded down the road five miles, when Boon saw the sign before the driver did. "That's my stop. I'll get out here. Thanks."

"You that kind of guy, huh? Well, you can just get the hell out." Boon got out and the truck peeled off. The driver was responding to the sign with four big letters on it, B A B Y, held by a pretty young woman by the side of the road.

"Morning, there fine one. Where's home?"

"Don't mess with me. I have a baby."

"I see that. That's what the sign says. I'm not going to mess with you. How old is the baby?"

"Six months."

"And how old is the baby's momma?"

"Eighteen."

"OK. What are we doing here, at this early hour, by the side of the road?"

"I need a ride. You can't help me. You should leave. I'll never get a ride if there's a man with me."

"Well, I'm Boon and I think maybe we should work together on getting you somewhere else. Makes sense to me. I don't think this is a good place for you to be."

"Why not? I do it all the time. On my way to play music." She pointed to the violin case at her feet. "I've got kids to feed."

"You have other kids?"

"I do. My older three are with my Mom."

"You're eighteen and you have four kids. How can that be?"

"I'm fertile?"

"Sorry I asked. None of my business. Does your Mom know you're out here?"

"Sure. She made me breakfast and saw me off. We do this all the time."

"Tell me, is the baby's father in this picture?"

"No, no fathers in this picture. My own father isn't in the picture, never has been. It's my Mom, she's on disability, she and I make a go of it. We do all right."

"I see that. Do you have a name?"

"Yeah, but I'm not giving it to you. You need to go, so somebody will pick us up."

"This music. How's that work?"

"I get to SF and do the stands. Make enough to last a couple of weeks."

"You must be good."

"I am good."

"You know, I'm kinda not feelin' real swift just now, been sick, maybe I could use a tune or so. Do you think you could trust me to hold that baby, seems to be asleep, while you rip off a bit of violin for me? I know it's early and we're standing by the side of the road, but, hey, it happens where it happens. Let's hear somethin'.

We could be standin' here for an hour. Let's make use of the time we have. It might draw a crowd. Who knows."

"Now?"

"Now."

She hesitated, then handed him the snuggled baby. Boon was lying on his side now on a bed of tall grass, curled up with the baby. She took out the violin. She didn't warm up; she began to play a Beethoven violin concerto. It was long and perfectly executed.

Boon was sitting up, the baby cradled in his lap, transported. He couldn't believe it. She was amazingly good.

When she stopped, he asked, "You're professionally trained. You belong in a symphony orchestra. How did you learn to play?"

"This is my Mom's violin. She taught me. She used to play, but can't anymore."

"Why not?"

"She's disabled. I told you."

"What's her disability?"

"Parkinson's, complications. Some mental."

"And she's taking care of your three kids?"

"Oh, she can do that. She's fine, but she can't play the violin anymore. She had me when she was forty-one, so she's older now. She loves being a grandma. She's proud of me."

"She should be, good God, girl. We have to make a plan. You sure I can't get a tag for you and this little thing?"

"I'm Hannah and that's Kitten."

"Kitten."

"Well, it's Katherine, but we call her Kitten."

"OK. Hannah. I have a plan."

"Yeah, I'm sure. Guys always have a plan. Goes with the dick."

"Now you listen here, Hannah. I'm not hitting on you. I'm an old man. Get that. I'm not going to mess with you, good Christ. You have a brain. Use it. I'm offering to help you and I strongly recommend you just say thank you and let me do what I can. This isn't rocket science, Hannah. I'm sure I don't have to tell you this is a dicey damn deliberate business, standing out here taking your chances that somebody decent will pick you up. Hey, I'm an optimist, but I'm also realistic. Things go both ways; that sun comes up and it goes down, you know that."

"Yeah, well, all I see is a guy who just got off a ride. I don't see a guy with a car."

"You got a cell phone on you?"

"I do. But you can't use it."

"Why not?"

"Because you'll probably call the law."

"That's right. That's exactly what I'm going to do."

"You're an asshole. Take off. I don't need your kind of help."

Boon sat down. Hannah nursed the baby who was now awake. A car pulled up.

It was a sheriff's vehicle. Boon stood.

"If you'll put your hands on the vehicle, sir." He patted Boon down. "Got a call from your last ride. Not a happy man. I'll need to see your identification. What seems to be the problem?"

Boon explained as the deputy listened. "Now if you'll just wait while I run this, we'll see what we can do. Do you have a name for the woman?"

"No. Just met her. Thought I might try to help her." Hannah came up and was now standing beside Boon, rocking the baby in her arms.

The deputy returned. "Mr. Boon, you are right. You certainly are in a situation here. We have a report on you. I'm sorry to have to tell you this, right here, but there's been a death in your family, and we need to get you in."

"Who is it?"

"Sorel V. Boon."

"That's my father. I'd hoped..." Boon sat down.

The deputy waited as Hannah put her hand on his shoulder, then he spoke quietly, "Now, Mr. Boon, we should just transport you now, if you'll come with me."

"I won't go unless they go, too."

The deputy turned to Hannah. "Ma'am, I'll need identification. Do you have that?"

Hannah dug into her backpack and handed it over. "Here."

"I'll have to run this. Just wait a minute."

He was back. "OK. Clear. We can go. I'm on my way off duty, but I'll hook you up. I've called in and we'll transfer you. I need a destination, Mr. Boon."

Boon gave him the address in Martinez. "That's where we need to go."

"You want to take her there with you, under these circumstances?"

"Yes. That would be good."

"Do you need to make a call, let someone know you're on your way?"

"No. It's too early. I have a key."

* * * * *

"Yo! Is there a doctor in the house? I need a doctor!" Boon slammed the front door of the adobe, hacienda-style house in Martinez as hard as he could. "Hey! Need a doctor!"

The man came running down a hall. "Dodd Boon, you bastard! Scare the hell out of me! Man, am I glad to see you! Hey! Cut the locks! Guess you and your sis can't be twinsies anymore." He was all smiles and hugged Boon. "Well now, brought the family, I see. Jesus, Boon, what *have* you been up to? I know some of what you've been up to, big news, but not this part."

"No, no, no. Hannah, my brother-in-law Dr. Hopper. Greg to you. Greg, this is my friend Hannah and her baby girl, Kitten. Just along for the ride, man, not what you think. We need to do an assist."

"Ah, a Boon charge of the light brigade. I see. OK, well, come on into the kitchen and we'll get a bite, some coffee, tea. See what needs to happen, here, Hannah, welcome." He pulled out a kitchen chair for her as the baby fussed and she began nursing her. "Healthy baby."

Boon sat down wearily. "Where's Dougie?"

"She'll be home pretty soon. Had an early surgery, something simple, but then she's off. Sorry about your Dad, Boon. Old Sorel fought like hell, but the cancer went everywhere, I'm afraid. Nothing they could do. I know it's no surprise to you; I was there when you called him about a month ago."

"Then you heard him tell me not to come, that I should keep looking for a job?"

"Yeah," Greg laughed. "He was somethin'. Loved the old guy, but, well, you know he's never been OK with what Dougie chose to do with her life, either. He always hated it that she 'worked in the mines,' as he called it. Of course, I'm doing that, too, which always made me suspect, as well. The man could not get working with minorities in suburban clinics. He wanted us in a big hospital doing open heart surgery every morning, I guess. Never mind that I'm a pediatrician and she's an oncologist. I honestly don't know if he ever understood what kinds of doctors we are. You can imagine what he thought of Torrey doing an MFA. Kept telling Torrey there's no money in it. Not wrong about that, you understand, but..."

"Where is Torrey? He's actually the one we need first. Or Heather, really. Are they still together?"

"Yeah. Ten years. They're expecting in about three months. Dougie and I are excited. Grandparents."

"I didn't know they got married. When was this?"

"Your age is showing there, Boon. They're having a child. They aren't getting married. Two different things these days." Hannah smiled at this remark as Greg continued. "They're still at Stanford. So you need Heather? What for?" Greg watched Boon grimace and stall on his reply. "You OK, Boon? You look pretty peaked. You OK?"

Hannah offered, "He's sick, I think. He said he didn't feel well."

"Boon, are you having some complications? What's bothering you? Tell the doc."

"No, no. I'm fine. What we need is an audition."

"An audition? For what?"

"We need an audition for Hannah. You see the violin. She's professional. She needs an audition. Heather. Get Heather to get her an audition. She can do that. She's got the contacts."

"Yes, I suspect she can, but is she really," he stopped and turned to Hannah, "Hannah, are you that good?"

"I think so."

Boon nodded, "She's that good, trust me. Get her an audition. Do this for us, OK? Call Heather, Greg."

"Well, fine. I'd be happy to do that, but right now?"

"Yeah. Let's get Hannah on her way. She has three other kids and a disabled Mom. We need to get her in front of somebody and home."

"You know, Boon, you aren't doing so well, are you? Let me have a look, check your vitals."

"Oh, no, Greg, just stay with this. I'm fine. Call Heather. Get somethin' arranged—here, there, wherever—and we'll get her a cab. We need to do this." He turned to Hannah and put his hand on her shoulder, "Hannah. You'll do this. Please. You can do this. Do Beethoven. Then Schubert if they ask for two."

"OK. I will. Yes. Thank you." She held eye contact with him and then added, "I think you should go lie down."

"I have to use the john." He pulled out his forty dollars and put it on the table. "Take this if you leave before I get back. Just play the piece you played for me and Kitten." He left and went down the hall to the bathroom.

Greg was on the phone with Heather when he and Hannah heard him fall. Greg hung up, went down the hall, knocked, then opened the door. Boon was unconscious on the floor. His head was bleeding where he'd fallen forward onto the edge of a towel rack. He'd then fallen sideways knocking three glass candle holders off the commode. Boon's opening remark came back to Greg as he called for an ambulance. He had burst into the house unannounced saying he needed a doctor. He'd actually said it three times. Dr. Hopper knew now that Boon surely did need a doctor; he did not, however, need a pediatrician.

Babette?

Yeah. Hi, Will.

Are you at a place where you can quit for a minute? I need to talk to you.

Yeah. Just let me shut down. Put tea water on.

You sound terrible, still, Babette. You look pretty ragged. You're not shakin' this, are you?

No, I don't seem to be able to.

Let's sit.

Something's wrong. What is it?

Arnold, Babette. It's on Facebook.

What's on Facebook?

He's not...with us anymore, Babette.

What? He moved? No, that can't be!

No, Babette. He passed away. It's true. None of us knew this. He had childhood leukemia. He's fought it all his life, in and out of remission. Some virus hit him, affected his heart, I guess, and he just couldn't make it, Babette. Yesterday. I checked; Facebook can be unreliable gossip, but I double checked. It's true.

No. This can't be! His girls! He has two daughters. No. This is...he was such a wonderful man. He was just here! I loved him!

I know you did. I wish I'd known him better. You had him helping with this book; I'm sure that meant a lot to him.

It meant a lot to me, Will. He made me realize every time he came over here that my book wasn't everything. He really did that for me. I have trouble, you know. He was just so engaging. I'm going to miss him so much. He would just walk in...

I know. You're so sick; I hated to have to tell you this today.

I can't do it anyway.

What?

Finish. I don't want to finish without Arnold.

How far are you?

Half way. I can't do it.

You're sick, Babette. You just lost a good friend. Just put it aside. You can get back to it. I think you need to rest. I'll stay awhile here with you. Maybe you should take a bath; I'll make you tea.

He's down, too. I can't do it.

Who's down?

My guy. In the book.

Oh, no, not this, not now. You're not killing a character?

He's sick, he's unconscious. The ambulance is coming.

You can't kill him, Babette. It's bad timing. You can't have that right now, Babette. We've been through this before. You take it all in. You do this, Babette. You can't have him die. I get this now: he's been sick for awhile hasn't he? That's what's going on. You have to get him better. Then you'll get better. Get him turned around, Babette.

I know. Arnold wanted him to find a woman. Arnold wanted a whole lot of things to happen for Boon; that's my guy's name. He's a far cry from that at the moment, but I guess, for Arnold, maybe...

Yes, that's exactly what you should do. That's what you can do. That's good. Do it for Arnold. But not tonight. Right now, let's have tea and get you to rest. I love you, Babette.

I love you, too, Will. Thank you for being here. It's so sad. He was so young and talented. I heard him play at The Forsyth...

I know. It's hard to understand.

I told him...I can't think this.

What? Come on, Babette. It's OK. What?

When Cira went back to her husband and ended it with

Arnold, I told him...

What? What did you tell him?

I told him to change his status on Facebook. I think that's the last thing I said to him.

20

DOCUMENTATION

· ·

You've got to read it to believe it.

—ED HARRIS

Donovan had a voicemail to call Marc Fisk. "Donovan King, here. What's up?"

"We got him. He's in Martinez at the Hopper residence—sister and her husband. Sheriff's deputy picked him up outside Santa Rosa. Sent you a fax. It's all there." Donovan called Helen and gave her the number where Boon could be reached, explaining to her very carefully that she mustn't miss a sale of sculpture now that Boon was located. If someone pressed her and wanted to buy, she should call Boon. She shouldn't give the number out to anyone else.

* * * * *

Dr. Douglas Boon looked at the results of tests on her twin brother. He was fine. He had pneumonia, he was anemic, he was worn out. His left foot was infected. He had a moderately severe concussion. He needed bed rest, good food and prescription medication. He had refused to be taken to the hospital, so the bed rest and good food was being provided by Douglas and Greg in the rose-wallpapered guest bedroom of their home in Martinez.

* * * * *

Heather and Torrey looked at an ultrasound of their baby *in utero*. It was a girl. They were going to name her Douglas and call her Didi. This child would be the fourth female in the family named Douglas, after a maternal ancestor from the late 1600s who was an alchemist. The original Douglas had changed her name and her appearance to male, so she could more easily practice medical arts. Her real name had been Esther.

* * * * *

Dr. Gregory Hopper reviewed the divorce settlement paper work. He and Douglas would go over it again together and finalize it. It was a mutually agreed upon, friendly divorce, citing the usual irreconcilable differences. Both of them had been seeing other people for years. They would continue to work together on the rare case, of course.

* * * * *

Hannah had a letter in the mail. She was to audition again with the symphony. It was her third audition. She was performing beautifully.

* * * * *

Donovan Trenton King had someone who wanted to be his friend on Facebook. His name was Trenton TeVelde King. Donovan went into shock and was unable to respond to the request. Within the hour, he was in an intensive care unit, giving cardiologists readings on a monitor.

* * * * *

Cindy read the results of her pregnancy test from the public health clinic. It was positive. She and Pete had already talked about it. They would have an abortion. They would have the required counseling sessions and go to college as planned. Neither of them planned to discuss this matter with their parents. Cindy was now seventeen and Pete was eighteen. They were seniors in the same high school.

* * * * *

Tinabelle had an email from Stephanie. It read: You might consider sticking with the circus, girl. Donovan and I have made plans. Thought you'd like to know.

Tina sent a quick reply: Nice act.

* * * * *

Jerald Redding received a personal letter from the Internal Revenue Service. He was being audited. This was no problem, of course, for a man like Redding who was meticulous about record keeping and honest. However, the sheer volume of materials he would have to secure and submit was overwhelming. He would have to hire help for this task, because Jerald Redding's net worth exceeded 85 million dollars. He owned small properties in four countries and banked in three.

* * * * *

Kendra Coppola James, art critic, reviewed the copy she'd written. It indicated that Doddson Kooper-Boon's show had been "abysmally uninspiring." She didn't like Boon's work and predicted that "we're, hopefully, seeing the last gasp of this sort of artist and this profile of waste-a-be art. We need to return to sanity. Outsiders are out." This would be published in the arts section of the Sunday paper with a photograph of "Vision," which Ms. James described as "hopelessly amateurish, reminiscent of a tilted gin bottle on three legs, an obvious sexual reference. Very immature." She had, however, been impressed with the gallery itself as a new venue, and carefully and wisely cited the "enormously capable and visionary presence of Donovan Trenton King from Payne Institute of the Arts as the darling man behind the scene."

* * * * *

Boon had the thing in his hand; he was propped up in bed. His brother-in-law had handed it to him. "Here's the brochure for the show."

"What show?"

"Your show, you know, the gallery thing. Doug and Torrey were pretty impressed."

"What is this? What are you talking about?"

"You don't know about the Good Fortune Sculpture Gallery opening? I know you weren't there; they looked for you, so they could tell you about Sorel, but decided it wasn't the best time, anyway, and left."

"What are you talking about, Greg? What is this?"

"You don't know. Well, I'll be damned. Donovan King? Doesn't any of this mean anything to you?"

"I know Donovan King, but not real well, I gotta say that. Bought me breakfast, helped me hang a sign, hung out with him for a night of the calliope. Circus. That's it. Left Portland, haven't seen him since. What's the gallery mean? Why is "Vision" on the cover? I couldn't find it. It was behind Office Supply Depot, but it was gone."

"It's a new gallery. All glass, above an antique store. I don't know. I couldn't go, had something on, myself. Big show. Sixteen or so of your sculptures, none of them for sale, ballsy deal, not having anything to sell. Fancy. Catered. Cellist. Champagne, the whole deal. Dougie said it was superb, that was her word. Torrey wants to buy "Vision," raved about it when he called me on the phone. Something about a telescope. I don't know, sometimes my kid seems a little loopy to me. Literary, you know. I'm like your Dad was, I guess; I don't get literary."

"There's nothing above that antique store, Greg. It's not possible."

"Look on the back."

It was a large photograph of Good Fortune Antiques with the new sign: to the marriage of true minds. A red roof over glass walls sat on top of the flat historic building. Underneath in small print he read: Helen King, proprietress. And under that it read: Signage by Doddson Kooper-Boon.

21

DO WE CARE?

A hero should always want something,
even if it's just a glass of water.
—KURT VONNEGUT

Boon didn't want the continual glass of water he was being encouraged to drink. He didn't want the food on a blue plastic tray with a napkin. He didn't want to take his iron, his vitamin supplements, swallow his giant antibiotic pills or eat the liver prepared especially for him. He didn't want his sheets changed. He didn't want the second shower in two days. He didn't want the television that was installed in his room turned on. He didn't want to call anyone. He didn't want to read magazines. He didn't want to have the dressing changed on his foot. He was rude: leave me alone.

He didn't want Greg and his sister to get a divorce. He didn't want to be there. He didn't especially want to *be*. He went down in Martinez. He slept, though he fought that, too. He needed to get on out, get back out, find his way in, see his way clear, go for the high road back to the sunny climb, that's what he kept saying. He babbled and then he slept. He dreamed about his father in a casket on a skateboard careening through rows of broccoli. He woke up once thinking he was asleep on a bale of trim. He awakened another time not knowing where the hell he was. It seemed like a nursing home; it was pink. He decided they were giving him psychotropics, the bastards. He was hallucinating, having conversations that hadn't happened, seeing things that weren't there: a brochure, a red roof over Good Fortune Antiques, photographs of his sculptures. Telescopes and Torrey in school and ballsy. He remembered Donovan; he was wearing a wig. Drugs, man. Bad shit, that's what Boon thought.

Dr. Douglas Mary Boon was not surprised. She was dismayed, but she wasn't surprised, since her brother was surely not at all accustomed to being incarcerated in a wellness establishment, whether it was a private home or not. He hadn't been in rehab, he'd never been in a hospital that she knew of, except for the caesarean section which produced the two of them. She'd seen her brother twice a year, always on his turf, at her request, which was a coffee shop of some sort, on some street, in the rain, somewhere in Portland. These visits never lasted more than an hour and were cordial, except for the recurring fact that he wouldn't take her money. She assumed, correctly, that Boon had never had a home in the traditional sense since leaving the dorm in college. He'd had what he told her were "lady stops," short alliances in bedrooms with females over the years, but he claimed that a couple of weeks was his limit. He didn't like houses. When she wondered why this was the case, Boon had told her he didn't see the point: what was wrong with the blue roof, sprinkled with stardust at night? She had pointed out that he did seem to prefer sleeping in an old car on occasion, but Boon claimed it wasn't true. The cars were for storage.

It was day five of battling Boon that the Drs. Boon and Hopper met for an early morning conference at their kitchen table in a house that was now on the market.

They were concerned about decisions which needed to be made on two fronts: one, the showing of the house and two, the progress of their patient. They concurred that his recalcitrance had resulted not in a gain, but in a slight loss of apparent health, and that specialists needed to be called in. They were concerned that he was losing more weight; his caloric intake was poor, as was his intake and elimination of fluids. The foot was much better, but his mental state was not stable. They agreed that he should be moved to the hospital for a battery of tests, most critical of which seemed to be an EEG. Perhaps the concussion had resulted in more trauma than at first thought, or perhaps ...well, they wanted him looked at. They wanted tests. They wanted non-family care which was harder to resist. They didn't know what else to do.

The telephone interrupted this confab, just as Greg was writing down his schedule for the week. He absent-mindedly asked, "Doug, you want to get that? It's not for me on that phone."

"Dr. Boon speaking."

"This is Helen King calling from Portland. I'm sorry to call so early, Dr. Boon. Do you know who I am?"

"Yes, Mrs. King, I do. We met briefly. You complimented me on my brown dress and matching shoes. The sculpture gallery show. I attended with my son. It was lovely, Mrs. King. Your shop is wonderful and we so appreciated the art." Dr. Boon was making a face and giving Dr. Hopper questioning looks, pointing at her watch. It was 6:00 AM. Why was she calling?

"I'm calling to see if I can talk to Boon. Doddson Boon, the artist. Is he available?"

"Mrs. King, you sound upset. Is something wrong? Boon's

here. I can get him for you, but can you tell me what's happening, why you've called?"

"It's Donovan, my step-son. I think you met him when you were here. He's in the hospital there and I want Boon to go help him. I can't come. I need Boon to go see him. He's bad. It's his heart."

"Let me go into Boon's room. He's been rather ill himself, Mrs. King, but I know he'll speak with you. I am so sorry to hear this about Donovan. He is a delight. Just wait while I walk back to Boon's room. Please don't hang up."

"I won't. Thank you."

"Boon. It's a phone call for you. Helen King. It's urgent." She handed Boon the phone and left, praying that he would handle it well.

"Helen, fair shine. What's up? You're early for a day of play."

"Boon. Donovan is bad. He's in San Francisco at that big hospital. I can't come. I want you to go see him. I don't have anyone else to call. Jerald's on a trip for business, but I talked to him just now and he said I should call you."

"Jerald Redding? Suit and tie? Ashtray man?"

"Yes, Boon. The man who bought the red ashtray. Yes. Can you go?" She was crying. She was crying for Donovan and she was crying because Boon had missed so much of what had happened.

"Well, surely and purely I will fly to his aid, dear lady. Now my sister, the doctor in charge, has just appeared at the door of my cave. I'll hand you over to her. You tell her where our Donovan circus man is and she can get me where I need to be. Don't give this another twist of your lovely curls, Helen, my girl; Boon's to the rescue. I'll call you when I have performed my mission of mercy. Here's my sis."

* * * * *

Drs. Boon and Hopper said nothing as Boon went in to shower. He went to his bedroom and packed up. He took everything he owned with him. He thanked them and asked for directions, all the information he needed to get to Donovan.

He left in a cab they called for him, looking pale and weak, but happier than they'd seen him in days. They hugged him goodbye. He thanked them. It was obvious to them both that he wasn't intending to come back. There were things they needed to discuss regarding his inheritance, but they felt it would wait; if Boon couldn't take in the sculpture gallery news, he probably couldn't handle the estate settlement issues, either. They would wait until he was stronger.

They went back into the house and Dr. Boon made the call to outline a plan. She informed the person she reached by phone at the hospital that one Doddson Kooper-Boon would be visiting Donovan Trenton King this morning and he himself was ill and needed to be retained for tests and hospital care. She gave the recent medical history and explained that Doddson Boon should be closely observed while he visited Donovan King and then met with privately on the subject of his own medical condition. It was rather convenient that the person to whom Dr. Boon was speaking was her lover of two years, Dr. Hanson Carttin, a psychiatrist of some notoriety in pharmaceutical maintenance. People loved him because he had saved so many lives or they hated him and thought he should be removed from the practice of medicine. He was controversial and both camps used the same nickname for him, "The One-Man Drug Cartel."

He was also notorious for the number of women he had befriended, meaning bedded, during the course of his professional career, every one of them doctors. Since Dr. Carttin did not prefer nurses, it was essential that he work in a major metropolitan area. Dr. Carttin assured Dr. Boon that he would do everything he could for her brother. He'd heard all about Boon, of course, and though he avoided what he called the "irredeemables," concentrating his remarkable skills on the "high profiles," meaning patients with trust funds and vitas who were far short of suicidal, he would undertake the task of fixing Boon. Anything for Douglas.

* * * * *

Boon checked in at the right desk on the right floor and was told Donovan King was in surgery, but someone would speak with him, a Dr. Hanson Carttin. While he waited in the hall, he used the cell phone Douglas had given him and called Helen, explaining that they were fixing Donovan up and he'd call her around noon, that she and Fox should carry on and not have a single worry between them.

The minute Boon saw Dr. Carttin, he gained his strength. His assessment of the man was deep, strong and fiercely resolute. Dr. Carttin was in his mid-fifties and decked out in a crisp, very crisp, charcoal gray casual suit with a starched blue and white striped shirt buttoned to the neck. His hair was dyed black and clipped meticulously. He had a light, perfectly even tan. He was wearing a silver bracelet which matched the one Douglas wore. No question: good-looking and nasty.

"Howdy! You're my sis's new squeezeroo! I'm Doddson Kooper-Boon, home from the hill."

"She told you that, but not with that exact word, I trust." They shook hands.

"Oh, no, she said you were good." Boon winked at Carttin. "Had that light in her eye she gets when she meets somebody new, but it was a little dim. Lasts about two years, tops, and then she moves on. Likes to keep younger and fresher in mind; I was thinking just this morning that she has that look of wanting to jump a rock star about now, menopause does that, and she's always been kinda wild compared to me. I'm the conservative one of the duo." He stopped a second and shook his head, "Surprised she backslid and took you on, since you're quite a bit older than the husband. You know, Dr. Hopper."

Dr. Carttin made no comment as they sat down in Carttin's office. He opened a drawer and took out a form. "Now, Boon, a bit of history. This won't take long."

"What are you on, man? That eyebrow sure has a buzz on it." Dr. Carttin had one arched eyebrow which nervously jumped when he was stressed. The man's face struck Boon as having had so much knife it looked like a Rodin sculpture. Boon's imagination took off and he imagined Carttin doing Mr. America poses in front of a mirror. Boon leapt to his feet and struck such a pose, hands fisted below muscled up arms tucked to the groin, head down, shoulders in, one leg bent dramatically. He sat down.

"What was that?"

"Oh, nothing, just an Iraqi stretch exercise I learned."

"You've been to Iraq?"

"No, have you?"

"No."

"You should go. Of course you'd miss night raids with my sister."

"Mr. Boon. You seem to be rather intent on making preternaturally lewd comments about your sister and sexuality. Tell me, did you share a room as children?"

"Oh, yeah. Sure. Quite awhile there."

"How old were you when this was happening?"

"I wasn't remembering much then; we were young."

"An estimate would be fine."

"In the womb, so I guess we'd call that prenatally, instead of preternaturally, for the form there. I see you're getting all this down. We were tight back then, sis and I were. It's unfortunate how being on the planet distances people, don't you think? We just haven't been that close since. Kinda sad."

"Mr. Boon."

"You should call me Doddson. That's my first name. It makes me more comfortable."

"You seem perfectly comfortable."

"I am." Boon had taken off his jacket and was rolling up the sleeves of his shirt. "You don't look so comfortable, though. Maybe you should med-up, man. I'm sure you have cozy-o's in the drawer there. Just take your time. I'm cool with it, Dr. Curtain."

"It's Carttin. It's French."

"Car Tan. Like car beige. That's what I'll call you, Carbeige. Too bad it's not a G. Would work better. But it does sound French if I do it right." Boon did his very best French imitation, theatrically using his entire face and pooching out expressive lips in a disgusting, saliva-spitting way to do it. "Carbeige."

"You seem poised to insult me."

"Poised? You jest! God, no. I'm a wastoid individual with broad streaks of good for nothing, remember? Homeless for thirty years. Makes sculpture out of trash twenty-four/seven, dumpster dives, lives in cars that won't start, gets foot rot, takes food stamps from the government, is lewd, nice word, I love lewd. Should use it more. Anyway, I'm a guy who doesn't make normal social connections, just loves everybody all the time: never married! never divorced! doesn't belong to a club! doesn't vote! no MFA, imagine that! Totally flat out broke and not in the slightest apologetic about it, so you could buy me breakfast when this ends, if it ever does, which I pray to god almighty happens and the sooner the better, anyway, nothin' to show for nothin' we could give a rat's ass about...your tie's on backwards, you know that?"

"I'm not wearing a tie." Carttin's hand went to his throat, nonetheless.

"You are. It's on backwards and it's too tight. At least that's what must be giving you the look of a man who's choking to death. You all right, man?"

"I'm just fine, Mr. Boon. We're concerned about you."

"I'm concerned about this desk." Boon stood and started moving it away from Carttin, diagonally into the middle of the room. "Better. Can't have that sharp edge protruding into your wealth baqua."

Carttin moved his chair up and sat down, not to be deterred, "Are you on any medications at the moment, Mr. Boon?"

"No, but you are. Say! What am I thinkin' here? I must be losin' it! I'm breakin' a hard and fast rule I set up for myself a long time ago, man. Don't hang with the crowd doin' the do. Rubs off, if you know what I mean. I think I'll leave you to your vices and go get breakfast. How about a five spot? I need coffee and something big and gooey and sweet. My sister and her damn green drinks and liver has just about done me in. Need some soul food." He stood. "Sure been swell, this has. I have to say. Never met a psychiatrist before. Always kind of thought I'd admire them, what they do and all, but I might have to adjust my attitude. Live and learn."

A twenty dollar bill appeared on the desk top and Boon took it. "Thanks, Hanson, buddy." He was putting his jacket back on. He stuffed the bill in the pocket, then put his palm to his mouth and gave it a big, wet lick, smoothing down his hair on the sides. "I'm bankrolled, thanks to you. Might be a nice star-belle down there in the cafeteria. Gotta look good." He started for the door, but turned slightly. "Hey, you take somethin'. Get yourself a glass of water. It's OK. I'm leavin.'"

22

THE JUGGLERS

· ·

Some people don't know this.
—WILLIAM STAFFORD

There was a good-looking woman in the cafeteria. It was Tinabelle, having green tea and toast. Boon could not believe his luck for a minute, but then saw the look on Tinabelle's face and knew luck was not at issue. Bad luck seemed more like it. She had been crying.

"Tinabelle, Doddson Boon, we met at the yurts. How about if the Boon joins the circus, might have an act or two up my flowing rabbit sleeves."

"Sit. I'm glad you're here." The voice sounded like she was telling him her car wouldn't start.

"OK. Tell me, tell me now, tell me true, girl. What gives?

What are they doing to our grand master?"

"We don't know. Helen called me. She doesn't know. They won't tell me anything. I'm not family."

"Well, you're his girlfriend, won't they take that into account?"

"I'm not his girlfriend, Boon. He doesn't have a girlfriend."

"He doesn't? Are you sure? I seemed to get the idea he might have two of them, actually. You and Douglas put someone named Steph..."

"Boon. I'm lesbian. Stephanie's certainly his girlfriend if you ask her, but Donovan won't even sleep with her. He's not interested. That's what he told me. That's what he told her. She's not listening. Can't blame her, I guess. If I were straight, I'd work it."

Boon sighed. Gosh, blows hitting from all sides. He went up the line for coffee, a sweet roll and a stack of bacon and returned to Tinabelle, who grimaced slightly at the greasy food. Boon justified his choices, "I've been so damn under the weather. I need this food, I have to say. Now what do they say for time? When's he coming out and coming around?"

"They don't know, or won't say. Last time this happened he was in a long time."

"What is this thing, exactly? What's wrong with him?"

"Heart. He has a bad heart, congenital anomalies, several problems, I guess. Aorta, for one thing; they did reconstructive surgery when he was about thirteen. Started high school late, in a wheelchair. It's some rare condition, bad. That's all I know. He's been on heart medication since I met him. He has to be careful with stress, overexertion. Has to watch his weight and watch what he eats. It's serious, Boon, that I know. One night he drank too much and told me he didn't expect to live past 50, if that. His Dad had it and died young, that's what he said. He's not supposed to drink."

"Well, I don't like any of this."

"Neither do I. I should call Helen. We need to go check and then I'll call her. She's beside herself."

"How did he get here? You weren't with him."

"No. I have no idea. Neither does Helen. He had Helen's name and number in his wallet and they called her and she called me. Donovan had given her and Jerald my number. That's all we know. We don't know if he was home or at Payne or where he was. He was in surgery when I got here."

"You know this Jerald Redding keeps coming up. What's Jerald have to do with Plan Z10?"

"Jerald? You don't know, that's right, how would you? Jerald and Helen are an item, Boon. Cutest couple. He gave her a diamond necklace from Tiffany's. You've missed some things, Doddson Kooper-Boon, but we can't do it now; let's see how Donovan's doing."

* * * * *

By noon both of them had called Helen twice with reassurance and they were finally able to call and tell her the truth: he was fine. He was in post-op. They couldn't see him because he wasn't awake, but that would happen. They would call her the minute they talked to him. The minute.

They went to a lounge down the hall from ICU where they were told Donovan would be returned to at some point. Tinabelle ranged all over the place, telling Boon about Donovan's past and his relationship to Helen and about the sculpture gallery and the opening, how much work Donovan had put into the gallery construction, gathering the sculptures, how it had all come together. She told him everything and he listened, unable to speak while she creatively animated every single detail of the opening, who wore what, who said what, the mime, the Tencel suits, the lighting, the food, the confusion about Douglas Boon, the starsplitter, the champagne. The only single thing Tinabelle didn't mention was the review of the show in the newspaper. She finally stopped, noticing that Boon had his head in his hands.

"Doddson Kooper-Boon. So you get this. Isn't it grand?"

He looked up at her. "Grand. No, Tinabelle, all I can think is tragic. If anything happens to Donovan, I'll feel responsible. He has worked so hard on my behalf..."

"That's ridiculous, DKB. Donovan works this hard for everybody. It's just who he is. You saw how he helps with the circus. It's not his job, it's not Payne, it's just something some of his students have an interest in doing. He doesn't have to do any of the things he does for us, but he does. He's funded us, helped train us, been on board for crisis after crisis. He's glued sequins on shoes, he's hauled in food, he went to the hardware store: you saw him do that the day we met. That's typical. He has projects like Boon and Tantamount all over the place; you and I aren't special. Donovan's a workaholic, Boon; he works. He doesn't really play and he doesn't date. He doesn't want to get involved with a woman and have the subject of children come up, since he feels he can't have them, much as he'd like to. I tell him to go ahead, fall in love, marry, adopt, science has all sorts of solutions now, lots of options, but he hasn't listened to me so far. He just works. He's driven. I think he feels he's racing the clock, that's my theory. And he's probably right. You know, Donovan is one of those guys who is always right, always making a contribution. He just is. He doesn't make mistakes. He's right on, all the time." She stopped and became thoughtful, then spoke very quietly. "I feel bad. I told him not too long ago, I was mad at him because he suggested revisions on a routine I'd worked weeks to perfect, I told him I'd like to see him stub his fucking toe, just once, that the perfection routine got old. And this happens."

"Now you're doing it, Tinabelle. He has a bad heart. He'll be fine. Let's stay with what we can stay with and not go running around the greyhound track after a decoy rabbit."

"I'm going to go check."

She returned looking glum. "He's awake, but they're not moving him yet. They keep asking if I'm family. I'm not and neither are you. I don't think they're going to let us see him, Boon. They said it would be morning. Tomorrow! I can't believe this. I'm going to have to just go, I guess. I take care of my aunt, she's alone in her apartment and not doing well. Bladder infection for the second time this month, poor thing. I have to get back and check on her. I guess I'll leave and come back in the morning. What are you going to do?"

"I'm staying. Leave me your cell number and I'll call you if there's news."

"OK. I'll call Helen and tell her you're staying and that you'll call her. I guess this is all we can do right now. I don't know how you're going to get in to see him."

"I don't either, but I'll think of something."

* * * * *

Boon slept the night on a couch in the lounge. He awakened every hour or so and asked about Donovan. He finally slept three straight hours and went to the nurse's station at 6 AM and asked again. Yes. Donovan was in ICU. No, he could not have visitors: family only. Boon asked if he could be given the number for Dr. Hanson Carttin, his psychiatrist. The nurse was more than willing to hand it over; Boon had been a nuisance. She gave him the phone.

"Hanson, Boon here. Know it's early, hope you're not in the clinches there, Hanson, with the you-know-who. Hi, Sis, if you're there. Listen, man, got a situation. Need your bludgeon with these people. Got a guy in ICU, as you know, Donovan King, sis told you all about this, I know she did. He's out of heart surgery and they won't let me in to see him because I'm not family. This guy has no blood family, Hanson, not a soul. Adopted. His adopted parents are in Geneva, Switzerland. I need to get in there and let the poor bastard know somebody cares about what he's going through. You know how wacko and unstable I am, who knows what havoc I'll wreak if I can't get my way. Might feng shui the nurse's station, if you know what I mean. Might start licking the walls or start photocopying strips of bacon. I have bacon in my pocket."

The two nurses overhearing this looked at each other with wide eyes and charts frozen in space in front of them. A phone rang and neither of them moved to answer it. Carttin had hung up on Boon; he handed the phone back, "You might answer that damn phone. Somebody could be dying. Jesus."

He sat down on the floor across from the nurse's station and waited, anticipating what marble face would do. He would call Douglas, if she wasn't there in bed with him. Then he would call Donovan's doctor. Donovan's doctor would call Donovan's surgeon. Donovan's surgeon would call who knew who. Who knew who would call somebody else and somebody else would call the nurse's station, and by Easter maybe he would be allowed to see Donovan King, who would, by then, be fully recuperated and visiting fellow filmmakers in Mozambique. He would wait it out. He took yesterday's bacon from his pocket and ate it, then sat there whistling a tune of air, flipping his head around in a posture of aggravatingly gleeful patience, tapping one tennis-shoed toe in time with the tune no one else could hear.

* * * * *

It took forty-seven minutes for the power wheels to turn. Boon was escorted into Donovan's room.

Boon approached the bed. "Donovan King, Boon here. You gonna pay for my coffee this morning? If you are, I could use some breakfast, too. Sure would appreciate it."

"Boon."

"Yo, Donovan. See you're in transition, man. How you feelin'?"

"Rough. I made it, didn't I?"

"You did. I'm just gonna take a seat over there and let you rest. I'll be here."

"No. Listen. You have to do something."

"Right now?"

"Yes." Donovan shut his eyes.

Boon turned to the nurse. "What the hell? Is he all right?"

She answered, "Yes, but make this short."

"Find Trenton TeVelde King. Capital T, small e, capital V, e, l, d, e. Facebook. Get Tinabelle to help you. Find him. Get him here."

"Who is this?"

"Says he's my son."

"You have a son? Talk about that in the universe of stardom!"

"Find him." Donovan shut his eyes.

"Sir, that's enough. Wait outside, please." The nurse went to the bed and adjusted the IV.

* * * * *

Boon called Helen. Five sentences: "He's fine. Sends his love. I need sleep myself. Will call later. Love to you, fair lady." No mention was made of another King in the wings. Boon told himself to wait: he didn't know what kind of bird he was, where he was roosting, what his flight pattern might be.

He called Tinabelle, "We're on, here's the go: we need to do something for Donovan. He's brain-working; I talked to him, and he gave us work in the department of importance. Lightning flash. I'll explain when you pick me up. I'll be out front. Can you come and get me right away? Hey, bring a juggler's laptop if you have one. We need internet. I don't know a damn thing about it; you'll have to help. Donovan said you'd be able to do it. Don't park, just pull under the portico. I'll watch for you, Circus."

23

IN COUNTRY

. . . .

We mirror our surroundings.

—Sarah Rossbach

Well, our Boon couldn't have it easy. No. The man named Trenton TeVelde King couldn't be nearby in a convenient environment, accessible with a simple phone call. Of course not. He wouldn't be right there on Facebook with a photograph and an address and some clue about his life. Of course not. He was twenty-one. That was it. No schools, no nothing. A birthday, which Boon scribbled down on a piece of paper and put in his pocket. No place of birth. That was it.

Tinabelle worked through everything she knew how to do and finally gave up, telling Boon he needed a hacker. Or he needed the police. It was her opinion that Trenton TeVelde King was either in hiding or hiding something, or both. She felt it was unnatural for a twenty-one year old, especially an American, to be so occluded online. Something was wrong with him. Something was wrong.

Boon called the police and talked to Marc Fisk in Portland, explaining the situation, surprised to find out that Fisk knew Donovan King. This was a help: Fisk ran the name and birthday and had a location within an hour. Permanent domicile, Perth, Western Australia. Dual citizenship. Easy. Just get on over there to OZ and get the guy and get him in front of his Dad at the hospital. No problem. There was an international phone number. Tinabelle offered to try it. They were at a coffee shop and asked to use the phone for an international call. She handed the girl a twenty dollar bill, explaining that it was an emergency. She would get the charges and give her more if necessary.

Tina presented herself as director of Circus Tantamount, seeking to speak with Trenton TeVelde about working with the circus. The elderly woman she talked to on the phone said Trenton wasn't "in country," that's how she put it, as if he were absent from a military site. He was in Germany. She had a number. She sounded distracted and in a hurry. Tina then called Germany and was told by a surly woman in a youth hostel that TeVelde was in America. He had left two weeks ago. When asked where in America, the woman said she didn't know and hung up.

Tinabelle finally decided to try to friend Trenton on Facebook. She typed in her name. She and Boon were eating breakfast when it came in: he responded and a flurry of transmissions ensued. Trenton TeVelde King was at Payne! He was in the library at Payne! They couldn't believe it! He had been to his father's office. He was hanging out, waiting to hear from Donovan, that's what he said. It was arranged: Boon and Tinabelle would come and pick him up. The two of them had readily agreed that they would wait to tell Trenton his father was in the hospital. They didn't want to scare him to death. It was working! How delightfully simple, that's what Tinabelle said.

Boon wasn't so sure. Boon saw it coming: too easy. He had a knot in his stomach that wouldn't quit; he saw trouble flying into their midst. He made a decision: he should go alone, line it out first. Donovan was in a fragile state. They needed more information. He convinced Tinabelle to drop him off at Payne. He would handle this. She gave him forty dollars for the task at hand and agreed not to mention anything yet to anyone. Too many unanswered questions. Tinabelle wished him luck and mentioned the cell phone, twice. He was to call her. She let him off in front of the library and reluctantly drove away.

* * * * *

"You are Trenton TeVelde King." Boon took him in. He didn't look like Donovan. He had sandy hair and freckles, was short and heavy set, wearing wire-rimmed glasses. He looked older than twenty-one.

"Yes. Who are you?"

"I'm Tinabelle's friend. She couldn't come. I'm Doddson Kooper-Boon."

"And?"

"And. Seems you are looking for a friend of mine, Donovan Trenton King."

"And?"

"And I am a friend of his."

"You are."

"I am."

"How do I know that?"

"You don't, son. You don't know shit. You are in a situation here, where you'll just have to trust me, I guess. I'm moderately trustworthy. Not the worst, not the best, but when it comes to Donovan, I'm good."

"Well that makes you pretty suspect in my book."

"It does."

"Yeah. Any friend of his can't be much. I thought the Tina-belle was probably his wife or something, so I let her spin, but I don't need some sleem friend of my father's in my face."

Boon glitched a minute on sleem, then responded, "Ah, angry young man, abandoned by the father who knocked up his ma and ditched. Is that what we're doing here?"

"You don't know anything about him. He's waste. I just found out. My grandmother let me in on it, finally. She's had his name all along. I kept asking and she finally told me."

"You don't sound Australian."

"I was born here and spent my first fourteen years here."

"Where was this?"

"None of your business. You don't need my life story."

"How's your heart?"

"My heart?"

"Your heart. Do you have any heart problems?"

"No, why would you ask that?"

"Son, I gotta say, you don't strike me as Donovan King's son. Now, I know that's not what you've been told, but you just don't."

"Are you calling my grandmother a liar?"

"No, I'm not. Where's your mother?"

"She's..."

"What? Where is she?"

"She's...gone."

"Well, do you know where she is?"

"Yeah. She's in a facility again in Perth."

"Facility. What's that mean?"

"It means she's getting help again. She's been in treatment for-ever. She doesn't really know me, never has. She talks to me, but she doesn't relate to me as her son. That's what he did."

"He made her mentally ill, I assume this is a mental problem, by impregnating her?"

"Yes. Grandma says she was perfectly fine until right after I was born and Mom was sent back to Australia. Grandma doesn't blame Donovan, she's really religious and keeps saying God has a plan, but I do. I came here to make it right."

"Your Mom was sent home to Australia and left you here, as a baby?"

"Yeah. It had to happen. I guess she was really bad."

"Who raised you?"

"Several families. I went to Australia when I was fourteen."

"And you've lived with your grandmother, your Mom's mother?"

"No. She takes care of Grandpa in a little apartment. He's frail. I stayed in a room behind the co-op. Did chores."

"School? Did you go to school?"

"Not in Australia. Not interested and I was busy, but then I learned about Donovan King, not hard to find, and came to get this taken care of, make things right, as I said."

"You know, son, that's not possible. You seem bright enough to realize that."

"He's some big shot faculty here and she's in and out of being fucked up. It's possible. I can take away his nice life. He's not a good man. I think he's shit."

"One thing. One big thing in this picture. We need a paternity test, Trenton. That would be first. Would you be willing to do that?"

"What's that going to prove?"

"It's going to prove whether or not you're the son of Donovan Trenton King."

"I have his name. She gave me his name. That's proof enough for me."

"Well it isn't proof enough for me and it won't be for Donovan and it isn't proof legally, Trenton. Get this: you are flying blind. I'm not saying you aren't his son; I'm saying we need to know for sure. It's simple. Facts. We need facts."

"Where is he?"

"He's away. On a trip. It's you and me. Tell me, what's your story? I know you don't want to tell me your life story and I don't need to hear that, but there's still chunks of daylight blowin' through this that I'm concerned about."

"What do you mean? I just told you everything you need to know."

"I'm not feelin' that, Trenton. Let's go here: what's up? You've been traveling. You just turned twenty-one. I'm a long way from twenty-one, what's it like for you? What are your plans?"

"Plans? I told you. I'm after him. Tell him off, make him pay for ruining her life."

"You want money, then?"

"That, but I also want to make him suffer, realize what he did to us."

"That sounds like a threat. Somehow it doesn't seem to suit you, Trenton."

"It is a threat. I want him to know what he did."

"I see. Well, beyond that, what's your story?"

"I'm an artist. I paint."

"Artist. I'm impressed. Not an easy choice, being an artist. I don't know about Australia, but in this country artists have a hard time of it: rocks and hard places all over from hell to cheezwhiz. Just generally speaking."

"Yeah. Tell me about it. I've been painting since I was fourteen and have nothing to show for it. All those years, a whole body of work cast into the void."

"Do you have anything on you I might see? I'm interested in art, believe it or not."

"No. It's online, though. I'm on a website for artists."

"I don't know anything about that, but I see a computer over there. Is there some way you can show me your work?"

"I guess. Why not?"

Boon stood while photos and art appeared on the monitor.

The artists were all young; Trenton's first name came up, followed by a short bio and images of a dozen paintings. He sat down when it was over and spoke to Trenton, "Young man, I have a suggestion. Tissue paper of a lampshade, but...where are you staying?"

"I'm out. I had money to get here, but that's it. I'm OK; there's a shed I found down by a loading dock with an old guy who said I could sleep there. He has me run errands for him."

"I'll bet he does. Well, I have a better idea. Tell me, how did you get money together to get from Australia to Germany to here? Seems like that would cost quite a bit."

"CRINGE. That's the website."

"CRINGE? What's that?"

"It's an artist-writer cooperative resource center. There's a man there, Nono, a French aboriginal who paid for me. He knows about my mother and when I told him what my grandmother finally told me, he paid my way. He's the director there; he's a crippled up rodeo cowboy. There's a fund. Said I should find my father. Said I'd have to get back on my own, but we said our good-byes. I won't be going back."

"He knows your work. Why did you go to Germany?"

"He said I had to go to Europe. Said I had to see Paris for him."

"And did you see Paris?"

"I did."

"What'd you think of the gayest of towns?"

"I liked it. I see why he thought I should go, because I'm a painter. He has all kinds of ideas about my work. He thinks I should be able to make it."

"Uh-huh. Well, I want to give a hand here, Trenton. Did you leave anything behind at the shed?"

Trenton thought about it. "Nothing I can't go back for later."

"Then I need to make a phone call to Tinabelle." He dialed and talked non-stop. "Tinabelle. Need your help. I need a motel, two beds in one room. Can you call and charge a room in my name? Need to be close to hardware store delivery, need to make that run. Then call me back and we'll take a cab. Trenton and I need to have a place to stay until Donovan gets back from his trip. Coupla days, isn't it? Until he gets back? Yeah, coupla days. Yeah, you're right about that. Call me right back, OK? Thanks." He hung up on her, knowing he'd better avoid her obvious questions, such as what the hell he was doing. He wasn't sure himself. He was having the response Tinabelle had when she looked at Trenton's Facebook page: something was wrong. The word rodeo was really, really bothering him.

* * * * *

"Donovan."

"Hi, Boon. Where'd you come from?"

"I'm around. You ready to blow this joint?"

"No. I'm not, Boon. They stood me up this morning and I'm not going anywhere for a while. Did you find out anything? Did you find him?"

Boon handed Donovan the piece of paper with Trenton's birthday on it. "Look at this."

Donovan looked at the birth date and smiled. "Not my son."

"How do you know?"

"Because. I encountered Lana TeVelde only once; it was on my birthday, at a party in Boston. I drank too much. The next morning she cried and cried and after that passed and she settled down, I left. She stayed around Boston for another few weeks, a real party girl, Australian, pretty, an art student, but unstrung, way unstrung, alcoholic, all kinds of afflictions, and I heard she left Boston. Never saw her again. The birth date here is a good year past what would make me this person's father. Frankly, I'm surprised Lana even remembered my name. She only met me that one night. Not proud of this, Boon."

"You're positive."

"Yes, no question."

"OK. You need to rest. You can get this off your mind, but I have to get going, here, Donovan. You carry on, man. Get some strength back and then I need to be getting down on my knees and thanking you for doing a whole hell of a lot for me. I'm still shakin' my head, Donovan. You are the man. But right now, I've got the old Boon plate heaped high with a few other things that need a fair amount of chewing. I'll be back. You talk to Helen?"

"Yes. We talked on the phone. She and Jerald are coming tomorrow."

"Well, good. Later, man. Suck up that pure oxygen."

* * * * *

The motel room was abuzz with more activity than Boon could handle. He opened the door, took a look, and almost shut it and took off.

"Tinabelle. Trenton. Man, what is this?"

"Hi, Boon. Brought food. Thought you might need something to eat, you and Trenton."

"What's the cat?" It was a fuzzy, totally black kitten.

Trenton explained, "He was hanging around outside, a stray. I asked at the desk and they said he's been around for a few days. When Tinabelle showed up with food, we brought him in to feed him. I'm going to adopt him. We named him Woolie."

"Tinabelle. Could we have a conference? Outside. Trenton, would you excuse us a minute? Tinabelle and I, well, we need a quick chat; you know how men and women are."

"Sure." Trenton was holding Woolie and scratching his ears.

They stood outside, walking down a couple of doors. "What, Boon? What did you find out? Did you talk to Donovan?"

"Yes. Not his kid, Tinabelle."

"That's obvious. No way. I knew it."

"Yeah, well, good for you. But what do we do now? Lots about this kid I'm not understanding." He ran it by her as succinctly as he could.

"Well, sounds simple enough. I'll call this Nono guy. Verify. Find out more. Does sound like a lot of money to put out to get him here. Might be a money scam. Donovan isn't wealthy, but he does have a bank account, that's for sure."

"You do that. It's a busy start to a standstill drill."

It took some time as they stood in the front office of the motel to use the land-line phone, but she finally reached CRINGE in Perth and had Nono on the line; she was frankly surprised such a man existed. Even though the phone had awakened him, he immediately had a question for Tinabelle, who introduced herself as a friend of Trenton King who was calling from San Francisco, California, USA.

Tinabelle listened and then exclaimed, "Who? What?" Tinabelle looked shocked.

Boon heard Tinabelle say, "Sir, you'll have to explain. I need to know more about this. I just met Trenton and I'm trying to help him."

Boon watched, trying to figure out what they were talking about. He leaned over the back of a chair he was holding onto, feeling tired and worn out. He needed to lie down. Tinabelle was finally ending the conversation, "Thank you so much, Nono. You've been so helpful. I'll have Trenton call you. In just a few minutes. Please be there on the phone. I know he'll want to talk to you." She hung up.

"What? What'd he say?"

"Oh, man, do we have a problem, Boon."

"No kidding. What?"

"Well, Trenton's on the square, except for one small detail."

"What's that?"

"He has a family. A wife, Elita, and a one year-old child, a girl, Boomy."

"He left them behind?"

"No, Boon. He brought them here. At least Nono hopes they're with him. He left with them and he had them with him in Paris. That's the last Nono heard."

"Jesus Christ. They might be in that fuckin' shed!"

"What shed?"

"We gotta get on this, Tinabelle. Let's go."

They went into the motel room and Tinabelle pointed to the phone on the bed stand. "Call Nono."

Trenton was surprised. "Nono?"

"Yes, Trenton TeVelde King, Nono. I just talked to him. He needs to hear from you. Right now. He's waiting."

Trenton stood and started to leave for the front office to make his call. Boon restrained him by grabbing his arm. "You're making the call right here, Trenton. There's a phone right there by the bed. Use it. We need to hear this."

"You do not. This is my friend and my business."

Boon was stern, even menacing. "Wrong. You've made it our business, Trenton. Now make the goddamn call. My patience is stretched thinner than a spider's web, I'm tellin' you."

Tinabelle added, "He's more than your friend, Trenton, come on."

Boon put his hands out questioningly, "What's that mean?"

"It means that Nono is family, Boon. Elita is Nono's daughter. He's worried about his grandbaby. Nono is Trenton's father-in-law."

Boon sat down on the bed and flopped sideways onto the pillow and closed his eyes.

Tinabelle came over and asked, "You all right, Doddson Kooper-Boon?"

He whispered, "Fair shine," and stopped.

She lifted his legs up onto the bed and sat on the very edge watching him. She took his hand and watched his shallow breathing. She stood. "Boon?" When he didn't answer, she leaned over and said it again, "Boon, answer me." She called an ambulance.

24

MISSING THE ACTION

· ·

*Let us consider for a moment what most of the trouble
and anxiety which I have referred to is about, and how much
it is necessary that we be troubled, or at least, careful.*
—HENRY DAVID THOREAU

Once again, a great many things happened without Boon. He
was on the planet, people came and went, he even signed some
papers, but he was clearly not participating in life as he knew
it. He was hooked up and the doctor, a Nan Drummond, an
individual of enormously powerful presence and very apparent
expertise, had ordered that Doddson Kooper-Boon was to be
incarcerated—his word, not hers—in the hospital until further
notice. He was suffering from exhaustion, his blood pressure was
erratic, he was anemic, he had arterial blockages, he had compli-

cations from a concussion. She didn't like the looks of his EKGs, his EEGs, his urinalysis, his blood work or his feet. She liked her patient just fine, but as she told her friend and colleague, Douglas Boon, "Your brother is unwell."

Once again, he was being told a great many very interesting things while he was unable to really process them. The first was the arrival of Helen and Jerald, acting as if they'd been married fifty years, wearing weddings rings and planning a trip to Scotland. They gushed over him and chattered about the gallery he had never seen and his work, which he still wasn't sure existed anymore. They left holding hands; it was weird, too much to take in.

Next, Tinabelle came dressed as a clown and did a performance for him which was fun, he guessed, but mainly she succeeded in making him feel he'd died and joined the big circus in the sky. She did tell him, after the show was over and she'd removed a matted, red wig, that Trenton and his family were living in an Airstream trailer in the backyard of the house she and Leisle rented in Berkeley from Leander. Woolie was with them and got along famously with Heat and Chill, and the baby, Boomy, was darling and the wife, Elita, was delightful and looked just like Eva Darnett. Nono and Mary J were thrilled. The sheer number of proper nouns in this speech flummoxed Boon, as did the fact that there was no mention of Donovan. When he asked, Tinabelle brushed it aside, as if the man hadn't nearly died, as if he'd really just been in Mozambique after all, and hadn't had someone claiming to be the fruit of his loins appear out of nowhere. She left, leaving Boon seriously troubled about his ability to understand what had happened and what hadn't.

Douglas visited, looking despicably ravishing with the despicable Carbeige in tow. Boon wanted to tell his sister that the decent thing she might have considered doing, with her poor brother sick to death in the hospital, might have been to show up looking like the fifty year-old she was, in jeans and a t-shirt or an old jogging suit, with her hair pulled into a pony tail maybe, towing the normal, middle-aged, bald, nice fellow named Greg Hopper. Or, speaking of doctors, maybe she could have decently checked in on him wearing her scrubs, on her way to surgery to remove a uterus, something to make him feel lucky he was a man. Instead, she looked as if she had just modeled for the cover of MORE magazine and hadn't had time to change. Her hair was three times thicker than he ever remembered it being, and cascaded down onto her shoulders like honey dropping off a big wooden spoon. She looked thirty, smelled like an English garden, radiated joy and had the tops of her tits showing above a sculpted designer suit which really didn't need the one button that held the jacket together: why bother, that's what Boon thought. The skirt was tight and short and the shoes were high and clacked annoyingly on the sterile floor as she walked vigorously around the room talking mainly about money. Carbeige sat and salivated in a chair in the corner, watching her ass, listening to her every word. He tugged on his shirt cuffs to maintain the requisite half-inch showing beyond the jacket sleeve; he was wearing black star sapphire cufflinks.

Douglas didn't stop: Oh, and by the way, the divorce is final, we're leaving for Mount Cinnamon, and oh, by the way, I need your signatures on these documents. A notary public appeared from nowhere and stood there. He signed for a bank account she'd opened for him, and had him sign a rich piece of paper which indicated that his portion—she did not say half—of the inheritance was $90,000. It would be routed to the new bank account. His sister leaned over and kissed him and said goodbye the minute the pen was lifted from the n on the last of many Boons, as if none of this meant awfully much. She walked out acting as if he'd just signed something saying he preferred chicken to beef for his next Thursday hospital luncheon, an exquisitely catered affair, for which Boon had learned his full signature was necessary: initials *would not do*. Finally, Carbeige shook his hand

and told him to "be well." When it was over, Boon pushed the button for the nurse and said he had a headache. It was a boomer. Boomy. Who named a kid Boomy?

On the seventh day, Boon met this child. He was back from minor surgery, but felt as if they'd removed his heart, his lungs and his head. He was reassured, however, by the things he could see: arms, hands, legs, feet and a dick. The threesome which appeared unannounced in Boon's room was a blurred assemblage of humans and flowers. The dark haired, tiny thing called Elita carried an enormous bouquet of red and yellow flowers which had enough greenery poked in it to landscape the salt flats. She set it on the table at the end of his bed, then moved it, saying it would block his view. He wondered just what view she was talking about. Trenton dangled the child over his bed, a cute bundle with two arms and two legs, which reminded Boon of a crib mobile.

This Boomy didn't like the looks of Boon and started to cry. He couldn't blame the kid. He himself hadn't had the stomach to look in the mirror in quite some time. He now had confirmation that it wasn't a good idea. Trenton positively enthused about the Airstream and Leisle and Tinabelle and Woolie and even the mysterious Leander, as once again, Boon wondered how all of these names had gotten into his cloud cover. And once again, there was no mention of one Donovan King, arch nemesis, the man Trenton wanted to see suffer. Boon decided maybe he didn't want to hear about the bloodshed, thanked them for coming, and took a nap.

Finally someone woke him up with something to say that Boon could understand. It was Torrey. He wanted to talk about "Vision." He wanted to buy it for Heather and give it to her when baby Douglas arrived. He didn't want anyone else to have it. He *had* to have it. He talked on and on about the details of the piece, the star-splitter poetry, the light, the power, the artistic integrity, the way it moved him. Boon drifted around in a euphoric cloud of re-being as Torrey spoke and finally asked Boon forthrightly if he could buy the piece right away. Boon mumbled unceremoniously that he could have it. When Torrey insisted that he buy it, Boon, trying very hard to hold back tears, gruffly told his nephew that it wasn't for sale: it was a gift and it was meant for Torrey and his family. Then Uncle Dodd, as Torrey called him, indicated that he really was pretty damn tired and had to get some beauty rest. Boon did sleep, and he slept very well: his first piece had found a real home. Someone thought so much of it that they had been willing to *buy* it! He felt quite proud that this first someone was a relative, a kid he'd always liked, who had grown up behind his back.

Donovan Trenton King. Day ten. He stood at the door of Boon's private room with a nurse. He had been transported from another, bigger, better hospital miles away. Boon could see the rim of a wheel. Donovan had been brought down the hall in a wheelchair, but now walked into the room and sat down. The nurse followed and he nodded to her: she could leave. "Boon, are you ever going to get out of here?"

Doddson Kooper-Boon, rarely a man at a loss for words, could not, for the life of him, think of anything to say. He was in shock. He couldn't understand how Donovan could look so different, so pale, so thin, so much older, so sick. Black circles rimmed the entire circumference of his eyes. He had a tremor in his right hand. His long hair was gone; it had been cut straight across in a jaw length jag with one side tucked behind his left ear. He was very visibly medicated. The nurse stood at the door, a sentinel, to Boon, of doom. He now understood why no one had mentioned Donovan: not one of them could assure Boon that he was still alive. He looked as if he could go at any time. Boon wanted to cry, to reach for Donovan's hand, to make it go away, but he didn't. Instead, he rallied and quipped, "They need the money. They'll keep me here as long as they can, Donovan, the bastards."

Donovan spoke, "I lied to you."

Boon felt the here it comes and took a deep breath. "You did. Well, Donovan, that's something people do, you know. I've been known to do it myself. Not a good thing, but it happens. Not the end of the world, fair shine."

"Listen to me."

"Sure thing. I'm right here. Confessional is open. What is it?"

Donovan just sat there, looking at his knees.

Boon prompted him, "I suspect you got your dates wrong. The kid is yours, isn't he?"

"No, he isn't. I was right about the dates, but I lied about other things."

"OK, Donovan. This sounds like a hard deal for you, but let's get through it, get it over with. You've got to get over yourself. Looks like a hurdle. I'll help."

"I know why Lana gave Trenton my name."

"OK. Why is that?"

"She thought I was a good man, an exceptionally good man, a noble man."

"Well, I would sure say she was right about that."

"She wasn't. She was wrong."

"Why?"

"Because I didn't sleep with her that night. I slept overnight with her, I held her, but we didn't have sex."

"Because she was drunk and you didn't want to take advantage of her."

"I was drunk, too."

"Well, you must have been sober enough to understand what shouldn't happen."

"What couldn't happen."

"Right. Never a good idea. Nobody remembers it in the morning, anyway."

"But that's not what happened."

"What happened, Donovan? Christ."

"I am probably the only man who ever turned Lana down. She was really a wonderful woman, Boon, just the most beautiful woman I've ever known, in so many ways. I met her that night and I loved her. Instantly."

"And then what?"

"I didn't tell her."

"Donovan, this is tough. Yes. I get that. You didn't tell her you loved her. You didn't sleep with her. You rejected her. You let one get away. It happens; I'm the guy who would know, luck has it as gospel."

"No, not that."

"Jesus, Donovan, what's the straddle?"

"I didn't tell her I'm gay."

Boon reeled. His head spun. He raced through the reference section of his interior library. He took his time and took his own counsel: when you don't know what to say, repeat, repeat, "You're gay."

"I am."

"Well, this is news. I didn't know that."

"No one knows."

"How can that be? Tinabelle? Why wouldn't you tell Tinabelle?"

"I haven't told anyone. I don't know why. Well, there are reasons."

"You might tell me what those reasons might be."

"It's complicated."

"It usually is, Donovan, at least in my experience."

"I don't know for sure, but I think my father was gay; he slept with my mother, his cousin, but the records indicate that he was gay. I lied to Helen; it seems it was the man, Yost, who was his lover, not Pauline. I suspect he was bisexual, maybe, I don't know. There are several possibilities, of course; he was very young when I was conceived. I didn't find this out until recently, of course, from court documents and prison records, so it has nothing to do with..."

"What does it have to do with?"

"I just knew, at about thirteen, that I was gay. I hid it, have hidden it all my life."

"Well, you've done a damn good job of that. I had no idea—not that I care one way or the other, Donovan, Jesus."

"My parents, the people who adopted me, were sophisticated, intelligent, open-minded people. They would have had no problem with it; I just don't know why I couldn't tell them, or anyone. I dated and had what everyone assumed was a normal life. I was popular. Well-adjusted, they would call it. I excelled."

"Obviously. And you had relationships with men."

"No."

"Why not?"

"I just didn't. I was afraid when I was younger, the whole AIDS thing, especially with my heart. Now I teach young people; it's dangerous."

"So you haven't had sex in your entire life?" Boon regretted this awkward, stupid, unkind, unsophisticated, cruel remark, of course, the minute he said it, but it was too late.

"That's right."

Boon closed his eyes and lay there trying very, very hard to get rid of the idea which had come into his head. He didn't want to go there. No! He had wondered why Donovan had done so much for him. No! Boon opened his eyes. "Let's get this covered, my man. Am I someone you've been interested in, as frosting on a certain kind of cake?"

"No, Boon. I did what I did for you because I think you're a great artist. I admire you a great deal, but I didn't fall in love with you. That's not in the picture."

"But you have fallen in love?"

"Yes, three times."

"And you've never acted on it, ever?"

"Never."

Boon didn't know what to say. He could understand homosexuality perfectly well. He knew lots of men, fewer women, who were gay. It wasn't an issue for him. Never acting on the feeling of falling in love, however, was an issue for Boon; he had always acted on even the slightest pretense that he might, if she were the last woman on earth, eventually fall in love. In the meantime, he would take her to bed. He couldn't imagine. "I can't imagine. It's sad, Donovan. It has to change. You work at a very liberal institution; you aren't the sort of man who would hit on students, whether you were straight or gay. And the AIDS thing is, well, this is the modern age, Donovan. It's handled well by intelligent men like you and the kinds of partners you would choose; you know this."

"It's too late, Boon. I won't be around long enough."

"That's bullshit, Donovan."

"Yeah. Well, think what you want to think about it, but have a look. I have to take care of some things fast. That's why I came, Boon."

"Have you met Trenton?"

"No. I gave Tinabelle money and told her to handle all their needs. She isn't to tell them it came from me. I don't see the point in getting involved. I'm not his father."

"But you loved his mother. What if you're the only man who actually loved his mother?"

"It was one night! It's not enough, Boon."

"The hell it isn't. Some people, Donovan, go their entire lives without somebody loving them. You may know more about this than I do, I grant that, but damn it, the kid is a good kid. I saw his work. I saw his family. This is an exceptional person, Donovan; I know, I know, everyone is, but Trenton is gifted as a painter and he's had a challenging life from the sounds of it. The kid has a lot of courage."

"I know that. And I'll leave money to make sure he's supported for the rest of his life."

"It's not just your money he needs, Donovan."

"Well, he doesn't need me as a father."

"Why not?"

"Because I'm not his father! A dying, gay man. Not his father. I'm not related."

"Interesting, coming from you. You were raised by people who weren't related. Where the hell would you be today if people who didn't know you hadn't adopted you and loved you, Donovan? Jesus Christ. What difference does it make? He's here. He thinks you're his father. Why can't you be his father? Obviously, his real father will probably never, ever be found. What difference does it make who his father is? You loved his mother, Donovan. You played in a field of glory there for one night of holding her. That's what matters, right there, as far as I'm concerned."

"He has a wife and a baby. He has a family. He doesn't need a father. He's on his way with his own life. He's young; he'll be fine."

"Bullshit. This is making me mad, Donovan. Christ. You know, I had an instant take on you that you were a good guy. A really decent human being. What I see now, right this minute, is a selfish man who has shut himself down all his life and is pounding the lid on even tighter. This is bullshit, Donovan. Get off it. You may be dying and you may not be dying, who the hell knows. I don't, and I don't care. You are missing something, big time, Donovan. Road goes both ways. The kid needs a father. Apparently you need a son or he wouldn't be here, that's my take on it. God damn it, it would be good for you. Gay men are great fathers; I know several of them. I swear to God, Donovan. I wish I'd fucked his mother, or held onto her all night for tears and drunken nattering. I'd take him in a heartbeat. I'd be all over this. I'd be proud to have Trenton as my son. I don't know how the hell he managed to get all this way with a wife and baby, and I've been out a long, long time. The kid is an amazement, Donovan. I tell you what, you bastard, if you don't pick this up and do the right thing, I will."

"You'll be his father?"

"No, Donovan, I can't be his father. I didn't even know his mother. That would be you, Donovan."

"So what do you mean?"

"Well, I'll tell you what I mean. If you don't tell Trenton the truth and happily offer to take on the role as father and grandfather in this scenario, I'll tell him the truth and I'll do it."

"You're coercing me."

"You're damn right I am. And, just so you don't think I'm some poor starving artist who couldn't buy the grandkid a birthday present, I just inherited 90 grand. I can do just about as well as you can in the finance department. Well, not nearly as well as you can, but I'm in the running. Plus, I'll sell my work, thanks to you, Donovan. I do thank you for everything you've done for me, but you aren't finished. You have more work to do, Donovan. You can't sit around in a fucking wheelchair and feel sorry for yourself until you croak. It's a damn dumb thing to do. Rally, man. Talk to Tinabelle about this, the sooner the better. Find a nice guy to love. You're young; get laid. Be a father to Trenton. Watch Boomy grow up. Live, god damn it, Donovan." He paused, softening his diatribe, and concluded quietly, "Clean up your act, man."

25

SMOKING

. . . .

Let me just stand here a little and look my fill!
—Mark Twain

Boon decided to disappear. He would leave the old home town, the place of his birth, the San Fran. He wouldn't tell anybody he was out of the hospital and he wouldn't tell anybody goodbye. He wouldn't go to the new bank account and he wouldn't call his sister, wherever she was, probably still in the Caribbean. They released him at 7 AM with a clean bill of health, and print outs of dietary restrictions, which he threw in the trash can on the way out. He walked due north and hitched his first ride. He would book; he would turn rides like thunder.

He didn't talk much to anyone on six rides, except for the thank you and the fair shine, and he didn't tarry between them.

He had one destination in mind and one only: Good Fortune Antiques, or, more specifically, the sculpture gallery. He hit Portland and did a quick stop by Colora, hunkering down over a plate of French fries and a shared cheap beer with Wee Willie, helping him load a dozen new two-by-fours into a pickup, and headed across town on foot.

Ah, the sign. The bride and the groom. To the marriage of true minds. He noted the flowers in the planter and the red trimmed windows. He stood awhile on the sidewalk and for the first time in twenty-two years wished he had a cigarette. He looked around and saw a young man smoking across the street. He went over and asked, "Mind if I bum a smoke? Just got out of the hospital and need to celebrate." They stood there silently smoking, Boon looking now at the back of the sign; he felt a sudden urgency to get inside. It was late. He was afraid Helen would close up at 6:00 and he didn't want to disturb her after hours. He put out the cigarette and kept the half, slipping it into his pocket for later. He said his thanks and strode across the street and went in.

Nobody was at the cash register, but he could hear voices in back. The place looked different, mainly because of the spiral staircase and a new chandelier. He went up. He sat down in a corner and he cried. Thirty minutes later he was lying down, resting, thinking, wondering, ruminating, obsessing, worrying, and rejoicing when she found him.

She screamed.

Boon sat up and spoke, "Sorry I scared you. It's OK."

"How did you get in here?"

"I walked in the front door. I'm a friend of Helen's. Is she here?"

"No, she's in Scotland with Jerald. If you were a friend you would know that. Let's shut off the lights and go down. We should go down; I need to lock up."

"Maybe we shouldn't." Boon was giving the woman a Boon-over. He had made one of his spontaneous decisions: play it. She was a beaut. "I like this place."

"Well, good, but we're closing. You can come back, Helen will be back on Saturday. That would be good." She started down the stairs.

"I think I'd like to just spend the night here, if that would be all right with you."

"It would not be all right, obviously. These sculptures are very valuable. Please, you'll have to come back later."

"I don't think so. Tell me, are you staying in Helen's apartment?"

"It isn't Helen's apartment anymore; it's mine."

"And where does Helen live?"

"With Jerald, in his condo, obviously."

"Where's Fox?"

"There. They have a housesitter. Why am I telling you all this? God, please, just go."

"Nope. I'm in for the night. Long day. Just got out of the hospital and came up from San Francisco and I'm flat beat out."

"You're not going to make me call the police."

"No, I wouldn't make you do that, but if you do, talk to my buddy Marc Fisk. That's CSI. He'll tell you I'm a serial killer, but that he has hopes for my rehabilitation any second, that I'm probably pretty harmless at the moment, just coming from the lobotomy at the hospital, and all."

She smiled, "Funny guy. Who are you?"

"You first, pretty lady. I never give my name to strange women. Never know: stalkers. Women can be deadly. You carryin' a knife? I see the boots. Probably a martial arts goona." She did look athletic, but too feminine and probably too mature for such shenanigans. She was probably thirty, petite and way too sexy for her own good. The longish, curly bronze hair and big brown eyes did it. Boon swooned a bit; he admitted it to himself. Might be in big trouble here.

"Oh, God, you are going to give me a hard time, aren't you? You say you know Helen? I find that difficult to believe. She's, well..."

"Old. Yes. I dig old. She and I have been around the block, honey. There are things about Helen you don't know. Man, can she drive a hard bargain. Charged old Jerald five dollars for something worth fifty-cents, if that. He dug it, though."

"Come on..."

"Sure thing. Where we goin'? You want to take me out to dinner? Swell. I like the idea. All I've had is half a beer, half a cig and half a plate of fries all day."

"I'm not taking you out to dinner and I'm not listening to you joke around in a disgusting way about Helen. I like Helen. I like her immensely."

"Well, so do I. Big influence in my life, Helen has been."

"Really? And how would that be?"

"She traded me a red ashtray for salt and pepper shakers once. Very important transaction; the clouds parted and there was a glory rainbow on the whole parade. Jerald was there playing Sherlock."

"Oh, god. You were in the hospital for mental, weren't you, not a lobotomy, that's not done... but something. Weren't you?"

"I were." Boon kept a straight face.

She stood there looking at him as long as she could stand it and then laughed. "I'm Brett."

Boon stood, bowed and introduced himself, "And I'm Doddson Kooper-Boon."

"Oh, God, you aren't."

"I are, fair shine. I are."

"Oh my God."

"You certainly are devout, I must say. His spirit must be moving around in *your* breasts."

She shook her head, trying to ignore the comment, "You did these?" She waved her arm around to encompass the sculptures.

"I did."

"You did the sign."

"I did."

"God! And you just show up like this!"

"You know, this God fellow: are you calling for him? Is he hearing you? Do you think? Is he going to show up, too?"

She laughed, "I'm sorry," she was giggling now. "This is just so funny. I've heard so much about you."

"All good, I'm sure of that, well, relatively sure; the Doppler effect might come in to play, I'm not sure. Now, I have not a dime on me, so could you spring for supper? I need to eat, doctor's orders, and then I need to sleep, doctor's orders. If you could see the doctor I'm talking about, you would move your pretty little self in the direction of a restaurant. Dr. Drummond is probably watching you as we speak. She's sixteen ISIS operatives all rolled into one." He pointed at Brett as if he held a machine gun and moved it back and forth, spraying her with ammunition.

"Don't do that! I hate that! Why do guys do that?" She went over and shut off the lights. "I suppose we could go eat, but we have to go down and you'll have to wait while I make a phone call."

"I have just the thing to tell him."

"What?"

"Tell him you just met the love of your life and it's over. You should say he meant a great deal to you, use the past tense, and then say he's a darling man, that you'll always remember him, then use his name, delivered poignantly, with a sniffle, and then hang up. It's worked on me."

"Sorry to stifle your creativity, and your machismo, but I have to call my mother. She and I had plans to watch *Wheel of Fortune*; it's her favorite show. I was supposed to get take-out."

"Well, hell, we can do that. I can handle two dames at once. It's been awhile, but I think I can remember how it works. Just have to slow things way down."

"Man, you do not quit! I don't think so. I think Mom will be just fine. She rags on me all the time about not having a damn date. I'll tell her I have a damn date and she'll open a can of soup and sit around all night long seeing me married with her grandchild by the weekend. That's how her mind works."

"I like this woman." Boon was, of course, talking about Brett.

* * * * *

They walked to Hide-Away-Away, a funk-end restaurant three blocks away, and had a quick meal. It was a business dinner, apparently, as Brett filled Boon in on the many details of running the new establishment which featured his art. She summarily dismissed any personal questions and went into a professional art curator, antique store hotshot routine that didn't quit, even with a glass of wine. She had things lined out for Boon to do. He had decisions to make about buyers and prices. He had calls to return. He had to advise on shipping. Two colleges wanted to speak to him about loaning pieces. He should get online and deal with the controversial blogs regarding his sculptures, much of which was the result of two critical reviews: one good and one bad. Blogging was critical to effective networking. He would have to consider the marketing tactic of announcing a new work in progress to keep people interested. He should grant an interview and have his photograph professionally taken in his studio. He really, really should have a website designed and have a more efficient network. She mentioned links. The word network was used so many times during the hamburger and pasta salad that Boon thought maybe she had a network tic. He ate and he listened and he watched her, deciding she was just nervous. Terribly nervous. He drank a second glass of wine.

She was finished and paying the check when Boon decided to get down to business. "You mentioned you don't get out much."

She teared up. "Damn."

"I see. Well, here's what I think. I heard everything you said about the gallery and I'm impressed with everything you know about selling art and whatnot; Helen has found a jewel, that's for sure, but Brett, this is a no-go."

"What do you mean?"

"I don't do the gallery, network, marketing thing. I never will. You'll have to do that part. I just roam around and collect stuff and shove it together and that's it. I don't do the whole art scene, Brett. I won't be blogging. I don't even know what it is."

"Well, that's OK. There are ways around that."

"What there isn't a way around, though, Brett, is this: can we go crawl in a bed at your place and sleep on it? And I do mean sleep. I just got out of the hospital, that's the truth, and I am really exhausted. I need a shower and sleep."

"You can't be serious. We just met."

"I don't care. Do you care?"

* * * * *

They walked to Good Fortune Antiques in a barren silence, entered, and Boon hung back wondering how Brett would handle things. He didn't have to wait long.

"Now, Boon, just go on in and shower and get on to bed. I have to finish up out here—I didn't close properly—and then I'll be in."

He did as instructed. He showered and crawled into bed and was asleep within three minutes.

He awakened at 5AM; the clock glowed the time inches from his face and he couldn't remember where he was. He rolled over and hit something at the foot of the bed, sat up and looked in the dusky light. It was a body, curled up with the corner of the bedspread over it. It was Brett, fully clothed of course, hugging a pillow and sound asleep. He got up, quietly dressed, grabbed his back pack and left the apartment. He walked to the cash register at the front of the store and found a red marking pen, then went up the spiral staircase to the top, flicking on the light.

He set his backpack down and walked around each piece, remembering what he had been doing, who was in his life, where pieces for assemblage had come from. It seemed that thirty years of his personal history sat in the room, spotlighted and tagged. He looked carefully at each sculpture and wondered who had cleaned them; they'd been outside, yet each one of them was polished up perfectly and there were no missing or loose pieces. Someone had spent a great deal of time getting the sculptures ready for the show. He assumed that someone must have been Brett. He walked over to "Vision" and wrote on the tag with the red marker SOLD: Torrey Hopper, Palo Alto, PAID. He printed his initials carefully after the last word. He then went to "Reason" and wrote SOLD: Dr. Donovan Trenton King, Payne, PAID, and initialed it.

He looked around at the other fourteen sculptures, trying to choose just the right one. He sat down and thought about it. He stood and walked around. He started to choose one, then sat down and deliberated some more. He finally chose "Light" and wrote SOLD: Trenton TeVelde King, PAID, DKB. He then went to "Joy" and wrote SOLD: Tinabelle/Circus Tantamount, SF, PAID, DKB. He then went to "Healing" and wrote SOLD: Douglas Boon, M.D., PAID, DKB. He chose "Balance" for Greg Hopper and fixed up his tag. He went to "Wisdom" and wrote SOLD: Mr. & Mrs. Jerald Redding, PAID, and initialed it especially flamboyantly. He thought of Cindy and Susan, maybe if he included Jim? He didn't know if it would be OK; it might cause problems. He decided to just do Cindy, and chose a smaller sculpture, one of his early pieces, which he had titled "Youth." He was twenty-four when he did it. He fixed the tag, formally indicating the recipient as Cynthia Michelle Forbes. He thought of other people, mostly women, and didn't know. He considered one in particular, but she was in Texas and he hadn't heard from her since she left Portland. Wasted effort. He decided on Lou. Lou would appreciate a sculpture; Lou had the house for it. Boon chose "Music," Lou was a music man, and wrote on the tag SOLD: Lou Prachek, Portland, PAID, and initialed it.

He then went to "Beauty," one of his most elaborate pieces, one of the most expensive pieces, because it was done with polished marble bits and shaped into the torso of a woman. It was the most labor-intensive of all Boon's sculptures. He wrote SOLD: Brett, Good Fortune Antiques, PAID. He didn't know her last name. He initialed it and added a heart. He shut off the light and went downstairs, returning the red marker to the drawer and snagging a book of matches. He left the shop and stood outside under the sign contemplating the day. He pulled the crushed half cig out of his pocket and lit up. He smoked. He needed coffee. He smudged the butt on the sidewalk and walked over to put it in a trash receptacle when he noticed a yellow road turtle loose in the gutter. He picked it up, slipped it into his backpack and walked away.

26

COFFEE HOUR

· ·

Damn this nostalgia! I swore I'd never
bemoan mistakes I made.
—David Memmott

Once again, people were looking for Boon. The cell phone
Tinabelle had given him was in the bottom of his back pack and
kept buzzing, but he ignored it. He didn't have anything to say to
anyone; he had no idea how to use the thing to get messages and
he didn't care right now anyway. He was on the go again. He had
to get across town to Highland Drive.

He rang the bell, listening to the harmonic wind chimes
making music on the south deck of the rambling, low, greige
house with natural cedar trim. He waited at the leaded glass door
and rang again, looking around at the yard which was so aston-

ishingly landscaped, with new trees and plants every time Boon visited, which was rare, admittedly. He noticed a new Japanese maple; that would be the perfect place for "Music," right there, under its delicate red leaves. He set his back pack down and went over to the area around the tree and began weeding. He took out his jackknife and deadheaded a few flowers and was really making a dent in things when Lou called out to him.

"Doddson Kooper-Boon! Is that you? Whatever have you done to your hair!" Ah, Lou. The voice: Boon had an average male voice, but whenever he was around Lou, he suddenly felt he had a deep, deep baritone, because Lou's voice was soft and feminine. Not gratingly high, no, but higher than what anyone would call average. Boon had never met an actual gay man with such a voice, other than Lou, but it was Lou's voice and his mannerisms which were aggravatingly stereotyped in sitcoms and movies.

Boon stood and greeted his friend, taking in the black silk bathrobe, matching cuffs and, especially, the French press coffee maker in his hand. Lou had a newspaper tucked under his arm and had obviously been on the east deck having coffee in the early morning sunshine. "Good, fair day, to you, Lou. Pockets of miracle-making all around this tree. There's going to be a sculpture right here, a gigantic wonder of musicality and drama."

"How divine, positively! Is it yours?"

"It is."

"How exciting! Did I pay for it?"

"You did." Lou had paid Boon many times over for the sculpture as far as Boon was concerned. He had picked him up one night in front of a restaurant, brought him home and let him sleep off a battle royal with a skunky little number who was rebounding from a nasty coke habit, an argument which Lou witnessed. She was hauled off by two girlfriends and Lou took Boon to his house. The next morning, Lou had come into the room with a breakfast tray and they'd been friends since. He had never made a move on Boon, although he once in awhile slipped and called him angel, which Boon slapped down hard every time, telling him brutally to keep it in his pants. They had known each other almost twelve years.

"Stop that terrible weeding you're doing. Marshall does it for me. Come in. We have to catch *up*! The salon styling is such an improvement. You do look terrific without the dreary, dreary length. Handsome, handsome, handsome man."

"Yeah, right, Lou. Leave me alone. Go get some clothes on, you look like a drag queen with all that wavy hair running around, wearing some kind of a damn dress. Jesus. Then make coffee and we'll talk. I'll take this pile down to the green bin."

When Boon entered the house, Lou was in the kitchen, now in tight Levi's 501s and a white t-shirt, barefooted, piling food onto a cutting board. A bottle of champagne had been opened and two fancy glasses with silver rims sat on the breakfast nook beside a pitcher of orange juice. Boon saw croissants and ham and three kinds of cheese and star fruit slices. He thought of Dr. Drummond's dietary restrictions and started laughing.

"What's amusing, Doddson? You seem to be in a startlingly good mood."

"Oh, nothing, just happy to see the grub. What's the champagne?"

"Celebration. Haven't seen you in awhile. Something divine must have happened by now that we can celebrate. And if not, we do it anyway! The night is young!"

"It's early morning, Lou, you loop."

"Is it? Wonderful! I've been up all night; I wouldn't know."

"Why have you been up all night? Is someone here..." Boon looked nervously down the hall toward Lou's huge, elegant, entirely mauve bedroom. He had peeked in once and it scared the shit out of him.

"No, no. Marshall came by and surprised me with Ylo Ylo and Irma; it was my birthday! It was lovely!"

"OK. Ylo Ylo and Irma. Marshall. Don't fuckin' tell me. You turned, too?"

"Oh, no, no, no. We're just all wonderful friends."

"Well, happy birthday, you old reprobate. How old are you?"

"Forty-three. I know you can't believe it, but I am. Forty-three. Looks pretty fab, doesn't it?" This was an understatement. Lou looked like he'd always looked to Boon: youthful and in enviably perfect shape, and he was prettier and even blonder than Douglas, which was saying something. Her looks were augmented by technology; his came from nature.

Boon asked, "You and Marshall are still friends? How's that work? Last I saw you, you were devastated, that was your word, and thought Marshall had run off for good. You were bawling your eyes out, Lou, and said you knew you'd never see him again. It was pathetic."

"Well, it just came into being that a gorgeous new friendship blossomed. We manifested a miraculous recovery, Boon."

"Well, good for you. Says something about your character. I like Marshall."

"You can't have him. How are you faring in that department, Doddson? Have you met her yet, Miss Stellar Attraction?"

"Hard to say. Spent the night with a real beauty just last night, dripping in red curls and big brown eyes, goddess body, boots. Hot little art curator who loves my work, apparently."

"Oooh, tell me, tell me!" Lou mixed champagne and orange juice.

"Yeah. Hot. She slept with your buddy, right there in the same bed, after knowing him only a couple of hours."

"OK. OK. OK. Tell it, tell it."

"Happy to. Now don't get excited, but I took a shower, alone, and went to bed and fell asleep. I woke up this morning and there she was, still in her clothes, even her boots, curled up on the end of the bed, hugging a pillow, covered up with a corner of the bedspread."

"That's it?"

"That's it."

"You need therapy."

Boon laughed, "Naw. Sun shines whether it happens in a bedroom or not, Lou, you know that. She's too young for me, anyway. How you doin'?"

"I need therapy, too, I suppose. I've been spending all my time working and don't have one single prospect. I haven't been out in over a year. I think it's over for me. Expired sell date."

"Oh, for God's sake! But, oh well, that's fine by me, both ways. I don't have to hear about your love life, nothing that interests me, and, actually, I'm here to talk about your work, Lou."

"I don't want to! I'm drinking sunrises and eating food. I'm taking a day off! I had my shower, read my paper and had planned to go to bed. I do need sleep, you know. I'm happy to see you and visit, that's great, but I don't want to work. I have to make a couple of calls, but other than that, I'm taking the day off."

"You aren't. You have to work. This is good, by the way, a sideboard fit for kings. I needed this coffee, too; you make the best coffee in Portland, Lou."

"A compliment. I understand now. You need help with money."

"I do."

"Well, how much do you need? You've never asked before; let's get this done and then we can talk about other things. I'll write you a check. Happy to do that."

Boon went to his back pack and pulled out the folder Douglas had left him from the bankers and handed it to Lou. "I don't need a check. I need to know what to do about this. You're the only finance guy I know and you know me; I think Rousseau had the likes of me in mind when he connected finance to slavery. Give it to me straight. I don't want all that financial advisor lingo you use. I hate it. I don't know anything about it and I don't want to learn."

Lou looked through the folder. "Doddson."

"What?"

"This has to be handled carefully. It may seem like a great deal of money to you, and it is, of course, but it must be handled well."

"No shit. I know that. That's why I'm here. What do I do with it?"

"Well, that's up to you. I need to hear some of your ideas about how you intend to make this money work for you. I need to hear your plans, your goals."

"Well, I picked up a road turtle this morning and I plan to start a new sculpture called "Travel.""

"And where will you be doing this?"

"I have no idea. Yet. I'll find some place."

"Doddson."

"What?"

"You can't live like that anymore."

"Why not?"

Lou stood and walked around, thinking of his answer. "Because, Doddson, you have been given a gift. And with that gift comes a responsibility. I know you want to make this inheritance from your father do good work in the world, Doddson. This isn't a great deal of money, but you still don't want to be like the 400 people who have more money than half the rest of our country combined, who hoard their money in a great many places, in a fantastic variety of ways, and aren't reinvesting conscionably. Their money isn't circulating and working for the greater good, Doddson. I choose quite deliberately to work only with people who want their money to do something important: to feed people, give them jobs, products, services, education, which includes supporting the arts, housing, medical care without, I might add, destroying the environment. My clients and I are working against poverty consciousness in this culture; we're a wealthy nation, we just don't have our wealth circulating. I know you. You actually think about these things! You need to use this fund to create a reasonable environment for yourself so you can do the work you do. This is important, Doddson."

"But what's wrong with the way I live? It works for me."

"There's only one thing I can say to that."

"What's that, Lou? You seem to be on the pontificating star point here today; shine it on me."

"It worked for you. Past tense. It's not going to work anymore."

"Why not?"

"Because it's dishonest. You can't live like a bum when you aren't a bum. It's gone, Boon. I know it's hard for you, but this gift requires that you adjust."

"It's money. I need some of it. I don't need all of it. You can do something right with the rest of it and I can go about my business."

"Right. But you need a place to live and to work. You need to feed and to clothe yourself first, Doddson, and then use the rest of it to work for others. Then you can more significantly make the contribution you were born to make: art."

"I can't do all that."

"Why not?"

"It makes me crazy."

"Explain, please."

"I can't create and be thinking about all that stuff. I can't have a place to live and go shopping and pay bills and confine myself in some hole and get any ideas about anything. I've seen it happen to people; they are so busy, busy, busy they can't live. They can't think. They certainly can't create. They aren't breathing, you know. They are busy. They don't have time. They don't have time for each other. And then there's the flip side, the consequence of busy, which is melt down, depression, stuck on the couch unable to do one damn thing from the stress of all the things that need to be handled. I can't live like that. Cramps my style. I'm telling you, Lou, I won't buy in. I saw it happen to my parents and their friends and my friends and their friends and I'm not up for it. I want to work hard, and I do, and I want to make a contribution, obviously, but I don't want to become part of the problem, just another complainer about how much there is to damn do. You just mentioned it: working all the time, haven't been out in a year. I know you work on your music probably more than the money thing, but still, what is that?"

Lou didn't answer. He cut a croissant in half and stuffed it with ham. "You have a hair cut. How did that happen?"

"I was with a woman and her daughter and a friend of theirs did it."

"And where are they?"

"They are with the husband who returned to take over. Got the booteroo. What's my hair cut have to do with anything?"

"You can change, that's what it has to do with, although someone else apparently made the decision for you." Lou paused and now had the look on his face of a man with yet another speech to deliver. "You're, what, fifty years old, Doddson. You have reached the point of maturation, as a man and as an artist, which requires that you change. You describe the extremes, that's relevant, but what you must have the courage to do is to create a balanced life. Art is your life; you can do it. Now you're being encouraged, even forced, to do just that: achieve some balance. This inheritance is a gift from the universe and it has a message attached."

"And what's the message? What does the universe want from me?"

Lou hesitated and then quietly spoke, "The universe wants you to clean up your act, Doddson. You wanted it straight, there it is." He looked at his watch and put his coffee down. "I have to go back to my office and make those quick phone calls. Excuse me."

Lou left down the hall and disappeared into a room Boon had seen only once and never wanted to see again; it was filled with files on three walls, two computers and all sorts of machinery.

There was some kind of electronic white noise sound in the room and two of the machines worked without human contact, spitting out paper. The whole room disturbed him.

Clean up your act. Boon remembered of course, instantly, saying these very same words to Donovan. He walked out onto the deck and sat down in the sun, buzzed by champagne and stung by Lou's words. He stood. He felt strangely nostalgic. He went back inside and put the folder in his back pack. He ripped off a sheet of note paper from a pad by the kitchen phone and wrote Lou a note:

> *Thanks, man, see you later. Get some sleep, then look up a friend of mine. His name is Donovan Trenton King, teaches at Payne in SF. Tell him Boon sent you. IMPORTANT: Do it today. Happy Birthday. Great coffee. DKB*

He left through the back door, hopped off the deck and walked to the alley. He turned right, headed for downtown Portland as clouds rolled in.

27

COFFEE HOUR TWO

. . . .

We cannot accept that we simply don't know what to do;
we cling to the idea that one should make choices
on the basis of knowledge.
—ANDREW SOLOMON

He swung by Bobby's on the way downtown and found a
young girl exiting the apartment who informed him that her
family had moved in six months ago: no Bobby, no mother of
Bobby. Boon sat on a big rock in the courtyard and contemplated
his next move. He saw a chain link fence bordering a slough littered with trash and got up to find an entrance to the wooded
area. He found one, and walked through the murky sludge and
down a hill to a creek, where he relieved himself and watched
clouds roll around in the sky. It was starting to rain, so he made a

decision: the bank. He would go get twenty bucks and buy some adhesive, maybe some wire. He had to start gathering supplies, get started, maybe go to Colora and rummage around, but first, the bank. He wasn't sure, but he guessed maybe he had banking business to do.

He presented at the teller cage dripping wet, handed over the bank folder and asked for twenty dollars. The teller looked at the documents, punched keys, and looked at her monitor, asking for his ID. She filled out a slip of paper, handed the folder back and gave him a twenty dollar bill with an odd look on her face, "Thank you for banking with us, Mr. Boon."

Since she had actually spoken to him, he felt encouraged to ask, "Tell me, do I have to come in here every time I need cash? Is there a way I can do it without coming into the bank?" People were waiting in the line behind him.

"Certainly, sir. I think you should speak with someone. The glass office right across the lobby there. Miss Young can help you."

Miss Young was anything but young. Boon walked in and handed her the folder.

She looked at it. "How may we help you, Mr. Boon?"

"Well, I need to be able to get cash once in a while and I wondered if there was an easy way to do it, or if I have to come in here every time."

"Yes. As you know, this is a savings account. We can transfer funds and open a checking account so you can write personal checks, and we can give you a debit card for accessing either type of account. You might wish to have a separate debit card as well for this account."

"A separate card?"

"You have a debit or credit card, I'm sure. Everyone does."

"I don't. Tell me, how does the debit card work?"

"Mr. Boon. May I see your identification, please?" He handed it over and she picked up the folder. "Would you excuse me a moment?" She went to a different office and ran a check on

Doddson Kooper-Boon. She found no record of a credit history or a banking history of any sort. The funds had been transferred from the home office in San Francisco to a newly opened account. She was, of course, suspicious.

She returned and sat down. "Mr. Boon, might you provide a local character reference for us? I'll need you to fill out this form. It's quite simple, just your social security number, address, beneficiaries."

"I don't have an address."

"Where do you live?"

"Here, in Portland."

"That address will be sufficient, then."

"But I don't live anywhere. I'm out."

"Pardon?"

"I don't live anywhere. I'm out."

"By this you mean you are without a domicile at this time?"

"Yes. I have been for thirty years."

"But there's an address on the driver's license."

"Walt's. I had a studio there, but don't anymore."

"Mr. Boon. I note that this transfer of funds just recently occurred. It's apparently an inheritance, since there's a death certificate attached."

"Yes, my father, Sorel Boon."

"I see. Our condolences, Mr. Boon. Might I make a recommendation?"

"Sure. That's why I'm here. I don't know anything about banks."

"I might recommend that you transfer a smaller portion of these funds to a checking account and I'll give you a debit card. Then you may access funds from an ATM machine. It's quite simple and would secure your nest egg."

"Nest egg."

"The bulk of your inheritance, until you decide how to invest it."

"I won't be investing it. I want someone else to do that."

"That's wise. Professional financial management is recommended, always. Do you have a consultant in mind?"

"Yes. Lou Prachek. Louis Allen Prachek on Highland Drive. I don't know if this is his bank or not."

She typed in the name and ran a check at her desk. "Yes, we have Mr. Prachek as a client. Perhaps I should recommend that you make a phone call and consult with him. I'd be happy to give you a moment to do that." What Miss Young did not mention was that Lou Prachek had six accounts and was, surely, one of the bank's most viable clients. He was known for managing sustainability portfolios.

"No, I just talked to him. He's been up all night celebrating his birthday; he's sleeping. I don't want to bother him. We talked about this. He said I should clean up my act. He'll take over. I think, since he banks here, I could just put the money in his account and be done with it. Can you do that?"

Miss Young took a moment. "How much would you like to transfer?"

Boon hesitated. "I don't know, maybe $80,000? What do you think?"

Miss Young sat there. She spoke. "Mr. Boon. I do think we might have to awaken Mr. Prachek, unless you can give me someone else to call who might verify your status. Perhaps a health care professional?"

"A doctor?" Boon paused and realized where Miss Young's thinking had gone. "You mean a shrink?"

Miss Young was nothing if not well-trained to be PC with clients. "Certainly not, Mr. Boon. But I do need a reference of some sort."

"Well, my psychiatrist is in the Caribbean, Mount Cinnamon, with my twin sister, Douglas, at the moment, so he's out. I guess Marc Fisk."

Miss Young frowned at this information, but recovered. "And who is Marc Fisk?"

"Police department."

"Here in Portland?"

"Yes. He's CSI."

Miss Young blanched the tiniest bit and excused herself once again. Boon went over to the free coffee bar and helped himself to awful coffee and four stale cookies and sat munching away at her desk. When she returned, he asked, "Well, how's Marc?"

"Detective Fisk is fine. He sends his regards."

"Did he mention that I'm a convicted felon, that there's an APB out for me as the suspected Rogue River killer?"

"He did not, Mr. Boon. You needn't chide me; I take my work seriously. And for your information, the Rogue River killer was female and was sentenced to 50 years some time ago, which I'm sure you know as well as I do. Now I will process this, if you'll kindly wait." She was leaving the office.

Boon asked, "What exactly did old Fisk say? I hope he didn't coerce you; the police, you know, can be threatening sometimes."

"He said, Mr. Boon, let's just see if I can remember this all correctly, he said that I should do whatever you ask, that he's known you for over twenty years and that he knew your father had passed away. He said you were a man of good, if not potentially great character, an accomplished artist, a man to be trusted. He also whistled when I intimated that you had inherited a considerable sum, and joked that he would be hitting you up to pay off his mortgage. Apparently the two of you are a comedy act. Nonetheless, I will go get this started. Please, help yourself to more coffee and cookies."

She really wasn't gone all that long and Boon left with his twenty, a banking address c/o Lou on Highland Drive, a debit card and a pin number. Miss Young had refused to allow 6666, so it was double 0 double 7. She had given him a banker lecture; she was apparently retained by the IRS as well, because she advised him to keep receipts of his major purchases and to never, never fail to get a receipt when he used an ATM machine. He simply *must* keep track of his expenditures.

He left, feeling sick from too many cookies and too much coffee, settled in on top of champagne and acidic orange. He decided to go get a milk shake and to get his act together. How he might do that was, at the moment of standing on the Portland city street, in the rain, with a roiling gut, an utter mystery. Boon couldn't understand it. Never had he found himself on such a cushy life raft and yet he realized he had also never felt so rudderless, so adrift, so marooned in a deep sea of not knowing what to do next. He saw Poppy's Ice Cream Deli down the street and focused on the milk shake. It was his one good idea.

28

BREATHE

. . . .

What did I do to deserve this?
—Brett Maria Foster

It was not good. She awakened to her cell phone ringing. Doddson Boon was gone. The caller ID indicated her mother, wanting the report.

"Hi, Mom. Early. Have to get to work. What's up?"

"How was he?"

"Who?" Brett hoped playing dumb would make the question go away.

"Your date."

"Mom. He's the artist at the gallery. He's fifty, Mom. He's too old. He wasn't that kind of a date. It was work."

"You can't do that, Brett. You're divorced. You're not getting any younger. You cannot persist in being so particular. He sounds like a nice man. Successful."

"Mom. I have to work. I do. You know my boss is gone, so I'm on my own. I'll see you after work."

"Well, if he comes back, take another look, Brett. Fifty isn't that old. But remember, make sure he doesn't have a drinking problem. Watch for that."

She showered, changed into a shift and flat shoes, yanked her hair back with combs, decided to skip make-up for the first work day ever in the history of Brett, and went to open up. It was pouring down rain and dark. She turned on all the lights and hit the button for music: harp. It didn't feel right, so she selected Celtic, something a little livelier.

The Good Fortune phone rang just as two customers entered the shop. She smiled at them and indicated that she would be with them shortly and answered the phone: it was for Doddson Boon. He wasn't in. Could she take a message. She could. He was to call Donovan King immediately. She hung up. It rang again: it was for Doddson Boon. He isn't in. May I take a message. Yes: have him call Tinabelle. Pronto. She hung up and was four feet down the aisle when it rang again: Doddson Boon. He isn't in. The message was that he should call Dr. Hopper immediately. She turned down the ringer and vowed to let it go to voicemail. She had customers.

They wanted to see the sculpture gallery, so she took them up, turned on the lights and stared at the tags saying Sold in bold red lettering. She kept her cool and chattered about the work, what was left of it to sell, and tried to breathe as she noticed the tag on "Beauty." The customers were distraught, explaining that they had been told about "Vision" and wanted to buy it. Perhaps they could contact Mr. Torrey Hopper and purchase it from him. Brett demurred, stumbled, stuttered and blew it: she admitted she didn't know Mr. Hopper. The customers were disgusted that she was a new hire who evidently didn't know anything and asked when they might come back and speak with the owner. That would be Monday. Brett was able to give Helen the weekend before addressing these two vicious beasts. They left in a huff, proclaiming that the culture was entirely bereft of competent employees in every arena of human life, but most specifically, the small corner of the world which housed Good Fortune Antiques.

Her cell phone rang. It was her mother. "Mom. Don't call me. I'm really, really busy. What?"

"Make sure he isn't a veteran. That PTSD thing is a nightmare. And no alimony. You don't need a man who's sucked dry by alimony."

"Mom. Bye. Love you." She hung up. The UPS driver was standing waiting for her signature. She signed and told him to bring the delivery in, pointing to the area near the cash register. She soon learned she had made a mistake. He brought in at least twenty parcels, which blocked the aisle entirely. She started taking them into her apartment when her cell phone rang. Her mother. She ignored it and reviewed the UPS delivery. Everything was from Helen; everything was from Scotland, except for two packages from Wales. She was dismayed. Helen and Jerald said they would be on a buying trip and would send things, but this was a lot to process all at once. She wouldn't be able to put anything out, unless they had given an indication of selling price. She would be busy.

She couldn't get the sculpture out of her mind. She was halfway up the spiral staircase to go have a closer look when FedEx arrived. The man said he had a delivery which probably should be brought in through the back door. She went through her apartment and unlocked the door to the alley and watched as he backed in and started to unload his truck. All of his truck was loaded with packages for Good Fortune Antiques. When he left, Brett surveyed her small apartment. The only really usable surface left was the bed.

She heard customers come in the front door and decided to close the door to her apartment and shut out the entire problem. Out of sight out of mind. Forget it for now. Run the shop. "Hi! Welcome to Good Fortune Antiques. What a great day to be inside."

"You don't need to sell us anything. We know what we want."

Brett had a premonition: clones of the first two customers, except for the fact that they weren't dressed as well. "Excellent! How may I help?"

"You can open your cash drawer and give us everything you have in it."

Brett went into automatic. "But it's morning and there's not much cash at this time of day." She felt like two people; the poise of the other Brett was amazing, possibly because she determined that they weren't pointing anything at her except greed.

"Just get it."

She went to the drawer and pulled out the bills: she knew how much was in the drawer. She always left $250 from the previous day's till. The deposit, which she made every two days, was in a bank bag in her apartment.

She handed it to the man. "That's $200, that's all I keep in the drawer."

"Where's the rest of it?"

"In the bank. I made a deposit last night."

"Lift the drawer. Let me see."

He was close and breathing on her neck as she lifted the drawer for the fifty dollar bill. The man took it and they left.

She called the police and reported the theft. She sat down on a stack of UPS boxes and cried. Her phone rang and she ignored it. She knew if her mother got the slightest hint of a burglary, she would appear, dressed in her combat fatigues, sniper rifle at the ready. The rifle would be a mere accessory; Brett's mother could kill two people at once with a single look. She was justifiably famous for this ability. Brett's life was littered with dead boyfriends and a dead husband who had encountered the supernatural visual powers of Brett's mother.

There were questions, forms, details, the replay, the descriptions of the perpetrators. No, she could not come to the station; her boss was out of town and she needed to run the store. They left.

The F blinked on the phone: voicemail full. She took down the messages, every one of them for Boon, including the police, a detective Fisk, which caused her grave concern, of course: she had spent the night with a criminal? He had joked about it...god. She left the ringer off and opened two UPS packages, one jewelry, the other candelabra, when she noticed the voicemail was full again. She retrieved the messages, all for Doddson Kooper-Boon, artist at large. She decided that was it. She would ignore the phone. If he showed up, he could deal with his own damn messages. Helen had her cell number; she would stick with that. Maybe she should call Bea and have her come to man the store with her for the day. The more she thought about her morning and her night before, the more nervous she was about being alone. She called her girlfriend and made a cup of tea, repeating relax, relax, relax. She wanted to go up and look at the tags on the sculptures, and then find out who all these people were. She wanted to read her tag again.

A young woman came in. "Hi. I'm Cindy. I'm a friend of Doddson Kooper-Boon."

"Hi. I'm Brett. May I help you?"

"Is he here? Mom read in the newspaper that he has a gallery here."

"He isn't. His sculptures are upstairs."

"Oh, fantab! Can I go see?"

"Sure. Let me come up with you." They went upstairs and Cindy dropped to the floor, sitting with her legs crossed and started sobbing uncontrollably.

Brett knelt beside her, "Cindy, what? What's wrong?"

"He did it! I've got to find him! I'm...Momma said I should find him. This is so important! I'm going to have a baby and I need to talk to him."

Brett sat down, sighing. Good God, what a man, to do this to such a young girl! Awful! Just awful! What a shit!

Cindy continued to sob and to babble about Boon, "He did it! I cannot, cannot, cannot believe it! I have to find him! Where is he?"

"I don't know, Cindy, but I'll help you find him. I will do everything I can to help you."

Cindy settled down, blew her nose on a red bandana and said, "That would be great. I have a pickup parked outside with black trash bags in the back. They need to be brought in."

"And why? What's in the bags?"

"Boon's studio. All his supplies and his "Love" sculpture. It isn't finished. It's awesome. You have to see it! I have to look at these. Can you get the bags and I can look at sculptures and then I have to get back to school."

Brett left feeling absolutely overwhelmed with the sheer magnitude of deplorability that must surely fill Doddson Kooper-Boon to the very brim. What a bastard! "Love" sculpture! She looked sixteen! Pregnant! In high school! Horrible, horrible, horrible! If she ever saw him again! Oh! Would she have something to say! Disgusting man!

She unloaded the bags and took them into the back room and stored them behind a screen to the side of an antique horsehair couch. She didn't want to see them and she certainly didn't want a "Love" sculpture by a disturbed man in her apartment.

She went back up to the gallery and found Cindy, again sitting on the floor sobbing, holding a sculpture the size of her back pack. The poor girl was gone.

Brett took the sculpture, noting the tag, and shook her head. The poor thing! She sat the sculpture down, turned the tag around and spoke to Cindy, "Now, Cindy, can you tell me a little more? How I can reach you?"

"He'll know how to reach us. He knows where we live. He lived with us. He and my mom had a thing going."

Oh, God. The mother *and* the daughter! "Oh."

"Anyway, Pete and I decided to have the baby after all and we're moving into the garage at Pete's parents' house. He's fixing it up, a nice bathroom and everything, and we needed to get these things of Boon's moved. Mom saw the write-up in the paper and thought this would be a good place for it."

"Wait, wait, wait. Tell me. You are having a child."

"Yes. We were going to have an abortion, but we decided not to. We're going to get married after we graduate and then go on to college. We're excited. The sculpture from Boon is so great; it's like our first baby gift."

"Wait, wait, wait. Whose baby is this?"

"Pete's and mine. Whose would it be?" Cindy shook her head.

"And your mother and Boon are an item, then?"

"No, Mom and Dad are back together. It's great. Mom's off meds."

Brett hung her head: too much information, way too much information.

"Well, congratulations on the baby coming. It's very exciting for you, I'm sure."

"It is! And I'm going to take this sculpture back with me and it will be our first really great thing in our new place. Pete will like this. He will. I love it! Don't you?"

Brett looked at it, "Yes. It's...fun, wild. Tremendous energy."

Cindy stood, wrestling to balance her back pack and the sculpture. "I gotta go. My math class starts in ten minutes. Give Boon a message for me, will you?"

"Sure."

"Tell him we love him. If we hadn't met Boon, I don't know what would have happened to us. It was awful and he turned it all around. He just saved us, really, he did, even Dad says so, and he isn't easy. Anyway, tell him to visit, so I can thank him for the sculpture. Tell him I'll make him mac and cheese. Tell him the tip money I spent that day buying him a cup of coffee was the best buy for a dollar I've ever spent, even though it cost me my job." She was crying again, overwhelmed by the considerable effort required to encompass a whole history of a family in a few sentences. "Tell him I love him. Tell him I'm glad he found a place to be."

29

BENCH PRESS

· ·

Of course, nobody's meditation is always enjoyable.
—SALLY KEMPTON

Well, now. Boon had a short nap. Boon was wet. Boon thought no thoughts. Boon thought about stress. Boon thought thoughts of dreaming propane sheep: sheep dreaming about propane. He thought about the glory of the rose, as a flower, as a religious symbol, as a sexual metaphor. He scratched on the top of a wooden bench, the very bench on which he had found the red ashtray, with his fingernail, in the rain, and decided that he liked the green slime the Pacific Northwest grew on surfaces in winter. He would like to use the idea of this slime in a sculpture. He thought travel, slime, roses, propane and finger food. He thought about weathervanes and the four directions. He thought about wind, flight, fancy pants and green chili peppers. He thought nervous breakdown, positive euphoria, testy doodling, hellfire and damnation and depression, in that order. He bench pressed nothing, lying down on the park bench at Ginn and Dayview. He lifted weights that weren't there, he imagined globes in each hand, Atlas grimacing with the sheer weight of the dual load. He was lying on the bench playing peekaboo with the sky, his hands over his eyes, then not, when a young woman asked him if he was all right. He said he thought so and watched a plane fly overhead and thought of the guy who did just this kind of watching to come up with a name for his band. He thought final chord. Glory chord. Clap your hands, make a stand, shout it out. He thought he would have to go. He thought he would have to leave Portland. He thought he would have to. He thought this as a thought incarnate. He felt the imaginary wall in front of this thought: it was a curvy wall. It was a sculpture. It had a name: Kelley Swartz.

Well, now. He assumed nothing. He didn't assume he should find her. He didn't assume she was alive. He didn't assume she would want to see him. He didn't assume it was worth exploring. He didn't assume he would know her if she walked up to the bench right now. He didn't assume he knew one thing about two things: her or himself. He didn't assume there was meaning left to wring out of a relationship that had lasted six months: six months of bedtime, primarily, interspersed with wandering around in a daze together holding hands and talking about art and life and how it was between them. How it was between them was something Boon still assumed: it was good. He couldn't seem to change this assumption; he'd tried, but it didn't leave him. She had left him, just one day sighing and casually mentioning she should go get a job, she had a friend of a friend of a friend in Someplace, Texas, big money, an easy play. If she was going to make it, she would have to do it now, ahead of turning thirty when her body would start going to hell. She was gone one morning when he woke up. She was twenty-eight when she left and Boon was twenty-seven. He assumed this was a long time ago. He assumed he had changed. She had changed. It had changed. He assumed he had to get some logic and throw it against the bulwark of nostalgia. He assumed he had to grab hold of reality and shake the dream loose. No.

He assumed the clouds had something to say to him: go to Texas. It began raining hard as Boon drifted with this idea and then it hit him. His father making paper airplanes for Douglas and for him. It was Sunday, the only day they had to spend time with him, just him, without their stepmother, who was glad to have a day to herself. They were in a park; his Dad was laughing. She was crying. Kelley was crying. He sat up, stricken with a grief he knew he must bear. His father was gone. His mother was so long gone; she had died when Boon and Douglas were eight. His stepmother was gone; she had died five years ago. No mother. Was Kelley a mother? Kelley was surely alive. The worst thought he'd ever had in his life came to him and he stood up defiantly against it. What if Kelley had, so far, lived a terrible life? What if she had not been as fortunate as he had been? He'd had a great life, a life he had chosen. What if she was miserable? Or sick, like Donovan? Or burdened? What if she was depressed or lonely? What if she needed help? What if, right this minute, Kelley was in terrible trouble? The very worst thought of all grabbed him by the ears and shook him: what if she thought he'd forgotten her? He didn't want to hear this: No! He'd worried about her since the day she left, but this new series of thoughts didn't add up to worry. This was panic; this was terror. This was a trip south as fast as possible.

He walked around the bench ten times and rearranged himself. Good. Now. Get going. Lighten, move ass, Boon. He smiled, finally, embracing the idea that women, not just Kelley, but women, oh hell, all people, were just wonderful. Wasn't the world just a dandy ball of fire wax and frills and girls and boys and whispers in the dark? Frills! Of course! Tuxedo! Boon knew now what the "Love" sculpture needed: riffs. He would find something, but right now: research.

Boon loved women unabashedly, of course, but there was one stripe of female that Boon was especially taken by, and that was the librarian stripe. He loved librarians, good old-fashioned women, they were always women, although he knew there were male librarians with brains who knew how to spell Buonarroti and what the literacy rate was in Puerto Rico, how much rainfall the Olympic Peninsula received yearly, which polymer adhesive might be recommended for application number 112, and where to find hairline copper wire. They knew the demographics of the Muslim brotherhood and the price of gold, butter, oil and wheat. They knew math, they knew their philosophers, they knew which Tolstoy had been relegated to the closed stacks and why. They knew which *colors* which masters used in their paintings, by period. They knew their way around every damn thing he'd ever asked them; Boon didn't believe in the internet. He couldn't imagine anything better than good librarians who had that stony-cold look service-minded intellectuals were supposed to wear: they knew how to help you and they helped you. No questions asked. He needed one of these paragons of instant knowledge now. He would go to the library and find one, one who had helped him before, an elderly reference librarian who wouldn't suggest that he use the internet. She would just shut up about it and punch it all in herself and hand it over. He had one in mind.

"May I help you?"

"You may, please, I need to try to locate a person, one Kelley Swartz, by name. That's K, E, L, L, E, Y and the usual Swartz.

"Do you have a birth date?"

"No."

"An address?"

"Texas."

"An approximate age?"

"Forty nine, maybe fifty."

"A middle initial?"

"N, I think, but I'm not sure. It was a funny name."

"Do you know the individual's place of birth?"

"Texas."

"Is there a particular town or city in Texas?"

"Houston or Austin. Probably Austin."

"Might you recall what the N stands for? Would it be Nicole, Nancy or Norwalk? I might assume Norwalk."

Boon's heart leapt. "Norwalk! That's her."

The librarian wrote an address down for him and handed it over. "This is all that's available. Now, it may not be current, of course. There's no way I can validate a current address, but this is the last one listed. Would there be anything else?"

"No, thank you."

He was stunned silly. He couldn't believe how easy it had been! Wow! He walked out and went to a truck stop on the highway and got his first long-haul ride south. He determined that as he traveled, he would throw away things from his back pack—Jim's clothes—as he moved south and collected pieces for his next sculpture and looked for riffs for "Love." He was in a hurry, but he would still collect things as they came across his path. "Travel" would be a sculpture for Kelley Norwalk Swartz. It would be his best work to date. It would be a huge hurrah of holographic hedonism. It would splash and splatter and shout and sing: Life is a glory wheel! It would be ten feet tall, a thin, undulating column, like a highway and the road turtle, painted metallic gold, with silver stars and myrrh dust, would be the crown. He might have to trade out for a bigger back pack. It did not occur to Boon that he could buy one.

30

FOUR-LETTER WORD

. . . .

What is it now?
—LINDA LAPPIN

Boon became a four-letter word in both Portland and in San Francisco. It was analogous to the parent of a small, winsome child, a parent who has had more than enough of a four-year-old with control issues; the parent who silently says "damn" at the tenth "No!" in a row uttered by this child, this adorable, beloved *thing*. Boon became a frustrating thing: an absent, unresponsive mad rag of a thing which had escaped. The sort of thing no one needs. Everyone was looking for Boon. They all talked to each other, 'round and 'round in circles, until finally they stopped pestering each other. Obviously, no one knew one damn thing about Boon's whereabouts.

Greg Hooper wanted Boon to be his best man. He was marrying someone Boon had never met, but that didn't concern Greg. He wanted Boon. As far as he was concerned, Boon was the only sane, perfectly reasonable Boon he knew, had ever known. Torrey was a Hopper with recessive Boon genes, so he was fine. The wedding was casual, in a park, in a week.

Douglas wanted Boon because she wasn't getting married and wanted Boon to commiserate. She knew Boon hadn't exactly appreciated her darling Hanson, that he would secretly rejoice, but she needed family. Dr. Carttin had changed his mind, and his body, during their trip and had been discovered in a hotel room in bed with someone else. The woman was not a doctor; she was a waitress. It seemed especially bad form from Douglas' perspective, because the hotel room these two occupied was also hers. She had to pack her bags while the lovers lay there watching her. As she left, saying nothing, the good doctor said, "Take care, Douglas, darling." She had flipped him off, very skillfully. She was a surgeon and used her beautiful hands well. She had two more weeks off, so she wanted Boon. While she waited for him, she decided to stay in her apartment and grieve, not for Carttin, she wouldn't waste a minute on that, but for her father.

Marc Fisk wanted to talk to Boon, not to get funds for paying off his mortgage, but to see what the hell he was doing. He wasn't on the streets; he'd looked for him, asked around. What mansion on what hill had he bought? Just how much money had he gotten, exactly? It was curiosity, plain and simple. CSI work, unbeknownst to the general populace, could be boring in the thankful spaces between major crimes, and Marc Fisk was bored.

Cindy wanted Boon because she'd stocked her mother's pantry with sea shell pasta and a great gourmet cheese sauce in a jar for a special version of macaroni and cheese. Where was he? He was always hungry and she wanted to feed him. She also wanted to tell him that she and Pete were going to name their baby Kooper, whether it was a boy or a girl, if that was all right with him. She also wanted him to see their place and to thank him for the sculpture. Pete had built a stand for it, with a motion sensor light.

Tinabelle wanted Boon, ostensibly to return her cell phone, since it was apparent that he didn't know how to use it. Her real reason, however, was that she could use some help. She had Trenton and Donovan on her plate big time. Where was he? She was a circus performer; she wasn't a magician. She couldn't see behind the curtain; she didn't know what was going on. Rabbits were flying around in the air attached to sentences and there was no hat to catch them. Boon was wearing that hat; she knew it.

Helen and Jerald wanted Boon. They were distraught that they had missed him. Helen worried about Boon's health and was disgusted with herself for not paying him for the sign when they had visited Boon in the hospital. He was probably starving somewhere! Jerald reassured her, but had concerns as well, the most primary of which was that he had a large box of bibelots which he had collected for Boon and his sculpture work. Jerald was extremely interested in giving this box to Boon. Given Jerald's obsessive nature, the box weighed heavily on him. He moved it, he opened it and rearranged things, he talked about it incessantly. Helen finally had to tell him: stop it. You're driving me crazy. He'll surface when he surfaces.

Brett needed Boon for many, many reasons. She had a list: work in progress, website, studio, photograph, video. The photograph was the most essential thing needed: she was disgusted with herself for letting Boon get away. She had known she needed a photograph. She could have taken one, should have taken one, but she had been too nervous. At the bottom of this list were names and numbers of phone calls Boon needed to make regarding his work. Brett felt they were all urgent. She had pulled "Love" out of the trash bag and installed it in a corner of the gallery, labeled as a work in progress, artistically arranging prospective objects Boon apparently intended to use to finish it around the sculpture. It was interesting. She was pleased with her idea.

She had then called a website designer, a Jason person, who had asked that she visit his office where he did his work. Brett had appeared without a phone call and found Jason moving the mouse quickly to shut down a porn site on his monitor. Brett had responded without thinking that she, too, enjoyed light porn. Well, of course, it was a bond like none other, and the two were instantly attracted to each other. They somehow managed to get a website together for Boon's work, despite the competing theme of crotchless panties which presented during every session.

Not only did these two have big plans for Boon; they had big plans for themselves as a team, in bed and in cyberspace. For now, however, they were content to skip the bed and explore the exciting possibilities of office sex. Brett, of course, did not share any of this excitement with her mother. Brett had made a decision. She would never again tell her mother anything about a man in her life until she was at least six months pregnant. Her theory was that the impending birth of a grandchild, should that happen, would divert her mother sufficiently—hopefully firmly and forever.

* * * * *

It was a very good thing that Lou Prachek was such a vital, healthy, relatively young man because he had a long day ahead of him. He read Boon's note that morning and made a decision. He would forgo sleep and find Donovan Trenton King. He was excited: this must be the connection he was waiting for. Payne. Perfect. He was amazed that Boon had such a connection and had extended it to him; Boon had seen Lou's recording studio on the north side of his house only once and hadn't heard anything he'd recorded, but he had nodded when Lou said his work was experimental harmonics. He seemed to understand that Lou's passion, which wasn't money at all, but music, was important. And now he was recommending a connection. This was excellent: Payne was connected with film and theatre, both applications Lou envisioned for his work. Perhaps an adjunct teaching position would accrue. He made coffee and went to his computer.

Lou Prachek was an entirely honest man who found himself lying shamelessly to the woman on the phone in academic affairs at Payne. He was an old, dear friend of Dr. King's from NYU; he had learned from reviewing Payne's website that King was a PhD, had taught at NYU and was now the head of Payne's film department; he taught directing. The exclamation point Lou attached to this data was incontrovertible and duplicated. Excellent!! The woman advised Lou that Dr. King had recently filed for a leave of absence due to health concerns, and when pressed by an emotional Lou, she named the hospital where Dr. King was in a recuperative mode following heart surgery. The urgency which welled up in Lou after receiving this information was considerable, so considerable that he booked a quick flight, dressed in black, slipped two CDs of his work into a leather shoulder satchel, and headed for the airport. He would visit Dr. King in the hospital. He would take flowers. He would meet him. He would go now; who knew. He might be dying. Heart surgery was serious. It was at this point that Donovan Trenton King had yet another person praying for his recovery; Lou wasn't a religious man, but he prayed anyway: please.

* * * * *

Tinabelle was leaving Donovan's room when she saw the bouquet coming down the hall. It was an enormous thing which entirely occluded the person carrying it.

She stopped just a few feet from Donovan's door and waited for it, since she assumed such drama would be for Donovan.

"Hello, hello. You're here to see Donovan?"

"I am. I'm Lou Prachek. Doddson Boon sent me."

Tinabelle computed mega info with mega speed, of course. Boon. Gay man. Bingo. Man, the work of lightning speed, this Boon. She and Donovan had struggled through the out-of-the-closet talk the previous day, preceded with the disclosure that it was all Boon's idea, an awkward affair which ended with Donovan in tears and Tinabelle with the serious headache of a tragedian. It was the only day on record that Tinabelle wished she were a man. Donovan needed to be telling this to a man, not a firmly partnered, lesbian best friend with a major performance in three hours.

Well, here he was. Gay bells on. Stupendously attractive man, this Lou, and, well, wow. "I'm Tinabelle, Circus Tantamount. He's awake and feeling quite well this morning, but we're still advised not to stay long." Tinabelle was having a very difficult time imagining herself walking away from this new development. She wanted to usher Lou in and watch what happened, but she had an appointment with a realtor to look at a post-Airstream house for Trenton and his family.

She scolded herself for being a soap operatic and started to leave. "Ta. Have a great chat. Nice flowers." She giggled as she left, imagining the bouquet among all the others in the room, clearly making its statement. The statement made by Lou's bouquet was $250, at least, among other things, the most obvious of which was the A word: agenda. She turned after a few steps to look at the back side of the human bouquet, but it was gone.

Lou stepped into the room not knowing what to expect. There had been no picture with the bio on the website, only a series of video clips showing all sorts of people, evidently in student productions. He had tried, but he hadn't figured out if King was in any of them. He knew now that he was: he had seen this man in one of the videos, wearing a wig on a set, blowing a horn. However: in the video the man was well; the man in the bed before him was *so* not well. Lou's first response was that he, Louis Allen

Prachek, was an evil, opportunistic creep who should put the bouquet down and leave. He seriously considered announcing himself as a delivery person from the florist and fleeing.

He didn't do it, of course. "Good morning, Dr. King. I'm Lou Prachek, and apparently you and I have a mutual friend. He asked that I bring you flowers."

"Thank you. Who might this benefactor be?"

"Doddson Kooper-Boon."

Donovan laughed. He hadn't laughed in some time, actually, and he felt as if someone else was making the sound, it was so unfamiliar. "Boon."

"Yes. He came by this morning."

"Where was this? We're looking for him."

"Portland. I live in Portland."

"And you came here, just today, from Portland?"

"Yes."

Donovan lay there as Lou placed the bouquet in the center of a bank of flowers, arranging everything, fussing, taking his time to adjust. When he turned around, Donovan King had silent tears streaming down his face. Lou was so concerned that he walked over, pushed the button for the nurse, sat down in a chair beside Donovan's bed and reached for his hand.

31

SWEEPING

· ·

It keeps driving you to find worth in the worthless,
value in shard-like pieces:
broken plates, shattered acrylic toys,
bits of smoking shrapnel.
—Donald Mitchell

Boon slept through most of the trip south, sticking with truckers with sleeping compartments, explaining that he had been in the hospital and needed to rest. He did feel tired. He knew he was just stressed, but he felt the need to sleep; it would make the miles go faster. He bought himself food and paid for his hosts' food, along the way, finding the ATM thing pretty useful, and he collected objects between rides. He did find a few things: the head of a black broom, a small, dented brass urn, three bottle caps from an obscure Belgian brew, a fat plastic straw striped like a candy cane, a silver, antique button with a pearl in the center, a set of earbuds, which was a find because the wire was long and hot pink, a clear drinking glass, cheap, with deep ridges, which he would break before using in a sculpture. He found a flicker feather and a crow feather. He found a wet, dirty sweatshirt which was beyond being useful, but he yanked the cord from the hood and saved it. His best find was from a truck stop outside Albuquerque, New Mexico: a set of fluted white ceramic trays, still in a gift box with a see-through top, parked on a dumpster lid. They were wonderful; they were riff! He found a shoe and took just the leather tassel. He found a black stuffed cartoony bat key ring, which amused him so much he put the key to Greg's house on it, although he knew the house had probably sold by now. Still, it was the only key he had left, since Walt's was gone, and he felt empowered by the bat and its white, shark-like teeth. He found one plastic bead on the sidewalk going into the restroom in a town called Humble, Texas: it was in the shape of a heart, with the clear glass encasing gold. This final find, Boon took as a sign that he was close, as, indeed he was. He was on the outskirts of Houston.

He hitched the final few miles with a guy in a little pickup, who said he would drop him at a bus stop if he wanted to go into Houston, that he himself avoided the city like the plague; he was on his way to Beaumont where he had a job prospect. And no, he wouldn't know any street addresses anywhere because he had just moved to the area from Oklahoma. Boon asked the bus driver, who gave him a booklet of routes, which had maps, and said he should transfer to this bus, then that bus, then that bus. He gave him a transfer slip. Boon checked at phone booths and on the third try, found one with a huge, ratty phone book and looked up Kelley Swartz. Nothing. Not even a K. Swartz.

He found the address without much trouble. It was a small house wedged between two bigger houses. It was not in very good shape and there was a realtor's sign in the yard with a plastic receptacle containing sheets of paper describing the dwelling. Boon was taking one when a neighbor called out to him, "You won't want to buy that house, I am telling you. Bad karma."

Boon assessed this next door neighbor, a tall, lovely black woman carrying a box to her car. "And why is that?"

"It's a rental and it's been bad luck for everybody who's ever rented it. I think they're going to tear it down. We're hoping they put in a park."

"Do you, by chance, know a woman named Kelley Swartz? Or maybe just Kelley; she may have married and have a different name."

"No, sorry, I don't. Never met a Kelley. Actually never met anyone who ever lived there; kept to themselves, mostly, except for the kids, but we've only been here three years." She walked on to her car, got in and drove away.

Boon stood there. The house was probably locked up. He looked around. No one in sight. He went around to the back and found a backyard littered with junk.

He would look at it later. For now, he would try the doors and windows. He knew he was trespassing, but he didn't care. He wanted to get inside, not understanding this fixed intent; it just seemed a wise thing to do. Have a look around.

He found a cellar door and submerged himself in the darkness, imagining that it might access the house. He couldn't see, so he lifted the door from the inside, propped it open and surveyed the space. The ceiling of the cellar did have a trap door. He moved it aside and knew he could crawl through it and get inside. He went back and shut the cellar door, crawled through the hole and found himself in a small room, evidently a pantry or storage room off the kitchen. A plastic cup from Johnson Space Center sat by the sink. Boon looked around and decided to pull the curtain and shut the few blinds so he could move around and see what he might find. He knew he felt uncomfortable in the house, just generally, and he was wise enough to know it wasn't because he was trespassing or because the woman had said it had bad karma. His own intuitive feelers were perfectly sufficient to convince Boon that the people who had lived in this house, at least the most recent ones, had not been well. As he surveyed the place, however, he determined that the house had been neglected and abused for many years. Sinks and light fixtures were broken; the toilet bowl was brown with stains and had no seat and no flushing mechanism. The tub was without caulking and was edged with an inch of grime against the wall to the shower stall with a plastic sliding door hanging off its runner. The shower curtain, once white, was black on the bottom third. The stench of dog poop and urine was overpowering. The carpet was soaked with stains. There was food in the fridge, covered with mold. The freezer contained a ham. Boon looked at the date without touching the unopened package: three years ago.

Every wall, ceiling and surface was brown with encrusted fly specks. It was easy to figure out that the last renters had moved without much notice: trash was everywhere and a great deal of broken, mismatched and filthy furniture remained. He opened the door to the garage and was appalled: the entire floor was strewn with garbage buzzing with flies, as if the renters had stood, just where he was standing, and thrown things out onto the floor. Nothing was even bagged and the pile was three feet high, four and five feet high in places. He looked up to see trash bags filled and stuffed into the rafters.

One thing disturbed Boon more than anything else: there were toys. Toys for little kids. The backyard had two small bicycles, one with training wheels. He was dismayed that young children had lived here, in this filth; obviously, they were not cared for properly. The single most prominent feature in the trash heap was the pizza box. There were, literally, hundreds of pizza boxes; most had been delivered. These people had lived on pizza! And pop. The cans were everywhere, in every room. He tried to determine the number of people, the family unit, which had last rented the house and felt that it was a man and a woman, given the clothing he saw lying around, and the shoes, and maybe three young children, a mix of boys and girls, given the kinds of toys. These realizations affirmed Boon's vow to never live in a house; houses were hidden, secret places. There was no way to know what went on in houses, not just this house, but all houses.

Boon thought drugs. Was this a drug house? Obviously adults who were impaired lived here and there was no sign of alcohol consumption. He decided to go upstairs. There was a half loft. The stairway was steep and the handrail was sticky with grime. The room was littered with junk, a big metal desk, army green, and a broken office chair. For some reason, these objects made Boon rule out drugs. He turned to look at a recessed area with shelves and there it was: a stained glass window, in a hole someone had quite evidently cut especially for it. It was thin and narrow, about 12 inches deep and 30 inches long. He looked at it carefully and wiped his nose, sweating in the heat to which he was unaccustomed. He felt like sitting down and spending the rest of his life weeping over this strip of stained glass. It was the most exquisitely beautiful thing he had ever seen. It was perfectly done; it was a work of art, stashed away in a bad karma house of neglect and ruin. He did weep, sitting there clutching his back pack. He wept for the beauty of the birds and leaves and clouds in the window, so intricately done with the tiniest pieces of glass and he wept for the woman who had told him one day she wanted to learn how to make stained glass windows. He had taught Kelley; he hadn't taught her to do this window, this well, but he had helped her learn about materials and design. It was so certainly hers and no one else's; it was neutral, an entirely monochromatic gathering of subtle shades of white, beige and gray. Kelley didn't use color; she was hyper-sensitive to sound, light and color and some of Boon's early work was too garish, what Kelley called "too loud," for her. Over the years, Boon's work had toned down and he had thought of her while doing "Vision" and "Beauty," his only monochromatic sculptures. The revelation of the moment was that "Travel" would be monochromatic. It would have to be.

His next thought was more timely and practical and it was followed by action: he took the window out of the frame, wrapped it in the one t-shirt of Jim's he still had, tied it onto the back pack with the pink cord, yanking the earbuds off and leaving them on the floor, and left through the cellar. His rationale for the theft was that the house would be torn down. He couldn't leave the window, but he didn't take anything else. He left the real estate flyer on the kitchen counter.

32

HOUSTON IS NOT PORTLAND

. . . .

We've looked and looked, but after all where are we?
—ROBERT FROST

Boon reviewed his history, his sense of place, his idea of belonging and decided that Houston, Texas, was a dandy city, but wisely determined that it was very different from Portland, Oregon, the small Pacific Northwest city he'd lived in for thirty years. He had to assess the two places in terms of size at first: Portland was soft and small and cool. Houston felt huge and spiny and hot. San Francisco felt smaller, more manageable than Houston, but he knew it was only because he'd been born and raised there. He knew San Francisco. He did not know Houston. He would carefully and respectfully get to know Houston. He pondered this and decided that different cities required different adaptations. He rented a motel room for one week and decided to eat right, rest, use a telephone in the room and research the task at hand, which was, of course, locating Kelley Swartz. He now felt he had a reason beyond his own fears and nostalgic pre-varications: he had a work of art to return.

He was looking for a woman, a woman who hadn't seen him in over twenty years. This fact presented increasingly as some-thing of a nightmare to Boon. He kept looking at himself in the mirror in the motel room and finally decided he looked sloppy and worn out. His hair was growing over his ears. He had a month's worth of stubble. He had a hole in the sleeve of the shirt he wore and the canvas pants, Jim's, didn't exactly fit. The belt he wore scrunched the waist in, but he looked ridiculous. He looked like he was wearing someone else's clothes because he was. He hated the tennis shoes, always had. He kept telling himself that he was becoming unbecomingly vain in his old age, but then, for some reason, he thought of Lou, and decided to yes, clean up his act. Lou never looked this rough, this tortured into physical existence, ever. Lou wasn't a dandy and really wasn't especially vain, even though he joked about it. Lou was respectable and took care of himself. He was modest with his clothing, but he took care with how he presented himself to the world. It wasn't about money, Boon decided, it was about self-respect.

He trimmed his hair and shaved, which helped. He then took off and went on a buying spree for clothes at a second-hand clothing store which had caught his eye on day one. It looked like a good place and it was. He took his haul, which came to $35.75, including a nice pair of real shoes with laces, Rockports, and went back to his room. He dressed in dark brown slacks, but changed to jeans, a real shirt with buttons, and a brown belt, the end of which didn't curl out from his pants the way the last one had. Over it, he wore a vest, a fine canvas and leather braided affair which he truly fancied. He had traded the black pack for a brown leather one. He looked polished and professional, by Boon standards, which was far from Lou standards, but what the hell. That's what Boon thought: he wasn't gay. He looked masculine and purposeful.

This is the figure that presented to Miss Frannie Hines of Gig Gallery, Houston. He introduced himself as an artist from San Francisco, Doddson Kooper-Boon. He felt the slide on the hometown was justified: what person from Houston knew or cared about Portland, Oregon? He had a piece, an early work by an astonishing artist, which he wished to return to said artist.

Miss Hines looked at the stained glass panel and shook her head, "It's pretty, but I'm not familiar with this artist." She hit a keyboard and shook her head. Boon was dismayed, since Gig Gallery claimed to be the premier gallery for stained glass in the world. Of course he realized this was pure conjecture on the part of the Gig people, but nonetheless, he was disappointed in them. "What's the name?"

"Kelley Swartz."

"I'm sure she would change that name." She was at the computer again. "It isn't, well, you know, poetic."

Boon couldn't understand how a woman named Frannie Hines, which made him think of her as Fannie Hind, an end-all name, could afford to be so judgmental. "Well, right you are, fair one. Had she married me, she could have been Kelley Kooper-Boon, which does have a certain ring to it."

Frannie became dismissive, although not entirely. "You might try Honey Help. Talk to Al. It's down the block on the corner." She pointed and went back to her computer.

Honey Help was another gallery, of sorts. Boon wondered what the premise might be, and decided eclectic was it. He saw not one single thing of any interest or value to his personal artistic sensibility, which he suddenly felt might be too narrow. The place was afloat with giant neon papier mache "things," utterly indescribable, beach balls wrapped with Christmas lights, driftwood trees, string assemblages that were impossible to look at and not feel trapped, and walking sticks, maybe 50 of them, all heavily veneered and topped with ugly heads of animals made from some material that looked like panty-hose. They had fake jewel eyes and were, to Boon, totally obscene. He checked the price tags: the cheapest one was $100. He looked at the stained glass things hanging in the windows and decided none of them would issue from Kelley's beautiful artistic mind, or her hands. They were crude and heavily reliant on wire, bells, balls, macrame and twigs. They were, to the piece, not instantly appealing.

He asked for Al. Al was busy; Al didn't want to be disturbed unless a customer was buying something. Was he buying something. No. Boon persisted. Frannie Hines had sent him. Well, OK, maybe. The teenager, male, was dressed as a janitor and acted like one. He was seeing dirt. He reeked of Pine-Sol.

Boon waited, wishing himself outside, wishing himself back in Portland, wishing himself under a rock or on a bench anywhere at all, when Al appeared. Al was not the expected person to emerge from the back of a gallery. Al would not be the expected person in any shop, anywhere in the world. He was at least 200 pounds heavier than Boon, black, and dressed in a green satin jumpsuit. He wore a pottery necklace of lime green, purple, orange and turquoise beads. He had a barrette in his short, graying afro, right in the middle, front and center. It was a turquoise plastic umbrella. Boon had to get hold of his sense of humor. He introduced himself, "Doddson Kooper-Boon, an artist from San Fran. Looking for the artist of this piece." He pulled the shirt away so Al could have a look.

Al looked carefully at Boon, then repeated, "Doddson Kooper-Boon. That's a Kissy Sway."

"A what?"

"Kissy Sway. Where'd you get it?"

"Old friend. Wanted to get it back to her."

"I'll give you 400 for it."

"Thanks, but I'm not interested in selling it. I'm interested in finding her. Her name is really Kissy Sway?"

"I guess so. Never heard her called anything else."

"Where is she, do you know?"

"Don't. Feather in the wind, that one."

"Could you describe her, so we know we're talking about the same person?"

"Tall blonde number, tattooes of birds on one cheek, all the stuff and nonsense, if you know what I mean. Sassy, but quiet about it. Pretty bad habits, I'd have to say, but I thought she was, oh, I don't know, kinda lost in the drift of the draftiness. Too much attention. You know she was a dancer?"

"As in exotic dancer."

"Yeah. Shit work. Arrested once, I heard, for the big down, but got out of it. She danced, I think until, I don't know, six years ago, maybe, way past midnight. Bonnet Club. A taut drum, Bonnet is."

"Taut drum?"

"Yeah. Mafcon. No moves without the man, if you know what I mean."

"Did she marry?"

"Marry? Yeah, sure. She had to, I'm guessing. Dan Reese wouldn't have it any other way, I'm sure of that much. She had a big ass rock the last time I saw her."

"When was this?"

"Fifteen years ago."

"Where was this?"

"At Bonnet. I took a buddy there. He was in town from Baton Rouge and had to go to Bonnet, some basic need to be met, if you know what I mean."

"And you haven't seen her since?"

"Naw. Saw her work once, always panels like this one, when she had it in a local show, years ago. I thought she was good and bought some of it. It sold pretty good for me. I bought one my-self; still have it."

"But you haven't seen her or her work in fifteen years."

"Right, maybe closer to sixteen now, although I heard she quit finally. Another guy I know, Herco's his name, dug her deep and was pissed when she quit. He died last year of an overdose, damn him, or we'd ask him."

"Do you know where she went?"

"Hard to say. Attached to that Reese, she's probably locked up in a bedroom with an armed guard at the door; I heard that's the way he often expresses his love and respect for women, and Kissy was one he actually fell in love with, so who's to say, but guys like Reese I do not like. Guys like Reese don't seem to understand what the word restraint means, as in restraining order. I don't like to talk this way about people but, I gotta say, from what I've seen and heard of Reese, I stay clear. Way clear. I'd advise you to do the same." Al wheezed under the sheer weight of speech, body and beads. The pottery orbs on the necklace were the size of golf balls.

"Heard. But tell me, if you wanted to find Kissy Sway, where would you look? You probably know this town as well as anyone. I'm assuming you're not recommending that I go to Bonnet."

"Jesus, no. You'd be a mark the minute you walked in the door. No, I'd look at Linda's Hope House."

"What's that?"

"Streetfront rehab for problems. I'll write down the address. Hard to find, for obvious reasons. There won't be a sign, probably not even a number. You'll have to figure it out. Now don't give this out to anybody, you hear? If she split with Reese, and is still in Houston, she'll be connected with Linda's. I don't know, but Linda knows dancers and the like and will at least have some idea of what happened to her. Linda does a lot of cocaine-plus rehab, multi-diag mentals, AIDS, a social worker type. Mother Teresa, except evangelical. Hands out Bibles by the case. I'm gonna sign my name on this, a couple of the women there send stuff over for me to sell; all this stuff is from places like Linda's, mental health places, AA people, Al Anon, coalitions. You hand it over to the first person you see there or nobody will even open the damn door wide enough for you to get in. I've never been there, but I've heard. Never met this Linda, but don't be put off. She's a hundred and fifty years old from what I hear and acts like she's senile, but she must not be. Heard of the turnarounds and she does the job. But hand this over; the place is barricaded. That's what I've heard." He nodded and started to amble into the back room with an asthmatic wheeze. He turned around and spoke to Boon, as if he knew Boon would be just standing there, not inclined to rush right over to Linda's. "Don't you wonder why I just gave you that address? Some brown town yokel dressed like a seventies cowboy?"

Boon was taken aback at this assessment of his attire, but asked, "Why did you, Al?"

"Because, son, I know who you are."

"You do? How could you know that?"

Al laughed and clapped his big hands, pleased with himself. "I am CO-nnected, my friend. I am One On the Spot. I hear the speech the minute it's made. I know the minute my grandson says poinsettia for the first time. I know when the next raindrop will fall: damn near never, it's Texas. I know everything that happens everywhere."

"Well, that's impressive. How do you do it?"

"Internet. Facebook. Blogging."

"Then you could check and see if Kissy Sway's on Facebook."

"She is, probably, everyone is, but she wouldn't use her name. Won't do you any good."

"But how do you know who I am?"

"I know because of your website. I put in a request for a price on a piece, but nobody's gotten back to me. I have a big house, a mansion, truth be told, and I fill it with investment art. It's my hobby. I'm a silviculturist by trade, and have gardens, twenty acres, trees. I like outdoor sculpture and I saw something on your website I kinda fell for."

"I don't know what you're talking about."

"Well, maybe we better find out about this. You said you were Doddson Kooper-Boon, San Francisco. I assumed you were jerkin' me, because you're really from Portland, Oregon, that's what it says."

"I am. I just didn't know I had a website."

"Well, there can't be two Doddson Kooper-Boons, hell if, that's all I can say. You have a website, man. Should have your picture on it, though."

"Which piece were you interested in?"

"Spirit. Big grasp of the universe."

Boon smiled. "You can have it, Al. It's my contribution and my thanks. Contact them and tell them to ship it to you, that you paid for it. Here, let me have a piece of paper, I'll give you a receipt." Boon grabbed a piece of paper which already had something printed on it and wrote "Spirit" SOLD to Al, Honey Help, Houston, PAID and signed his full name and the date. "Since you know everything about everything computer, I'm sure you can get this to Good Fortune Gallery, or wherever, however. I don't know anything about it, but get "Spirit" onto your place, put it in the trees. Maybe someday I can visit and check it out. I appreciate getting it to a good home. What's your last name? I better put that down, too."

"It's Aloysius Browne. Appleseed, they call me. Candle Mansion. Everyone knows where it is; it's on the registry. Can't miss it. Say, where you stayin'? You need a place?"

"No, thanks. I'm at the Travel Trail south."

"Well, just show up. I'm here on Tuesdays and Thursdays, otherwise I'm there. Find Kissy and show up, and thanks for the art, my man."

Babette.

What, Will?

Babette. You have to stop. I've been here three times a day three days in a row and you aren't here. You haven't even heard me come in, have you? You have to stop. Let's have tea. Stop. Tell me how it's going.

OK. Just give me a minute. I'll log off.

Is this thing almost finished?

What thing?

The novel, Babette. What's wrong with you?

I'm stiff. My back hurts and my arms are tingling.

Jesus, Babette. I don't understand why you push yourself so hard.

I don't push myself. It's going too slowly, actually.

How many words do you have?

69,888.

Babette. It's March 7th. Let's see, that's, what, 3,000 words a day, actually more because you babysat your grandson two of those days. Meribeth Tront says 500 a day, tops. This is ridiculous.

I'm not Meribeth Tront, Will. If I were Meribeth Tront, I'd quit. She has written 35 books and is ninety years old. If I were Meribeth Tront, I'd quit.

I'm not so sure, Babette. You seem pretty driven to me.

I'm not driven, Will. The story carries itself and it carries me with it. I don't have much to contribute at this stage, at least. It knows where it's going by now; I don't.

If I didn't know you as well as I do, I would think you were crazy.

Interesting. Fascinating commentary on the process, Will, as usual.

33

DOES HE NEED A DOG?

· ·

Here's to your 500 words a day, Meribeth Tront.
—Babette Bouche

The family therapist, Moxvil Levin, MSW, listened for an hour and suggested that his client get a dog. He felt a pet which required love, care and constant attention would mitigate the overwhelming concern the man sitting in his office expressed about the potential of dying tomorrow, or today, for that matter. He was pleased that his patient had a developing relationship with a remarkable individual. He was pleased that his patient had engendered an effective parental alliance with a young man who wasn't his son but who wanted to be, a young man who didn't bat an eye at having a gay father figure. He was pleased that his patient was getting healthier and planned to return to work part-time. He was not pleased that his client obsessively worried about dying. He didn't obsessively worry about his health; he worried about dying an instant and premature death.

Of course, it was Donovan Trenton King who sat in Levin's office. Trenton King had been in for three sessions, as had Lou Prachek, who only needed one, if that. Poor Levin, triple teamed as he was, shouldered through a long list of issues and finally had things settled down except for the Big Archetypal Death Deal, for which he recommended ongoing psychotherapy with a referral in place. Now he was pulling out the stops: get a dog. He put it this way, "In addition to regular sessions with Dr. Johnfield, I suggest you get a pet; I recommend a puppy, actually."

"A dog?"

"Yes, a dog."

"I don't want a dog. I've never had a pet. Too much work."

"Precisely."

"You think I need more work?"

"I think you need less work on the subject of Donovan and more work on the subject of others. You've done well with people, but you need to get a dog."

"I can't get a dog, with my lifestyle. I'm gone; I teach. I have health issues."

"Get a goddamn dog, Donovan. I don't need to see you again until you report back here that you have a dog. Simple. Get a dog. Get your life back. Love a puppy. Love yourself. You aren't dying, Donovan, but you're thinking yourself into a living grave, which is the worst kind. Get a dog. Now, I'll see you out."

Babette.
What.
You'd better come out front. Big surprise.
What?
Log off. Come. Now.
Boy, nice guy. Snap, snap. OK. What the hell?

Look.

I see it. What is it doing here?

It's your new puppy. Mathilda. She's a Weimaraner.

I know that. I don't need a dog.

You do, Babette. She will be a nice companion while you write.

Ridiculous. I don't need a companion while I write. It's a solitary profession, Will. You know that.

I have her sister at my house. We're going to have dogs, Babette.

Since when, Will? No.

Yes. I'd planned to give her to you for Valentine's day, but it was too early to wean her. She's a gift from me to you, Babette. I love you.

Well, I love you, too, Will. What's her sister's name?

Hermione.

My Christ, these names, Will. Mathilda and Hermione?

Math and Mione, that's what we can call them. Good names, huh?

Will, sometimes it is exceedingly difficult for me to believe that you are a poet. I am not calling a dog Math. I'll call her Tilda.

Then I'll call mine Hermy.

34

STEALING THE BIBLE

· ·

These things I command you, that you love one another.
—St. John 15:17

Everything he'd heard about Kissy Sway bothered Boon. Absolutely nothing he had seen or heard from the wrecked house to the Hope House didn't disturb the hell out of Boon, understandably. The tattoo on the cheek was news to him, and it bothered him. The name Kissy Sway bothered him, as did the description of Reese, the club, Herco, the streetfront, the "down," the bad habits, the armed guard, all of it. He reviewed everything and decided that there wasn't anything to latch onto that was positive about Kissy Sway, that didn't make him worry about her even more. The only things he'd heard from Al which made any sense to him were about Al and the window panel. And Doddson

Kooper-Boon. He decided he wouldn't run right over to Linda's Hope House. He had been spooked by the case of Bibles, the 150 years old, the word barricade. He thought he should think about things, so he bought take-out Chinese and went back to his motel room.

It was an odd thing to Boon that midway during this meal, the room seemed to flatten into a narrow space about two feet tall and three feet wide. He couldn't breathe. He stopped eating, hunched over styrofoam on his bed, put down the fork and decided to lie down. The oppressive feeling that something was wrong simply had to be dispelled instantly; he affirmed that he wouldn't be able to live with this for long. He thought it must be the MSG.

He was wrong, of course. He lived with it. It came in waves of complicated grief, vicious character self-assassination, rebellion against born-again Christianity and strict step-parental authority from his childhood, and worries about aging generally and everything else specifically. He felt remorse that he hadn't seen his father before he died, that he really didn't remember much about his mother. He worried that Douglas was making a mistake, that Donovan might have died. He worried about the state of affairs in the state of humankind worldwide. He worried about violence and the unequal distribution of wealth. He worried about his wealth, which he decided he might resent for a couple of reasons. Making that money probably shortened his mother's life; she threatened and then she committed suicide, a bitter consequence of what she told her parents, who eventually told her children when they were older, was loneliness, which translated into marital neglect in everyone's minds. Boon knew, as did his grandparents, that it was much more complicated than that—no one blamed his father—but they did know what she had been talking about. His father's life had probably been shortened by a constant desire to accumulate more of everything except children. The other reason Boon might have problems with the inheritance was speculative: he couldn't handle it. He amended that: he didn't think he wanted to handle it. So far, it wasn't looking so swift, the inheritance, wasn't. His work was suffering. He worried that his creativity was gone. He worried, unjustifiably, about hair loss and the bile which rose into his throat and burned. He obsessed about Kissy Sway and then extended it to all women. Something felt over and done with. He might be checking out. Maybe this was the end for him.

He went down. He didn't eat for three days. He didn't really sleep; he languished in a dreamless state of self-inflicted agony. He finally put a label on things in a broad, general way: he decided he was angry. He decided things were fucked up. He decided he'd recently learned too much about too many sordid, awful things, things he'd always known—he'd seen quite a bit of it along the way—but hadn't confronted sufficiently to ever go back. He had an enormously difficult time at this juncture trying to determine what going back meant. To what? To where? What did it mean?

On day six, Boon went out and had breakfast at a diner, went back to the motel room, retrieved the vest he'd thrown in a drawer, intending to leave it behind when he checked out, opened his back pack, pulled everything out and began assembling a sculpture on the bureau. He made an interior frame for the vest using metal coat hangers he found in the closet, then took the Gideons Bible from the nightstand in his room, and lashed it inside with the hoodie string and began. He named the fledgling piece "Salvation" and got out his one tube of glue, a Sharpie pen and his jackknife. The thing was curious as it began to take shape: it was the vest atop two tennis shoes, a visual representation of a chest in motion, perhaps. It was hard to judge, but Boon thought it was interesting and important, somehow, but granted: he felt this way about all his pieces at about this stage. He kept working on it and decided to incorporate the cell phone, which had stopped buzzing sporadically, in the vest pocket. He hoped to get it recharged so viewers of the piece could take the call if so inclined.

At various junctures, when he'd worked himself into a state of excessively high nervous energy, he went outside and walked a few blocks, around the Travel Trail neighborhood, mostly the parking lot, and found things to work with: a fake gold hoop pierced earring which had been run over, sticks, paper cups, a length of gold chain, a broken mirror, two rocks, a realtor's magazine, a pair of broken purple plastic sunglasses, and a beige rag, still folded and clean. He'd saved his take-out Styrofoam, tore it into strips, and used that. As he reviewed the developing piece, he saw the influence: it belonged in Honey Help. His artistic sensibilities *had* been too narrow; he was absolutely right about that! Something was freeing up for Boon and he began to get a glimmering, a gleefulness, a gargantuan glory glop of gratitude. It kept tapping him on the shoulder and he stopped for a few seconds now and then to look around the room. He was alone.

35

KNOCKING ON HELL'S DOOR

A great person is a group effort.
—Bob Makowitz

It wasn't a knock on the door; it was the phone on the stand by Boon's motel bed. It rang. When he didn't pick it up, it stopped and then a red light came on and blinked at him. He stood holding two pieces of wood together to wait for the glue to set and watched the red light blink. There was a knock at the door. He stayed right where he was, utterly disinclined to answer this knock. He watched the door, wondering if he'd locked it. Evidently he hadn't, because it opened.

"Doddson Kooper-Boon?"

"Yes." He was squeezing the balsa wood pieces so hard, they snapped in half.

"I need to come in and speak with you."

"Well, then, come in, fair shine. Who might you be?"

"I'm Adrienne Grigg, do you know who I am?"

"Well, you're Adrienne Grigg, but, no, I don't recall having heard the name or met the face, no." He pulled out a chair for her and she sat down. She was elderly and smelled of lilacs. She had a bun on top of her head, with messy tendrils hanging down and a crocheted back pack. She wore chamois boots with fringe, a long, tie dyed skirt and a thin, gray sweatshirt with the sleeves cut off. His first thought was a hippie version of Mrs. St. Nick, right down to the wire-rimmed glasses and the twinkly blue eyes. She had brought him warm cookies, that was his second thought.

"I'm here to speak with you about Kelley Swartz."

Boon sat down. "Yes." The heart raced ahead of the mind, body and spirit.

"Could you kindly tell me how you know her? Before we chat further, I'll need a reference point or two, if you wouldn't mind."

Boon swallowed. He thought about it. "But I don't know why you're here and how you found me."

"Surely you don't find me threatening or questionable in any way, Mr. Boon."

"No, but I'm not feeling comfortable." He wanted to say he felt like shitting his pants, but held himself back.

"OK, fair enough. Let's get you more comfortable. I work at Linda's Hope House. Al called and said you came around asking about Kissy. He'd already told me he'd located you, something about a website. He was trying to flush you out himself and was surprised when you showed up. He and I are, let's just call it renegades from the same rat race, and he let me know the minute you left. He assumed you wouldn't come to Hope House; he said you had that look on your face. When I asked him how the inquiry had come about, apparently the window there"—she pointed at the stained glass panel propped up against the mirror to the dresser—"I twisted his chunky arm and asked where I might find you. I see your phone is blinking. That means someone tried to call you. That someone was probably Al Browne, confessing the terrible sin of inflicting your privacy with Adrienne, the evil witch of motel row. Other than scrambling your brain for a few minutes, I don't expect I'll do a great deal of damage here tonight. It will be painful, Mr. Boon, quite painful, but not damaging. I suspect it will be a good thing in the long run, or I wouldn't have come." She smiled.

He liked her. He didn't like the word painful, used twice, but he liked her. "So, Kelley. She and I dated in our late twenties, in Portland, Oregon. She disappeared one day, to make her way here in Houston. I haven't seen or heard from her since."

"And what, if I may be quite rude to ask, do you want with her now?"

Boon sat there: good question, Adrienne. "That's a good question. I'm not sure."

"How did you come by the window; did you haul it here all the way from Portland?"

"No. I stole it from a rental house which is going to be torn down."

"Yes; I know the house."

"You do?"

"I do. I thought that's where it came from. I've seen it before, of course."

"That house was a mess. Did she live there?"

"Yes, but that was almost nine years ago."

"Wait, you've known her nine years? Wasn't she working at Bonnet Club then?"

"She was."

"Why was she living there? Wasn't she married to the Reese guy?"

"She was. She left him and rented the house. There was a restraining order on him; she filed for divorce, and she contacted Linda at that point."

"But she kept working."

"Yes, she worked for another five or six years; I'm not sure."

"She divorced a husband, had a restraining order put on him and kept working for him?"

"Yes."

"That's sounds crazy to me. Why would she do that?"

"She needed the money? Other reasons? You tell me."

"How would I know?"

"Well, I thought you might."

"Well, I sure as hell don't."

"Mr. Boon. Am I understanding that you don't know Kelley had your child, a girl?"

"What?" Somehow he spoke another word. "No."

"Yes, apparently she arrived in Houston pregnant with your child, Mr. Boon. I assumed you knew she was pregnant, although she never gave me that specific indication."

Boon breathed. He stood. He walked around. He sat back down. "Where is she?"

"Kelley?"

"Yes."

"We don't know, Mr. Boon. That's why I've come. You've gone to a great deal of trouble to get this far in your search; we're hoping you will succeed in locating Kelley. We're all anxious to locate her."

"What about the child?"

"The child is over twenty-one now."

"Where is she?"

"I don't know, Mr. Boon."

"God! What's her name?"

"Her name is Genevieve."

"Her last name?"

"Genevieve Kooper-Boon."

Boon was tearing up. "Why didn't Al tell me this? He knows about all this. He knows Genevieve, even!"

"He does, though not well. It's because Al is competent, Mr. Boon. He's a competent mental health care adjunct. He told you some history, some carefully selected history, knowing Al, and he decided I should speak with you since I'm trained to do so. He called me after he did some research and found out your father had recently passed away. We both decided to give you some time before hitting you with this. And, frankly, here's the main reason, which I trusted most; Al Browne thought there was a good chance you'd find her on your own. He said you were an intuitive adept, and Al would know. We waited, hoping you'd find her, or Genevieve, or both. We strongly suspect they may be together."

"Why do you want to find her?"

"Because Reese is also missing, has been for five months, and we're concerned that he may have been involved somehow. We just don't know. There's another woman involved, as well. Her name is Mindy Saterino; none of us have ever heard of her."

"A dancer?"

"I don't know. Terribly injured, apparently, we don't know how or why. We're concerned, very concerned, Mr. Boon. Please help us if you can. We received a call from Kelley, but the connection was cut off. All we know is that she may be in some trouble, and Mindy is hurt."

"What about the police? Aren't they looking for them?"

"Yes, they are, obviously. And there are several warrants out for Reese. To date, they have no leads to pursue. They assume he's left the country; there's no reason, really, to think he's involved with this now, but we can't be certain. We thought perhaps she would go north, to old connections. She isn't in Austin with her family there, we know that much. We just became so encouraged when you arrived. You may know of possible places she would go that we can't possibly know about."

"The police know about me, too, don't they?"

"Yes. I spoke with them and explained that if you left here, I was to be notified. You've been under light surveillance."

"I stole a Bible."

"You did."

"Yes, from the room."

"I think I should go out and tell them and have you arrested. Right now."

Boon smiled, knowing she was trying to make him feel better. "I'll put it back."

"Don't you dare. There are more Bibles. It's in the sculpture, I take it?"

"Yes. How did you know that?"

"Well, it's pretty obvious: you have everything else that isn't nailed down on it, where else would it be? And the shoes are a clue, wouldn't you think? I've never seen anything like this. Plus, you surely know the Biblical reference: this is exactly what Gideon did. He created an ephod as a snare. It kicks."

Boon really appreciated Adrienne. "You know, Adrienne, you've brought news that is hard as hell for me, but I have to say you're a shiny star-splitter, girl. I'm going to find Kelley and I'm going to find my daughter. You can count on that. You wanted to know what I wanted with Kelley. Well, I can tell you now; I feel I know you well enough to tell you the truth."

"And that is?"

"I've always loved her, always. Maybe I knew about the baby, maybe I really did, because I have to tell you, I haven't had a day in my life since she left that I haven't missed her and worried about her. I don't know why it's taken me so long, but I'm here. I'll find her. I have to."

Adrienne stood and gave him a hug, "Let me know. I have to tell you one more thing, Mr. Boon."

"What?"

"Genevieve looks just like you. We haven't seen her around here in a few years, but she's a Kooper-Boon, for sure. Al said the same thing."

36

TWO MINUTES

. . . .

The experts do not follow rules.
—Huston Smith

Adrienne was gone two minutes when Boon knew. They aren't here. During the third minute, he had the flash: she might be looking for him! Kelley might finally be looking for him! He went to the front desk and handed over his debit card and a twenty dollar bill and asked the girl, Sue, to please help him. He needed an emergency flight from Houston to Portland, Oregon. There was a family emergency. He also requested that she arrange for a rental car at his destination. He went back and packed, checked back with Sue, paid his bill, and took a taxi to the airport.

He arrived in Portland the next morning at 4AM. He drove to Jive Joe's since it opened at 4 and bought a cup of coffee and a breakfast burrito. He read the paper and waited, then drove to the police station and waited in his rental car. Marc Fisk drove into the parking lot at 6, returning from a burglary crime scene. Boon waited until he got out of the car, and yelled, "Hey Fisk, you wanna pay off that mortgage?"

"Boon, Jesus. What are you doing here? Did I see you just get out of a vehicle? A new Honda? What the hell?"

They went inside and Marc listened to the story. He typed things into his computer as Boon talked and kept nodding in an aggravating way, as if everything Boon wanted to know was right there at Marc's fingertips, just inches away from Boon's brain. "Nada."

Boon shook his head, "Don't tell me there's nothing. Can't be."

"You know, Boon, Houston's a lot bigger than Portland and has a really good, well-staffed police department. Why is it that you would assume I could find things they can't?"

"You want me to tell you?"

"I do."

"Because you have the gift, my man, and I have confidence in it. You can break rules; you can go beyond. If there's a single living soul who can shuffle this deck and pull out the queens, it's you."

"Well, that's flattering as hell, but I don't have a whole helluva lot here, Boon. Everybody has the names, the ages and the missing part."

"Well, that's all I know. I'm going over to Colora and line them out. Take them some grub and some brew. Maybe a big box of donuts and coffee. See if they've heard anything about a Kelley or maybe a Kathy, or a Mindy or Mandy. He started out the door, but returned, "Oops, not thinkin' here. There's a man in this picture and it isn't Reese. There's a jack in the deck."

"And who is he?"

"I don't know. Kelley's boyfriend, husband even, whatever. But she will have a man, trust me. I just got there."

"But isn't this a problem? What if..."

"You know Marc, I have no idea. Yes, I love this woman and always have, and I have a daughter I have to meet as soon as possible. Beyond that, I have no idea. I'm not tracking her down to set up ma, pa and the kid, who isn't a kid anymore. I mean, think about it. She's been dancing until six years ago. Is she with a guy? She is. Is she going to be interested in Booneroo? Probably not. She's raised our kid entirely on her own for over twenty years. I would say being pretty stand-offish would be a blessing, actually. If she doesn't shoot me the minute she sees me, I'll be lucky. Christ. I didn't know about it, but that doesn't mean I didn't do it, at least from the looks of it. They say Genevieve looks just like me."

"No! That poor kid! God! She's had a hard time of it! And she's a girl! It would be different if it was a boy, that would be bad enough, but a girl! It's terrible! She must be a total freak, totally shunned! Probably never had a date."

"Uh-huh. You are the comedian, Fisk. Just roll me out in the aisles every fuckin' time. Get your ass to work."

37

FLIPSIDE, BACKSIDE, SLIDE

My wings have stiffened, I'd better slow down.
—B WONGAR

Boon thought how predictable it was that he always arrived at Good Fortune Antiques just before closing and stood around on the sidewalk looking at his sign and lurking and wanting a cigarette. He felt tired and stiff and more than a little overburdened. He'd been to Colora twice and to several other points of reference in Portland. He had made himself visible; he had flapped his wings and crowed: I'm back. He hadn't been missed particularly, that was apparent. None of his alliances knew what he'd been through recently, at the speed of light, in a hospital, in a bank, in trouble, in Houston, in hot water, in a damn airplane for the first time in his life. He sat down on the sidewalk and considered just going back to Colora and sleeping for a week. Fisk could fiddle around with his play-toy computer and he would sleep. Finding Kelley, Mindy and Genevieve weighed heavily, so heavily that by this point in the afternoon, he was able to honestly not care if they were found this instant or not. Not would have to be OK. He wanted to check in with Helen so she could tell the whole world the errant artist had returned, and then he would go sleep. He and Helen had a thing: they could be brief.

Boon walked in and hollered, "Fair One of the light brigade! Yon Boon, home from the hill! Where are you, my princess, my divine queen of the firestorm?"

This escaped from Boon's mouth, at high volume, before he noticed the figure at a table near the back wall, her back turned to him. He panicked. He wanted to hide. He started to back away. Tall, blonde! It was Kelley! Jesus Christ! She was stacking books! What was she doing here? He pressed his body against the wall and willed himself transported to another universe, another planet, another city, state, town, another shop. Anywhere, somewhere. Please, no. I cannot do this now. I can't, I can't, I can't. Help me, help me, help, me. He had stolen a Bible. He was being punished.

"Good day. Might I help you? I heard you say something quite intriguing. Might you be looking for someone?"

Boon's eyes were huge; he could feel them stretched, bugged, bleeding in their sockets. The concern instantly shifted from ocular to cardiac. His heart had stopped. He fell against the wall, but caught himself. This was it.

"Are you all right?"

Boon, ever gracious and quick on his feet with verbal virtuosity, blurted out, "Who are you?" This was delivered in the tone of voice people use when they find an intruder in their garage, trying to steal their car.

"I might ask the same of you."

"I'm Doddson Kooper-Boon. Who the hell are you?" He wanted to say: you aren't Kelley and you aren't Brett and you're so fuckin' far from being Helen that it isn't funny, but he didn't. It might confuse things.

"Oh, wonderful! I've heard so much about you!" She hugged him. "I'm Lana TeVelde."

The blood drained, every drop of it, from Boon's body. It drained into a hole in the floor he felt he'd surely dug himself. He thought at this exact moment that he might turn to Jesus after all. His very life force had drained out of him, his heart had stopped, he was blinded, his ears were ringing and he had an erection. He needed to touch the hem of a garment and be healed. He stood there. He stared. He was evidently speechless, as he rocked on his big feet, then caught himself.

"You seem a bit unsteady. Perhaps a chair. I might suggest you sit down."

Boon had a silent retort: and I might suggest you put a warning sign outside. Danger: Approaching Most Beautiful Woman in the World. As he sat, he registered the name fully. He'd heard it and he'd thought Trenton's Mom, he actually had done that, but now it hit him: the mentally challenged, in a facility, Donovan ex, but not ex, Australian person. Well, Boon stared at her: just exactly what you need, Boon. You don't need anything right now but the most gorgeous female you've ever seen, recently escaped from a mental institution half way across the world, hugging you hello within five seconds of meeting you. Perfect. Who is fucking in charge here, that's what Boon wanted to know.

Lana read his mind, another bad sign. "I've been put in charge here while Brett is off on a honeymoon and Helen and Jerald are in Seattle at an antique show."

"Brett? Honeymoon?"

"Yes, she and Jason. So darling, those two."

"Isn't it a tad fast on the fair shine?"

Lana giggled. "Brett told me it was love at first sight. They actually met in his office over a porn site, believe it or not."

Boon believed it. If there was one thing, in addition to everything else, that he could have assured the multitudes he didn't need at that moment was any mention of pornography, in any context whatever. Somebody or something was clearly out to get him. He mumbled, "Well, good for them."

Lana forged ahead with her lovely Australian accent. "I do so adore your work, Mr. Boon."

"Just Boon. It's Boon."

"Boon. I am enchanted by your sculptures, every single one of them. I just cannot imagine where such a vast reservoir of creativity originates. It simply erupts in every piece; there's such visual thrust in the dynamic interplay of color and texture throughout. It gives me shivers, just talking about it." She closed her eyes and shivered dramatically. Her breasts moved, her butt moved. What was she wearing? Was she clothed? Yes: tiny sliver of a dress, very thin, clingy and peach-colored. A naked dress, cut on the bias. He got it: Miss Australia. Ten years ago. No, it would be more like twenty. He shook his head; if this was what mental illness did for you, he was in line. No wonder he looked his age; he was sane. Well, relatively speaking.

"So you're Trenton's mom?" Boon decided to focus himself on reality; she was a grandmother. Maybe that would help. "How is Trenton?"

"He's wonderful. You know, I presume, that I've not been in his life much and until now haven't really been able to get to know him. It's a deep sadness, sometimes, which prevails, but it's my hope that we can continue to grow together. You can't imagine how strange it feels to finally get to know your child after so many years. It's so terribly odd, how this has happened. I spend a great deal of time shaking my head—and being grateful." She paused as Boon remained quiet, and regained her cheerfulness. "Such a happy, happy family. That granddaughter of mine! She is charming! I'm staying with them in their new house for two weeks, then it's back home. My parents are quite elderly."

Boon remained steps behind, of necessity. "They're not in the Airstream?"

"No, Tinabelle found them a darling place which Donovan bought for them. A wonderful garden, just superlative."

"And Donovan?"

"Donovan's doing much better. My, that was a scare! He's so happy with his new puppy. And he and Lou, well, they are such an interesting couple. They share so much, yet have divergent interests; it's perfectly beautifully balanced."

Boon didn't understand balance at the moment. "Puppy?"

"Yes, they have a new Husky puppy. They named him Neanderthal. It was Tinabelle's suggestion. He's chewing on everything now, but he'll outgrow it."

Boon's head was swimming. He wondered if it was still attached to his body. He reached up to feel his throat.

"Do you have a sore throat?"

"No, no."

"I should offer you something, heavens, how desperately rude of me. Please, do come into the apartment and I'll fix you something refreshing."

"You're staying here?"

"Yes, the burglary, you know."

"Burglary?"

"Yes, poor Brett was robbed of $250 one morning. Helen and Jerald have restocked quite marvelously and they wanted someone to stay. And your work is so valuable, we can't leave it unattended. I'm happy to do it for them; I just spend my evenings reading anyway."

'What are you reading?" Boon hoped she would say *The Secret Life of Squid* or *Modern Goat Breeding*. Maybe *The History of the Grecian Urn*.

"It's a history of the life of Michelangelo. You know, I'm sure, that he thought painting ruined him, that he would have been better off taking a job making sulfur matches. I find that funny, don't you?"

"Funny."

"Now, all I have is gin. I make a mean little gin rick, Aussie-style. I hope that suits you, Boon. And if you're hungry, I have prawns; I could make us a light dinner. I do so love prawns."

He looked at her and he looked at the Bombay and he thought it would be best if he took the bottle, tipped it down his throat, drank the entire thing and instantly passed out. That would be plan A. "Great. Sounds great. Prawns. Prawns are good." He wasn't fond of gin. Was he saying so? No. A big fear thought swept in: she was a drunk. He would have his hands full. He would be in trouble tomorrow. She would be back in rehab. His world would turn gin black. Everyone would be mad at him for taking advantage of poor Lana. Did he care? No, he did not. She seemed fine to him, a bit charged, but all right. He would take his chances. He was thirsty. That was Plan B.

It was Plan C that commenced. Apparently Boon couldn't recall his broccoli revelation of not that long ago in Santa Rosa: the I Don't Want To Be Twenty Anymore revelation, which overcame him as he watched young people accomplish all sorts of things on two or three hours of sleep a night. He was sleep deprived, food deprived and emotionally overloaded. He drank the gin. He watched Lana fix the prawns. He had another drink. They ate, talking about his art and nothing else. He expostulated about the extended boundaries revealed during the invention process with "Salvation." He had no idea what he was talking about. He woozed in and out of sporadic thinking: mostly he was out, floating around in a reverie of marshmallow cream meanderings in a minty mist. Iceland.

He was thinking about Iceland, trying to put a chill down, when she announced a shift in the evening's activities, "Boon, you just lie back there on the couch and rest a bit while I clear this. I'll fix dessert and make our coffees. You must be so, so exhausted."

He remembered the pillow being put under his head, the smell of gin and lime, the kiss on the forehead and the darkness that followed. He died. He was dead for ten hours and awakened with one thought: had he slept with her? He looked around and saw no sign of her. He hoped he'd been on the couch all night, but he couldn't be sure. He sat up. Jesus Christ! Two drinks! Headache, headache!

His drinks had been topped double shots, unbeknownst to him. His only reassurance was that he probably hadn't had sex; he was far, far too hung over.

Too old for this, man.

He showered, recalling his last shower in the apartment. He seemed to be in a pattern of spending the night with beautiful women and not getting any. What was his problem? He dressed and tentatively opened the door and entered the shop. There she was, in a tight, black dress, already with a customer. She smiled and nodded at him. He mouthed a thanks, blew her a kiss and fled.

Where was he off to in such a rush? He had no idea. He had a rental car to return. He had to sit on a bench somewhere for a couple of days. That was Boon's plan, his only plan. As he stepped off the sidewalk to get in the car, a small black square on the sidewalk caught his eye and he leaned down to pick it up. It was a wet stamp, a one cent stamp with a picture of a native American necklace on it. He patted it onto his thigh to dry both sides and slipped it into his pocket.

The two bundles were on the back seat. He started the car and sat there, listening to the engine run, and decided he'd better lighten his load. He left the car running, pulled out the parcels and took them into Good Fortune Antiques, slipping in unnoticed by Lana who had her hands full, a rug draped over one arm and a teakettle in the other hand. Her back was to him and he noticed diamonds studding the high heels of her shoes and thought of the Simon song.

He went up the spiral staircase, flipping on the light. He unwrapped "Salvation" and he unwrapped Kelley's window. He looked around. "Youth" was gone. "Vision" was gone. "Spirit" was gone. "Healing" was gone. "Balance" was gone. He needed paper and pencil. He saw a small desk in one corner and then noticed "Love." His pieces were scattered around it; he peered at a small note at the bottom: work in progress, NFS. He took the note off, crumpled it, and put it in his pocket. He scribbled a note to replace it: finished, DKB, and stuck it into a hole at the top. He admired what Brett had done, and wondered how it had gotten there. It must have been Susan or Cindy. He liked the statement the assemblage made, although he picked up an eraser and put it in his pocket, replacing it with the one-cent stamp. He moved a few of the pieces around on the display until he felt it was perfect.

He then wrote a note for "Salvation" with the title, indicating that it was for sale. He put a price on it: Ten dollars. He wrote it out: ten dollars. He wanted to make sure they didn't mistake his intent. He then wrote a note for the stained glass window panel: NFS, NFS. NFS. Kelley Swartz/Kissy Sway Original. Property of Genevieve Kooper-Boon. Hang by silver chain in window six feet from floor, extreme right. Do not center. Insure for $10,000. He wrote it out: ten thousand dollars. He initialed it DKB and added the date. He then took another piece of paper and wrote: Next scheduled show: Trenton TeVelde King. He put it on the desk under a glass paperweight of a dolphin.

He stood at the top of the stairs and listened for voices; he wanted to make sure Lana wasn't at the bottom of the stairs at the cash register. He heard her lilting accent down a hall, moving away from him, and he scrambled down the stairs and left the shop, closing the door quietly. He had quite deliberately left all the lights on in the gallery. He looked up at it from the sidewalk outside and smiled, but there were tears in Doddson Kooper-Boon's eyes. He was overcome by a strong feeling that he might not be back, and the tears were coming because he didn't know why.

38

WAGON TRAIL

. . . .

Both of us understood what a privilege it was
to be out on a walk with each other.
—W.S. MERWIN

He found the bench behind a cabinet shop that had closed. He slept for two days and remembered why he didn't drink. It made him feel ugly and mean. It made him depressed, it made him aggressive when he talked, it made him feel worthless. Combined with the fearful encounter with Lana, when he'd assumed at first that she was Kelley, Boon was left without his sense of sanity and without any desire whatever to do art ever again. Everything was foolishness. Everything was fucked. He jumped at everything. He looked at everyone, simply everyone, to see if they might be Kelley or Genevieve or Mindy or some guy attached to them for some reason. He concentrated on men in suits, big guys who might own a club and do dirty business, although he knew it didn't make sense; guys like that would be walking around in casual clothes just like everyone else. Still, any male he hadn't seen before, which was most of them, was suspect. He trailed them all, anyone who caught his eye for any reason, and became an inveterate stalker of humanity. He did specifically single out tall or tallish blonde women and peered at faces looking for the tattoo and narrowed his focus considerably for Hispanic women who looked like exotic dancers and were injured. He didn't find a single one of them in Portland, but he kept looking.

In periods of respite from stalking, Boon did briefly consider checking in with his friends and family. He went over the possibilities, one by one, quite carefully and quickly. Lou was out because he'd be in love and twitterpated about Boon's money. He would discuss investments and use words like portfolio. Donovan was out because he'd cleaned up his act and Boon evidently hadn't. Who needed that? Cindy and Susan were out because Jim would be lurking and probably offer the bum some more of his old clothes. A boring, tense and long dinner might ensue wherein Susan would fiddle with his foot under the table and Cindy would gush about Pete this and Pete that. Douglas was out because she was with that ridiculous Carbeige and therefore without a brain. He didn't want to see his sister without a brain. Greg was out because Boon felt sorry for the poor bastard who probably would never get laid again: a divorced, aging fellow with no prospects. Somewhat like one Boon. No, Greg was not the upper he needed. Obviously the entire Good Fortune scene was simply stacked too deeply with good fortune for Boon to stomach: Honeymoon! Buying trips! Miss Australia! Mr. & Mrs. Jerald Redding, glowing with marital bliss at seventy! Depressing. Trenton he really didn't know, ditto his family, and his mother was there, as well as the baby. No. Tinabelle would be fine, but the retinue was over the top and there was Lee-something. He wasn't in the mood for loving couples of any sort, which also left out Torrey and pregnant Heather. He didn't need to see a pregnant relative right now. Damn Bobby had disappeared and the Armory wasn't doing bingo anymore. He'd learned that Jake was divorced and living in Tulsa.

He went to Colora Collective and checked in. He was told he could strip some copper wire and salvage catalytic converters from the pile in back if he needed his five bucks. No: he needed to talk. He took Wee Willie by the arm and hauled him out front and sat him on a bench. Boon paced around in front of the small man, who looked pale and frail, older than ever, and told Wee Willie his troubles, pretty much all of them. Willie had listened to these kinds of Boon melt-downs for well over twenty years and secretly felt Boon was the son he'd never had; he'd claimed him the first week he met him.

True to form, Wee Willie was instantly vastly commiserative when Boon finally finished, "No use in bellyachin'; you'll get over it."

"What about Kelley, though, what about my kid? Jesus, Wee."

"They'll show up or they won't. Nothing more you can do. You don't know anything about it. You don't know what's supposed to happen. Guess you should quit rantin' and rollin' around town like you *do* know. I got the reports: you're not doing a damn thing other than just that. Makin' a fool of yourself. Now, I gotta get this insulation paperwork together for Bonita. That woman drives the hard bargain; I don't know if we'd survive without her, truth be told. You get back there and get me some precious metals. Rent's due in three days and we're short."

"I'll pay the goddamn rent. How much is it?"

"We're short $175."

"Fine, you got it. And I'll do the damn catalytic converters. You can go out to dinner."

"I ain't goin' out to dinner, Boon. Off the grub, anyway. No interest. I'm readin' P.D. James."

39

CUE

. . . .

I conclude now I have no inner resources,
because I am heavy bored.
—John Berryman

He started going to The Grande, a short-shrift bar and pool
hall near the college.

He slept until noon on his bench behind the defunct Frank's
Cabinet Shop, and did nothing all afternoon except sit around
and watch his feet. He sometimes wandered around, spoke
briefly, if at all, to anyone, didn't check in at Colora beyond
paying the $175 and next month's rent, too, and definitely didn't
call anybody. He didn't check in with Fisk and he didn't go to the
Y to swim or to shower. He didn't collect things for sculpture.
He bummed smokes and coffee and ate only at The Grande, ar-

riving at 6:00 PM. He always slipped in the back, watched people playing pool a while, then went to the end of the bar up front and ordered a beer from the tap and a plate of food. After he paid for it, he returned to the back room, sat down on a long split log bench along the north wall and ate and sipped his beer. He liked The Grande because it held no peers. It was a new place for him; no one would ever find him. It was the college crowd, interspersed with a few demographic necessities: a couple of secretaries being "out," a couple once in a while, sometimes a professor or some other older person, but no Boon types. No one paid any attention to him, none, and he liked it. He sat each evening listening to chatter and smelling bodies and hearing noise and ate his one meal of the day. He usually left after an hour, returning his plate and half glass of beer to a bus table at the end of the bar. He then went back to his bench. That bench became a grief seat.

It happened in the third week of what Boon now called his Life of Missing, days of mourning the loss of an important friend. He knew he had started going to The Grande because he missed Wee Willie, who had been found dead of a heart attack at Colora Collective early one morning, just a day after the last conversation he had with him. He knew he was grieving, but he couldn't believe how hard it was to accept this man's passing. Willard Toflett had been the vision behind Colora Collective, the last one left of the three men who had started it in the mid-eighties, the smartest one. Willie had always been there, had put up with him, had given good advice, had kept him straight. And fed. He'd gone to Wee Willie's simple funeral; he'd paid for it, bought the flowers and had given the eulogy himself, breaking down at the end and barely finishing.

He'd done everything he could for Willie, but it was all too late. He should have seen it coming; he should have gotten him to a doctor. The last time they'd talked, he had noticed Willie wasn't quite himself and seemed especially frail, and Wee had said he wasn't eating. Boon couldn't shake the feeling of guilt. He might have been able to give the old man a few more years. He knew he had to let him go; he was old, but Wee Willie's passing cast the blackest pall on Boon's life he'd felt in some time. He was supposed to go through Willie's things in the room he'd occupied at the collective for years; he had volunteered to do it, but he couldn't get around to it. He hadn't been by the warehouse, even, since the day he'd taken the rent by and learned that Willie had died the next morning. He kept saying he'd do it tomorrow. He didn't want to see the room where he'd spent so much time having great conversation, listening to Wee talk about books. He knew he would find the P.D. James book and he was afraid Willie hadn't been able to finish reading it.

It was a Tuesday, a dark, rainy Tuesday of no consequence whatever, except for the fact that he had to eat. He was losing track of the days; he couldn't even remember how long it had been since the funeral. He arrived at The Grande early, soaking wet, and got coffee. He felt shaky, a little weird, as if he might be coming down with something. He ordered nachos and a beer after he'd dried off a little and went back to the log bench. He was eating nachos, prying chips from globs of cold cheese, when his eye caught the move. A pool cue shot back in the hand, threaded now against the back of the body for a shot. His head jerked up. He put the chip down. He stood. He had instant chills. He watched the difficult final shot of the game. In. He looked at the player, who was now knocking down the pool cue and putting it in a case. A man walked up and gave her three bills. She was leaving, taking a last drag from the cigarette and putting it out on the cement floor with her foot.

Boon followed. She was tall, wearing a sloppy sweatshirt over loose jeans. She was overweight, not obese, but lumpy. Her blue-black hair was cut in an unflattering, layered chop-bob which hung to the sides of her face. She wore no make-up and combat boots. When she was outside, she cleared her throat of smoker's phlegm and spat on the sidewalk. She took out another cigarette and lit it with a Zippo. As it snapped shut, he knew for sure; he knew the hand that snapped a lighter shut in just that way. He knew the pool player who handled the cue in just that way. He knew: this is Kelley Swartz. This is Kissy Sway. Four feet away, on this very day, in the rain in Portland. Was he sure? He was not. No tattoo, no tattoo, no tattoo. It could be Kelley, the classic face, plus twenty years, could be hers, but he wasn't sure, then he was sure. He followed her. He watched her move. He thought about how to find out. The obvious did occur to him: walk up and ask. Are you Kelley Swartz? It seemed a little rough, mostly on him.

Three blocks down the street, she turned on him suddenly and said, "You are following me and I don't appreciate it."

It came out with no thought or effort on his part, "Kelley Swartz."

She looked at him.

He saw her recognize him, though she didn't say anything. "Kelley, I'm so glad to see you." She didn't respond; she just stood there looking at him. "Why didn't you come back a long time ago, Kelley? Why didn't you?" He just stood there, wanting to hug her, wanting the smiles, wanting the happiness to start showing.

"Kelley?" He said it softly, feeling he'd sounded accusatory.

She stepped toward him and hugged him, "Boon. It's been so long, Boon." It was very brief, this hug, and she stepped back from him. "Can we go to your place and get through this? I came to find you, but now that I have, it's hard, Boon."

"I know."

40

MOTEL, OH!

One of the lies would make it out that nothing
Ever presents itself before us twice.
—ROBERT FROST

Awkward was a word, and a feeling, familiar to Boon. He had been an awkward child. He had never been athletic; PE teachers and coaches had all considered him awkward. He had gotten himself into awkward situations, usually with women. He was in one now. She had asked if they could go to his place and talk. He was in her car. He was pointing at an ATM. He was using it. He was pointing at a motel. He was registering as Mr. & Mrs. Doddson Boon, something he'd done several times over the years. He was unlocking the door to the room. It was unbelievably awkward.

He sat in a chair as Kelley looked around the room. "You look great Kelley. Different, but great, just great." He felt the flatness of this remark and wished he'd kept his mouth shut.

She didn't answer. She started to undress. The black wig flew onto the bed, revealing long blonde hair, graying in front, cascading down to her shoulders. The sweatshirt came off. Boon was stricken with the most serious fright he had ever felt in his life. Under that sweatshirt was a small, lithe body and voluptuous breasts. The entire sweatshirt was padded. What stood before him was a blonde in a bra wearing huge jeans. The jeans came off, obviously also a heavily padded garment. She stood there in a thong, bra and combat boots looking like Kelley, looking very much like Kelley. Her body was beautiful, but no longer perfect. Her face was beautiful, but there were crow's feet and smoker's lines. She looked her age. She looked fantastic. She pulled a long white men's shirt from her bag and put it on.

Boon shook his head. "God, Kelley, what are you up to? Scare me to death."

For some reason, the presentation in front of him instilled more fear than desire. In fact, there was no desire for anything except an explanation. "Tell me what's going on, Kelley. What the hell? Where's Genevieve? Where's Mindy?" It was right here that Boon remembered the guy, and everything went entirely black: a monochromatic nightmare of distinctly horrible possibilities. He honestly felt like leaving, right then and there. He didn't think he could handle it. He could live for the rest of his life with the image of the woman before him now and be perfectly happy.

She sat cross-legged in the center of the bed, boots and all, asking him to check and make sure the door was locked. He sat down in the chair and she asked, "Where do you want me to start?"

"Start with the day you left me; you were pregnant, Kelley. Let's start there." He felt cruel and cold.

"I didn't know I was pregnant when I left. I had been working a month, at a small place called Rita's, when I started getting morning sickness and had to quit. I was renting an apartment with another, older dancer, Rhonda, and she saw me through the pregnancy. After Genevieve was born, I lived on public assistance, of course, and worked cleaning in the apartment complex, Genevieve strapped on my back. I lived there until she started preschool, then I started dancing again. I had good sitters and kept her out of daycare. I had a boyfriend, John, who was a great help, until he met someone else at a club where he played music and left us. Genevieve was heartbroken and so was I. I quit for awhile and lived on food stamps and general assistance, but it was too hard to make a go of it, and I started dancing again at Bonnet Club. I had trouble; you know I can't stand noise and crowds. I don't know how I did it."

"What happened to the tattoo?"

"How do you know about that?"

"Just what happened to it?"

"It was fake. I didn't wear it all the time, but it became a sort of signature thing."

"Reese."

She scowled. "Am I telling you things you already know? Obviously, you asked about Genevieve and Mindy. Don't drag me through this if you know the whole story, Boon. Spare me."

"I don't know the whole story, only parts of it. I just came from Houston. Adrienne, Al Browne."

"Ah. So you know I'm missing, that you know. I tried to call Linda's and let them know I was out, with Mindy, getting her to Oklahoma, but I lost the connection. You know why I'm disguised, then, at least part of it, don't you?"

"I'd guess Reese. But first, where's my daughter?"

"Our daughter is in Superior, Montana."

"Are you sure?"

"I'm sure. I talked to her this afternoon."

"What's she doing in Montana?"

"She lives there, in a trailer on a ranch. They're building a house."

"What's that about: who's they?"

"She met a guy in college, at the University of Idaho. He's from a ranch near Superior. They're engaged. His name is Harold Johannsen. I met him last Christmas; he's a wonderful person, exceptional in every way. They're building a house."

"You said that. It sounds good, sounds like she's in a good place with good people. Now, Reese."

"Not a wonderful man, Boon. He wasn't wonderful when I met him, and he sure isn't now."

"Did you love him? Do you love him? You married him!"

"No, never, and that's the problem."

"You decided you couldn't be with him, so he threatened you? The restraining order? I don't understand why you would keep working for him after you put a restraining order on him. Or how you could marry him."

"Genevieve. When you meet her, you'll understand, Boon. She looks like you; she's built like me. She has your personality. To him, she was a commodity."

"What did he threaten, Kelley?"

"He threatened to take her out of the country. She was fourteen when he made this move; he'd been pressing me to marry him and I married him that same week. He had no personal interest in her, except as a pawn to use against me. You have to understand something: Reese isn't interested in sex. He's impotent, in many ways. He's interested in control. He's very powerful; he could have taken Genevieve easily and had her gone forever. Very easily. Eventually, I moved out and I made a deal with Reese, until I got Genevieve through school, out of Houston and connected with a strong support group."

"What was the deal you made?"

"I'd work the club and do whatever he asked as my boss, but he couldn't approach me outside of the club. He would sign for the divorce. He agreed to that."

"Kelley. Where is he? Where's Mindy?"

"I have no idea. I think he's probably out of the country. I don't hear from him, but, still, I don't take chances. I took Mindy to a hospital and now she's in rehab in Oklahoma City, so it's OK, Boon; the Mindy thing is just so part of the business. She'll get through it, so it's over. And I found you."

"But it isn't! You're in disguise; you're not taking any chances. That doesn't sound like it's over to me. I still don't understand what the hell you're doing."

"I decided to travel as a pool shark. The disguise helps the game, too, you know. I don't earn as much when I look like Kissy Sway, I'm sure you get that. Compared to the club, small pool rooms aren't so hard for me and they're off the track. But Reese knows Kooper-Boon, Genevieve's real last name. I came here to find you; I was afraid he might trail me, or have someone else do it, and that he might find you before I did, but I took my time anyway and stayed low and careful. Reese always said he'd track me down if I ever left Houston, that he would find me. I just know too much about him and he'll never give up, restraining order or not, and in his twisted way, he loves me. There's no get-ting around that. He just can't change or won't change. I've come along the coast in a rental car. I abandoned mine in Oklahoma City. I've been staying in hostels and had to sharpen my pool game, the only thing I could think of that he knows nothing about, and you do. He knows about you, though, knows I came from Portland. I haven't breathed your name since I got here. I haven't looked for you; I hoped you would find me. I didn't know how, but you did, thank God."

He asked again, "Why didn't you come back a long time ago, Kelley? Why didn't you let me know about Genevieve? Why didn't you?"

She took some time to answer. "I thought about it, many times, Boon, but I knew you were brilliant, that you were a great artist, even back then, and I didn't want to stand in your way. It's why I left in the first place, and then, as things happened...I knew my life dancing, a child, would keep you from being who you were meant to be. I wanted more for you; I wanted you to marry a respectable woman who could help you live a wonderful life. You're from such a good family; I'm not. I wasn't right for you. And you didn't try to contact me, either, Boon, did you?"

"No, and I don't understand why not. I don't. I've never for a moment forgotten you, Kelley. I've worried about you. And, Kelley, you are a respectable woman: you were then and you are now. I've never married or had a relationship like the one we had since." He got up and walked around, trying to lighten things, to get past the why-didn't-we, the accusations, the excuses, "How long have you been here?"

"Three weeks."

"That's when I brought your window back."

"My window?"

"It's in a gallery here. I stole it from your old rental in Houston, on Median Road."

"You didn't."

"I did."

She sat there staring at him, tears brimming, "I loved that window. You taught me. It's been so many years ..."

Boon stood up and went to get her a glass of water. Then he lit a cigarette from her pack on the nightstand and offered it to her, after taking two long drags himself.

He sat down, fortified by nicotine, waited for her to gain some control of her emotions and to finish the cigarette, before asking the hardest question of all, "So, Kelley. You have a man in your life now."

She set the glass of water down and looked at him. "Yes, I do, Boon."

"And where is he?"

She sat there with such a serious look on her face that Boon felt like repeating the question, pushing her for an answer, but he just sat there, too resigned to the coming bad news to say another word. "Nic's here, in Portland. He flew in two days ago."

"Where in Portland?"

"At The Benson."

"The Benson. Not hurtin'. Why doesn't he, this Nic, go around with you sharking?"

"He's reassured by the disguise and he knows I'm doing it to look for you. He has a disability, a bad leg, and doesn't do the standing around thing very easily and he's sensible; he knew this conversation had to happen and didn't want to be around for it. He's shy, trusting, confident. We've known each other awhile, almost four years now. We bought property in Alaska and that's where we're headed, permanently. He's a stockbroker, so he can work from anywhere."

"What about Genevieve?"

"What about her?"

"How does she feel about this?"

"She's excited for me. She likes Nic and she's just relieved that I'm getting out of Houston."

"Well, then, Kelley, I'm happy for you, too." He paused, struggling with the word happy. "I loved you, Kelley Swartz. I'm..."

He teared up and stopped.

"Go ahead, Boon. We need to see this through, as I said. I'm here."

"I'm so glad you're the mother of our child, Kelley. I'll meet her as soon as I can, you know that." He stopped again and she sat quietly, waiting. "I'm not much for this kind of thing, Kelley, I'm not good at this, you know that, you know me, but I loved you then and I'll always love you. I've thought about you and worried about you and missed you every day since you left. You just left. I woke up and you were gone. I haven't found anyone else like..." Now he was crying; he couldn't go on. He hung his head and sat there, hunched on his chair. Finally he whispered, "I feel defeat, Kelley, it's all over now; this is the sweet cheat. I loved you so much."

She scooted off the bed and hugged him, holding on awkwardly as he sat on the chair. She was crying now, too. Finally, she stood with her hand on his shoulder, trying to regain control. She steadied her voice. "It's OK, Boon. I cried a lot over us, too. It was special; it really was. When you meet Genevieve, that's the very minute you'll know what we really meant to each other and why it happened. Hang on to that; I do, every day. She's a joy; there's no better way to describe her. You'll see, and then you'll understand." She rubbed her forehead. "I wish I could make you feel better, Boon."

She sat back down on the edge of the bed and waited for a time, adjusting, allowing him to adjust, trying to remember to breathe deeply to relieve the stress. Finally, she was able to reach forward and tip his chin up, so she could look him in the eye. She smiled at him, a tender, sweet smile, and said softly, "Boon, honey, you have the surprise of your life ahead of you: Genevieve Kooper-Boon is so very much her father's daughter."

41

CRAZY

. . . .

Each story is an image of the whole story.
—Taigen Daniel Leighton

Of course, Boon was Boon. It would be someone female who'd known him a long time, Bonita from Colora Collective, who would line him out, get him off his morose bench of grieving over every damn thing he could possibly imagine, including the death of motivation to get to Montana. That motivation died an hour after it was born, after the talking was over and Kelley left and he was alone with himself to blame for everything. Montana sounded like the big sky country all right, someplace to send your spirit when you died. Death was big on Boon's mind; he liked sitting around and talking to himself about the end. He thought it was appropriate.

Bonita found him at The Grande, sat down beside him holding her motorcycle helmet, and started talking. She didn't care that he seemed to be only half listening. She was wise and knew something would drift in and settle, if not now, later. She watched Boon concentrating on her Harley boots as she gave the big speech.

"Now, Boon, you are riding sidecar on the road to the rest of your life, buddy. That's not your deal. You belong in the driver's seat. Now, I don't see any problem with sitting around grieving; I've been doing that myself, Boon, we all have, but we have a collective to run and Wee would be turning in his grave if he could see you sitting here in this dump crying in your cheap, damn beer, doing not one damn thing. I suggest, and it's only a suggestion, that you get off your dead ass and give a hand. I know you paid two month's rent, that's great, but that's not enough and you know it. You couldn't even get your lazy butt over to clean out Wee's room, for Christ's sake, what kind of respect is that? I did it, but you'll have to go through it again. I stored it all in the lockup. Now what that leaves is a nice big room with a bed and a long ass work table, a chair and a coffee cup I bought you. I want you to move in there and help out, which mostly means just being there. I ran it through all the guys and fifteen of us can't be wrong. They sent me: get Boon on board, that's what they said. You can do your art thing and man the glue stick. Damn it, Boon, we need a glue stick, bad. Leadership, man, leadership. Power to the people. You didn't die, Boon, Wee Willie did. Get that?"

Boon looked at her. He'd looked at her before, of course, for maybe seven years or so. He hadn't looked twice; she wasn't much to look at, but she wasn't hard to look at, either. Not bad, nothing terrible, perfectly nice looking, in fact nothing wrong with her at all, except that she was tough as nails, swore like a sailor, and wore men's clothing the way men wore clothing, revealing nothing. He'd never been told anything about her and had never asked.

He'd talked to her a few times and thought she had a good head on her shoulders and nice eyes. He'd noticed when she added a bright pink streak to one side of her long brown hair, he had noticed that, and thought it was smart, but hadn't said anything about it. She did the books; she hauled things; she took care of a million details. That's all he knew. She didn't live at Colora Collective; he didn't know where she lived. She rode a Harley to work. She didn't get paid. He didn't know if she had a family or anything else about her. She looked like a biker chick. That's what he'd always thought. She was forty-something-like and on the tall, slim side. He had seen her peel out on the bike one night and had one of those testosterone flashes: Jesus, what a woman, but that was it. Mostly, Bonita was one of the guys. He answered her, "Yeah."

"Man, that's it? That's all the eloquent, poetic, crazy Boon has to say to a damn good proposition from a damn good woman?" She stood, "Well, most men are plainly a waste of time; I grant you that, which is why I'm single forever, watch me. Most women aren't so swift, either, I'll grant that, too, but I guess I just overestimated another one of the slugs. I'll leave you sittin' here in your slime. Careful: you know, when the wind blows, things dry out and you might get stuck there on that bench. I've seen a lot of slugs die that way."

He stood, he reached into the air with both fists and pulled down, as if he intended to pull the heavenly graces down around them, and then he spoke "Bonita, Bonita. Tell me, since when do you warble? I see a shadow lurking behind Bonita and it's got a smirk on its face. You're yankin' me." He put one fist into the air and pulled again. "What's dazzle up to? I see a mountain of glory in the distance..."

She interrupted him, "See, there's the nutcase Boon. That's better. Why don't you just come with me, right now; I'll ride you over on the Hoot and you can have a look. I have another helmet you can wear. Let's go."

"Nope. Dame on a rainbow run, wisps of heather in the glade right here and right now, Bonita. I smell the heather and it's in bloom and I smell leather. Sit it down and let's hear the tale. I'm not moving 'til light shines." When she stood there, unmoved, apparently, he added, "I'll buy you a pilsner, big splurge, if that'll loosen the glory gills."

"Not much to tell, Boon. Geez, you've known me forever."

"Nope. Haven't known the now, egret, haven't known the now."

Bonita looked around at the nothing happening in The Grande, raised her eyebrows, shrugged, blew out a big, tired breath and gave it a go, "I'm a drummer in a band. VeraCruise Four. I came from right here. Went to college, in English, trumpets ablare, at PSU. My parents moved to Tucson, sick and tired of rain drops. I have a brother who's in the Navy, teaching, guess what, computer science, and a sister with three kids, count them, three, in Ashland, Oregon. She married an optometrist who is about as lively as the fourth plank there in front of your toe. So much excitement so far in this, that I'm sure you're shitting your pants. Wow, huh? I live in a dump over the hill there, all alone and happy about it, and cut and paste it together. Write music. Fight like hell with the guys in the band, but we're good. Nothing else. Play music, write music, such as it goes, work at Colora and read books, take odd jobs. I do canned foods and co-op cut that won't qualify for the food bank. I get food stamps, so ta-da, I live like a queen on pork 'n beans, peanut butter, tuna, Wheat Thins and York candy bars. Mint's good. After I eat, I work on my bike, but I'm not good at it. I only do it because I can't afford to take the damn thing in to a decent mechanic. It's transportation; everybody asks if I'm a Hell's Angel or something. Christ: wrong about that. I wouldn't last ten minutes with those guys; they'd see right through me. Bike nerd. That's me."

"Well, now. I'm perking, Bonita. I say we have another round, have a decent meal before the hour passes, shoot some pool and make this happen."

"Make what happen?"

"The deal, the proposition, the leadership, the glue stick, the art table. Climb the mountain, girl. You said it: we should do that, but I think we should dance around a little, make the moves a littler looser, a little closer."

"Somehow, that sounds dangerous, coming from you, Boon."

"You damn right it's dangerous. You said you bought me a coffee cup. Christ, the intimacy, the boldness, the potential in that is beyond anything I've ever experienced in a gift from a woman."

"You're full of shit, Boon. It's a coffee cup from fuckin' Target."

"Not to me it isn't. It's the Holy Grail, it's the Horn of Plenty, it's the golden goblet of medieval mead. It's yellow, or gold, this cup is, isn't it?"

"Well, yes, it's a kind of goldenrod color. How would you know that?"

"Oh, because you would be thinking, in your inestimable wisdom, this: buy a cup to cheer the bastard up. That would be yellow."

"Well, don't get too excited. It's a coffee cup."

"Yeah, yeah, but I am hearing you with the brushes at the drum kit. There's a beat."

"You're coming on to me! Over a coffee cup! A yellow coffee cup from Target! Man, are we desperate and pitiful, or what?"

"We are not. You have no idea what you're talking about. I could tell you about a red ashtray I found on a park bench. That red ashtray changed my life."

"A red ashtray you found on a park bench changed your life."

"Yes, it did. And a yellow cup is going to change our lives, fair shine, you'll see."

"This is absurd; it's a stupid cup, Boon. You're a wacko!"

"Should be. Hope so. Try to be."

About the Author

Llawren Bird hesitates when asked, "Where are you from; what do you do?" Though she now lives in the rural Pacific Northwest, she was born in Kansas, spent her early years on the reservation in North Dakota, graduated from high school in eastern Montana and attended college and university in Colorado. She's worked in Denver, Los Angeles, Guadalajara, and in many smaller, found communities. Her background extends from agriculture to advertising, college teaching and volunteering on behalf of the disenfranchised. A generalist, she moves through shifting paradigms as a contemporary and writes it down, telling the truth as she finds it in fiction, and only in fiction. She wouldn't write a memoir if you paid her.

redbat
books

For other titles available from redbat books, please visit:
www.redbatbooks.com

Also available through Ingram, Amazon.com,
Barnesandnoble.com, Powells.com and by special order
through your local bookstore.

www.ingramcontent.com/pod-product-compliance
Lightning Source LLC
Chambersburg PA
CBHW030640260626
47157CB00007B/2418